Sparks Out

A Grace Howard Mystery

By Kelly Adamson

Acknowledgements

This book is dedicated to the memory of my mother, Betty Maynord, who always let me stay up past my bedtime, as long as I was reading.

Special thanks to my writers group, Joan Kennedy, Lucy Merrill, Ken Bishop, and Krista Leamon.

Contents

Chapter 1 — Sparks

"There's a spark in all of us, my friends.
A spark of madness,
A spark of greatness,
A spark of the divine.

Kill it,
Waste it,
Or let it shine.
You got your spark and I got mine.
—Sparks (1986)

Grace had hated the smell of lilies ever since she killed the transvestite in Las Vegas. It was hard to believe they used to be her favorite flower. And today, a bouquet of Stargazers sat right in the middle of Sparks's massive desk. She could smell the awful things the moment she stepped through the door, out of the hot mess that was Alabama in August.

She tossed her purse and bag on the black leather sofa opposite the desk and wrinkled her nose at the big, flamboyant blooms. From a fan, no doubt. Sparks wasn't the type of guy to buy fresh flowers for himself. Fast cars and expensive guitars, yes. Flowers, no.

The card was wedged down in the vase on a plastic pitchfork. Grace plucked it out and read it. "Congratulations on your book. Love, Cassie, Vicki, and BJ."

Grace may have been working for Sparks for only a couple of months, but she knew who Cassie, Vicki, and BJ were. They called themselves the Sparklers, and they headed up Sparks's international fan club. The whole concept seemed bizarre to her at first, but they'd actually proved themselves quite useful, having spearheaded Sparks's online presence and "kept the dream alive," so to speak. And all gratis. That was, apparently, what devoted fans did. It had certainly made Grace's work easier. She smiled and tucked the card back in the bouquet.

"Sparks!" she called. "Where are you?" Her words bounced off the marble floor and high ceiling, echoing down the hallway.

No answer.

"Sparks!"

Still no answer.

She could feel her face begin to redden. She knew where this was going.

Last Friday was the first time she'd ventured any farther into the private area of the house than the rear kitchen that served the pool and veranda. On that morning, she'd arrived at nine a.m., as usual. Sparks was always there to greet her, sometimes still in sleep pants and tee-shirt, but awake, at least. Last Friday, for the first time, his office had been vacant. Just like the kitchen and the music room. But when she called his name that day, he'd answered.

"Grace, is that you?" The voice sounded muffled, hard to accomplish in this high-ceilinged Spanish Colonial mansion that Sparks Westergard called home.

"Yeah, Sparks, it's me. Where are you?"

"Down the hall. Just follow the sound of my voice. I'm so glad you're here. I've had a burst of inspiration and I'm champing at the bit to get to work."

He said he'd found the perfect spot to reflect on his charmed life, and had already filled up four of the little microcassettes she'd brought him.

This was welcome news for Grace, who thus far had spent a considerable amount of time each day trying to get the man to stay on task. She was there to help him write his memoirs, but in her first week, he insisted they go for a ride each morning in a different sports car from his extensive collection. His Maserati on Monday, his Pagani on Tuesday, his Bugatti on Wednesday, and so on. The rides usually lasted all the way into another state and back. Apart from the fact that he liked European supercars, she learned nothing about Sparks Westergard that first week.

The second week, he played the entire catalog of his band's music for her, personally. He played and sang nine albums' worth, some on the guitar, some on the keyboard, a few a cappella. From start to finish, from 1985's "Cut to the Chase" to 2003's "Below Decks." By Tuesday, she had a headache. That night, she told her husband, Nick, that working for Sparks was like herding cats. So what if she'd spent hours writing "Grace Westergard" on her notebooks in curly letters when she was thirteen? So what if his poster had been taped behind her bedroom door then? So what if she'd saved her allowance for a month to buy his live double album? Yes, *album*. That was a long time ago. She was a grown woman now. A professional. She was here to help him write his memoirs and further his online presence for his planned comeback. That was all.

So, last Friday, when he announced that he'd found his groove, Grace was delighted. She followed the sound of his voice through the arched doorway and down the hall. There in that moment, belting out one of his greatest hits, his voice sounded every bit as clear and strong as it had twenty years before. He was making a comeback, and she was going to be there. She felt that familiar little tingle run up her arms. She picked up the pace and rounded the corner just as he ended in a high-pitched, '80s hair band wail of her name, "GRAAACE, YEAH!"

"Oh, my God!" she cried, her voice lost in the larger sound of his.

Sparks Westergard stood dripping wet and very naked in the middle of a marble tub large enough to wash a car in. His long blond hair hung dripping over his shoulders. He was Poseidon without the trident, and in the second before she managed to spin around and put her back to him, the image was burned in her brain. He looked very good for a man in his fifties. Very good, indeed.

"Could you hand me a towel, Grace?" he'd asked, the very model of innocence.

She hadn't answered him, but stormed off down the hall to the sound of his laughter.

That was last Friday, and she was determined not to let him embarrass her today. He would pretend not to hear her so she would have to go looking for him. Fine. If he did his best thinking in the tub, so be it. She would pretend not to notice. She grabbed her bag, complete with the transcription of the cassettes from Friday, and started off down the hall to the marble bathroom.

She passed the archway to the kitchen on her right, with the lounge and pool beyond. The bright morning light danced on the water outside and reflected back on the blue interior walls. It danced on the long, granite wet bar. It danced on the stainless steel appliances that lined the rear wall. And it danced on the body of Sparks Westergard, who lay sprawled on his back on the tile floor.

"Oh, my God," Grace gasped, this time for a very different reason.

She dropped her bag. Its contents skittered noisily across the tile. She ran to him, fell to her knees and grabbed his wrist. He felt too solid, somehow.

Too heavy. Too motionless. She knew even before she felt for a pulse that it was hopeless. Sparks Westergard, king of '80s glam metal, was dead.

Chapter 2 — Cut to the Chase

The police arrived within four minutes of Grace's call to 911. She was waiting at the front gate and punched in her code to let them through. Her hands were shaking so badly that it took her three tries to get the numbers right.

She'd left the house in a hurry, needing air, needing to get away. But now she had to go back in, to show them Sparks's body—it seemed horrible to think of him that way—and to get Sparks's terrier, Karishma, before she started biting policemen.

The little dog was lying beside Sparks with her head on his arm. Grace hadn't noticed her until she heard her whine. She hadn't had the heart to move her, but now she would have to. Poor Karishma. Like most of the females in his life, she'd saved all her love and adoration for Sparks. But in her case, it meant the dog loathed everyone else. Grace knew the first person who touched her master was going to get bitten. It had taken Grace eight weeks of bringing the little dog turkey jerky every day in order to win her over. Karishma had gained a pound—a lot if you only weighed eight to begin with—and Grace had gained a friend.

"Wait!" she called, hurrying into the house. "Don't touch the dog!"

But it was too late. Karishma was snarling like a wild cat while a young policeman with a crew cut grasped his hand to his chest and cursed. The little dog stood sentry in front of Sparks, teeth bared. Grace scooped her up without breaking stride. "Come on, Sweetie. Let's go outside."

She was headed toward the pool when a commanding voice stopped her.

"Ma'am, I'm going to have to ask you not to leave the premises."

Kelly Adamson

The voice belonged to a stocky man with a red face and more hair on his upper lip than on his head. His cheap tie was loosened and the top button of his shirt was undone, most likely because it wouldn't fit around his thick neck. His accent sounded like he was from Boston, or maybe Maine. It was a sure bet that he came south for the winter once, and decided he was never going to shovel snow again.

"I'm Detective Morton," he said, "and I'm going to have to ask you a few questions."

Karishma began a soft growl as the man approached. Grace shushed her. She sank into the leather sofa with the shivering dog and waited while the detective fished in his pocket for a notepad and pen.

"What time did you find the body?"

Grace cringed again at the word "body," even though she knew it was correct.

"About nine a.m.," she said. "Give or take a couple of minutes. I called 911 right away, so they'll have the exact time." Her voice trailed off as she remembered that frantic call.

"Walk me through what you saw."

Grace cleared her throat, suddenly dry as dust. "Like I said, I arrived at nine. I didn't see any cars in the drive. I didn't see anyone or hear anything out of the ordinary. Whoever did it must have been long gone."

"Did what?" the detective asked.

"Well, killed Sparks, obviously. That's why you're here, isn't it? Or do they always send a detective when someone dies?"

Morton straightened and made a show of adjusting his tie. "I'm just here to find the truth, ma'am, and ninety-nine percent of the time that truth is a heart attack or some other natural cause. Sometimes it's accidental, like a drug overdose."

Grace sighed. It was an understandable assumption, she supposed, but Sparks didn't do drugs and never had, as far as she knew. Despite his long hair and jaded past, her employer was pretty conservative. Grace was a little surprised at first, but had to admit it made perfect sense. After all, the Reagan era was Sparks's glory days. The economy rose, the Berlin Wall fell, and he and his band were the kings of Sunset Strip.

His friends at the time had all hated Reagan for cracking down on the drug cartels, thus jacking up the local prices. But Sparks didn't care what they did with the Peruvian Marching Powder. His weakness had always been alcohol. Any kind, anywhere, any time of day. And blondes. He had managed to give up the first seven years ago.

"He's clean," she said, "but the autopsy will show you that."

"Mm hmm," Morton said, in a tone that showed he thought she was delusional. "Go on with your story, ma'am. You arrived at nine and then what? Which door did you use?"

She motioned toward the glass door that led into the office from the pool. "I always come in the back, because this is the door Sparks leaves open for me. But today I had to use my key for the first time. I guess I should have known something was wrong."

The pen scratching on the notepad stopped and the detective looked up. "You just used your key for the first time?"

"It's the first time I've needed it. Sparks is always here when I get here. I really didn't want a key at all, but he insisted."

The detective parked his backside on the edge of the desk, above a row of skulls that had been hand carved into the wood, and studied Grace like she was the bearded lady at the fair. "How long have you been married?" he asked.

"I hardly see how that's relevant."

"I just find it odd that you didn't want a key to your own house. There must be a reason for that. Call me curious."

Kelly Adamson

"I don't live here," Grace said, a little exasperated at this line of questioning and his mocking tone. "Why would you think that?"

The detective crossed his arms over his massive chest and shook his head. "I'll never understand these modern relationships," he mumbled. Then to her, he said, "If you weren't here last night, Mrs. Westergard, where were you?"

"I'm not Mrs. Westergard," she said, then laughed, thinking of all the times she doodled that very thing on her school books in the eighth grade. Inappropriate laughter, wasn't that a sign of stress? She supposed she qualified as stressed.

"My name is Grace Howard. I work with Sparks. I'm helping him write his memoirs." She paused. "At least I was. I guess I'm not anymore." The realization of her sudden unemployment was something else to add to her stress.

The detective blew out a breath that ruffled his mustache. Grace could tell he thought she'd been purposely playing him, trying to make him look foolish, or at least uninformed. She felt like she'd been called to the principal's office for writing "Grace Westergard" in her textbooks. She wondered if this guy had any friends.

"Ms. …Howard, is it? If you don't feel like answering my questions here, maybe we should take a little ride downtown."

"I am answering your questions." She straightened up, trying to keep the defensiveness out of her voice. "I've told you nothing but the truth, so help me, God. Dana—Mrs. Westergard—is in Biloxi. She goes there all the time. As far as I know."

"What does that mean—as far as you know? Do you think she lies about her whereabouts?"

"No, no. That's not what I meant," Grace said, feeling her cheeks begin to redden. "You're putting words in my mouth."

As a girl raised in the south, Grace knew that being rude was the eighth deadly sin, but a tiny part of her brain kept telling her *he started it.*

There was something about his nasally Boston accent and clipped manner that made her teeth grind. Her grandmother would have excused him, saying he was just a Yankee and didn't know any better. But Grace hadn't inherited her granny's compassion.

The detective cocked his head to one side and looked at her. She could feel his tiny, dark eyes boring into her skull.

Damn it. Why did she say that? As far as she knew, Dana was in Biloxi with her friend, Brittany, losing considerable amounts of Sparks's money at her second-favorite pastime, blackjack. Her favorite, Grace suspected, involved her personal trainer, Raul. But, if the woman was having an affair, it was her own business. Grace was determined to stay as far away from the whole mess as possible. She had tried hard to forget the afternoon she'd rounded a corner and found Dana in a lip-lock with Raul. She had surprised herself with her ability to move so quickly and quietly, ducking back around the corner and dashing down the hallway before the pair could come up for air.

That was over a month ago, and she almost convinced herself that she'd imagined the whole thing. She hadn't told anyone, not even her own husband, Nick. It was like a tree falling in the forest. If no one heard it, maybe it didn't really happen.

She summoned her pitiful poker face and said, "Dana gambles a little too much for my taste. That's all. But, to each his own. I guess she can afford it." She bent over Karishma, who had fallen asleep in her lap, and kissed her on top of the head. She could feel the detective's eyes on her. They were like laser beams. He went back to his notepad, scribbled a few things, then stood.

"All right, Ms. Howard, I need you to write your contact information here for me." He turned to a clean sheet and handed her the notepad and pen.

Kelly Adamson

"Name, address, phone, cell. I want to be able to get in touch with you easily, if and when I have more questions."

She stared at the desk and the lilies for a second, just beyond where he'd been sitting, then took the notepad. "Am I a suspect?"

"Ma'am, like I said before, this is not a homicide investigation."

"It will be," she said. "Sparks's computer is missing."

Chapter 3 — Nick

The rest of the morning was something of a blur.

Grace dreaded telling the fan club about Sparks even more than she dreaded telling Dana. She knew them better than she knew Dana, and liked them better, too.

She'd heard that Dana used to be a stripper, not that she held that against her. A girl's gotta eat. There was just something about her Grace didn't like. Maybe it was the whole Raul thing. All she really knew about Sparks's wife was that she looked like a Malibu Barbie, with waist-length blonde hair, visibly enhanced breasts and a golden tan she worked diligently to maintain. Her time in the tanning bed would probably leave her looking like a leather purse by the time she was fifty.

Grace's Scots-Irish ancestry made it physically impossible for her to tan. She gave up on that dream in her teens and now kept her sunblock close at hand.

A uniformed officer reported to Detective Morton that Sparks's cell phone had been stolen along with his computer. The only one he'd been able to find in the house was an antiquated flip phone, possibly dropped by the thieves. Grace was rewarded with a sour look from Morton when she told him the phone belonged to Sparks. He had an irrational distrust of new technology. The old Nokia was the first and only cell phone he'd ever owned, and he'd spent many times over its value buying new batteries for it. It had been worth it to him not to have to learn a new system.

Grace found this out when she tried to get Sparks to use a digital voice recorder for his memoirs. He told her he was under the impression she took

Kelly Adamson

dictation. She told him the only way he would find someone to take dictation would be if he turned his DeLorean into a time machine that could whisk him back to 1985.

They compromised when she found a pair of handheld microcassette recorders on eBay. Sparks trusted cassettes. Cassettes were tried and true technology, unlike computers.

Morton found Dana's number on Sparks's phone and asked if Grace wanted to call her. She almost laughed again. More inappropriate laughter. Why would she want to call a woman she barely knew to tell her that her husband had just been murdered?

While Morton did the honors, Grace took Karishma out back to the manicured lawn. It had turned out to be a sweltering, cloudless day, the aftermath of an August thunderstorm in Alabama. The only shade she could find was near the stone wall that surrounded the property. So she stood by the gate, took out her own cell phone, and called her husband, Nick.

"Stinky's Massage Parlor," Nick said. Grace started to laugh, but it came out as more of a sob. She gulped and sniffed and took a few deep breaths to get herself under control.

"You there?" he asked. "I think we've got a bad connection."

"No, I'm here. Don't hang up."

"What's wrong? Something's wrong."

She sniffed again, then it all came tumbling out. "Sparks is dead. I found him with his dog. The dog's not dead. And I think she's our dog now. She hates everyone else. The cops are here. They asked me not to leave yet. I would've called sooner, but it's been a zoo."

"Don't move. I'm on my way."

He disconnected. Grace immediately felt better. Nick was on the way. She knew it was silly to feel that way, embarrassing even. It was the 21st century, after all. But she took comfort in his presence, and she was pretty sure he felt the same about her.

At any rate, she didn't need him to be her knight in shining armor. Since their ill-fated trip to Las Vegas last fall, she'd made great strides in the self-defense arena. She never wanted to feel that helpless again. She bought a pistol—a pink and black .22—and took classes at the local indoor range. She practiced faithfully at least twice a month until she felt comfortable with it. Nick tried to get her to trade up to a 9mm, telling her she would have to be prepared to empty the little .22's clip into an attacker to get the stopping power of a single 9mm round, but she declined. She didn't want to learn another gun. She thought about Sparks and his old cell phone and smiled. She was going to miss him.

She realized her purse was still lying on the leather sofa, and she hadn't said anything to Morton about the gun being inside. Part of her hoped he'd find it. She had a permit. She wasn't doing anything illegal. And she'd like to see the look on his face.

The shade was shrinking. She moved closer to the gate to follow it, then put her back to the fence and looked out over the property. Sparks's house was in a suburb of Birmingham called Mountain Brook. The area was old, upscale and secluded, despite being only minutes from the city. It was where Birmingham's wealthiest lived. The bluebloods, the old money, heirs to coal mining fortunes or railroad magnates. The neighbors had probably all gotten the vapors when a long-haired head banger moved in. They couldn't say the property hadn't been maintained, though. Dana's third favorite pastime was spending money on the house.

An eight-foot high wrought iron fence surrounded the property for security, while an interior fence of stone enclosed the back yard and pool area for privacy. Skinny cedar trees lined the outside of the stone wall, poking their pointed heads over the top like nosy neighbors trying to see the pool. They were tall and perfectly trimmed, and more blue than green, some odd species that Grace had never seen before. They probably cost a thousand dollars apiece. The more expensive it was, the more Dana liked it.

Grace looked down at the blue-gray mix of sand and gravel under her feet. A low spot where the path went through the gate hadn't drained well after the rain last night. Now her shoes were covered in sludge.

The yard guy—or landscape architect, if you lived in Mountain Brook—had probably shown Dana two choices of gravel. One from Indiana that cost six dollars a bag and one from Italy that cost six hundred dollars a bag. It didn't matter to her if it became blue-gray mud when it rained. It was one hundred times more expensive, so it must be one hundred times better.

Grace heard the engine in Nick's truck before she could see it. The sound of the Chevy 350 rumbled through the densely wooded area like thunder. He parked outside of the perimeter gate where one of the officers met him. They talked for a minute and Grace wondered if they would let him in. Then the two men shook hands and strode up the front lawn toward her. She scooped up Karishma and hurried to meet them.

"How's your sister?" she heard the officer ask Nick. He was young, with a white-blond crew cut and a baby face, but biceps that made his short sleeves bunch up a little.

"Who are you?" Detective Morton stood on the veranda at the front of the house, his hands on his hips, his stance wide, like a man about to fight a duel at high noon.

"I'm Nick Howard. I'm Grace's husband."

"Have you ever been in this house before?"

"No."

"Good. Then you can stay out here with Officer Shipps. I don't need another set of footprints contaminating my crime scene. And you," he pointed at the baby-faced officer, "don't let anyone else through that gate without my say so. You understand me?"

"Yes, sir."

Morton motioned for Grace to follow him. "Ms. Howard, I need you back in here for a minute."

Nick leaned close and kissed Grace on the cheek. "He needs a laxative," he whispered. Karishma growled at him. Nick looked from the dog to Grace. "Don't tell me," he said.

"She's had a rough night. She's usually quite friendly." Only part of that was a lie.

Grace walked up the wide tile steps past Morton. "Oh, no," he said. "You're not bringing that mutt in here."

"She was inside when I got here," Grace said, "lying on Sparks. So any contamination she was going to do has already been done. Besides, you should be nice to her; she's your only witness so far."

They stopped in front of the desk, an immense piece of furniture Sparks designed himself and had commissioned for this room. Walnut, she thought he said, with gargoyles holding up each corner and a row of skulls grinning out from under the top. The carving was done by a man who called himself a whittler and lived so far back in the hills of Tennessee that the blacktop ended miles before his house. Sparks was so excited about the desk that he had gone personally to pick it up. His eyes lit up when he told her the story of getting the U-Haul stuck three times on the way to the man's house. When he finally arrived, the old man greeted Sparks with a shotgun and swore he had never seen hair that long that wasn't on a woman. He held the gun the whole time, even after he was paid, even while helping load the desk on the truck. Sparks loved telling that story and he loved that desk.

Grace could see into the kitchen, where Sparks still lay on his back. She wondered how much longer they were going to leave him there. A

Kelly Adamson

man knelt beside him taking pictures with an expensive-looking camera, while a woman dusted the granite countertop for fingerprints.

"I'd like you to take another look around and see if you notice anything else missing," Morton said. "Or anything out of the ordinary."

"Besides the dead man?"

Morton ignored her.

She looked around, really tried to concentrate, but it wasn't as if it were her house and her belongings. She had no idea what all he had. She looked in the music room. None of the guitar stands were empty. She looked in the garage. All the cars were there. There was a bedroom she had never been in. It was all dark wood and masculine colors. A pair of jeans and a faded Rolling Stones tee shirt lay discarded in a heap on the floor. Sparks's favorite tee-shirt. He wore it at least twice a week.

The nightstand held a paperback book about MTV in its heyday. Sparks and his band were probably in it. A pair of reading glasses lay unfolded on top of the book. Grace wondered if anyone had ever seen Sparks in his reading glasses. Now no one ever would.

When they walked through the marble bathroom, she saw the gray drawstring bag that contained the mini cassette recorder Sparks had been using. It wasn't evidence, but Morton wouldn't have let her take it. So she didn't ask. When the detective kept walking, she picked up the bag and tucked it under her arm, behind Karishma.

She had never been in the main part of the house and told them so. There was no point in her looking there. They would have to wait for Dana for that. She and her friend were on their way now, driving back from Biloxi and due to arrive before dark.

"Can I go now?"

"One more thing," said Morton, leafing through his notepad. "Did the victim often drink alone?

She cringed again, but guessed "the victim" was a step up from "the body."

"Sparks didn't drink. Not for several years now."

"Well, he did last night. There was a bottle and an empty shot glass on the bar."

Grace shook her head. "No way. Maybe it belonged to whoever killed him. Dust it for prints."

Morton snorted. "Don't you think the killer would have taken the shot glass with him if it had his prints on it?"

Grace ignored his patronizing grin and kept walking, stopping in front of the walnut desk. She could see the bar through the open doorway. "I don't see a bottle. Where is it?

Morton didn't answer.

"Sparks was a recovering alcoholic," she said. "He never allowed liquor in the house. Where's the bottle?"

Morton cleared his throat. "We're dusting it for fingerprints. And yes, you can go now. Just don't leave town."

Kelly Adamson

Chapter 4 — BJ

Nick's truck idled loudly as they waited in the drive-through at Jack's Hamburgers. Nick wasn't about to miss lunch just because of one little murder. Grace often teased him that he was like Jughead from the old Archie comics. If he didn't eat every few hours, he would dry up and blow away. He was blessed with a metabolism that allowed him to eat whatever he wanted and never gain weight. Grace called it a blessing. At six feet tall and 150 pounds, with a constant need for food, Nick called it a curse.

He pulled the bags in through the window and put them on the bench seat beside him. The smell immediately roused Karishma, her little nose working double time as she edged toward the bags.

Grace stretched her arms and tried to get a little blood flowing in them again. She'd held Karishma for the past two hours and was starting to regret fattening her up on turkey jerky.

Nick ate fries from the bag as he drove through the lot. They passed two police cars parked together. It made Grace think back to the flurry of blue uniforms that morning. She didn't know Mountain Brook had that many officers. Seven patrol cars were still at Sparks's house when they left. She wondered how many people were stealing cars or robbing jewelry stores in other parts of town. If they weren't, they were missing a great opportunity. There was certainly no one left to stop them.

"Where do you know that cop from?" she asked. "The one who let you in."

"Shipps? Our sisters were best friends in high school. Never saw one without the other."

"He seemed quite fond of Leah."

"Yeah, he always had a thing for her, but he was three or four years younger and she thought of him as a kid. That doesn't sound like a big difference now, but when you're fourteen and the girl you're hot for is seventeen, you're out of luck."

"I suppose." Grace tore a fry in half and blew on it, trying to cool it off for Karishma. "It's like the Stones song. You can't always get what you want."

"Am I supposed to be offended by that?"

"I'm not talking about me, silly. I'm talking about Shipps. Okay, that just made me think of BJ and the rest of the Sparklers." She leaned her head against the window of the truck. "Ugh. I'm dreading calling her. I really don't want to be the bearer of this bad news."

"Can't you let the cops do it?"

"No. I owe it to her to tell her personally. She's a nice woman and she's been nothing but helpful to me. And she's *so* crazy about him. I mean, unnaturally so. I don't want her to find out on the six o'clock news. That would just devastate her."

Their house seemed quieter than usual when they walked in. Grace turned a light on in every room, despite the fact that it wouldn't be dark outside for another four hours.

She settled Karishma on the couch with the gray drawstring bag full of tapes. It must have smelled like Sparks and the dog was fine as long as her furry little head was resting on it. When Grace tried to move it, Karishma whined and yipped in a pitch that made Nick cover his ears. Grace put the bag back. It was a small price to pay.

She put off the phone call until they finished eating. Or more precisely, until she finished watching Nick eat. Her appetite eluded her at the moment. She managed to choke down two fries and a few sips of sweet tea. But even that was a struggle.

Kelly Adamson

Nick finally said, "Aren't you supposed to be calling somebody?"

"I put my phone on the charger."

He took his out and slid it across the table. "Use mine."

"I don't know the number."

Nick walked to the kitchen, where her phone was charging. When he returned, he picked up Grace's limp right hand from her lap and placed her phone in it. Then he picked up her other hand and put his phone in it. She stuck out her tongue at him, and he kissed her on the top of her head. Then he started clearing the table.

Grace groaned. No excuses.

BJ was the only member of the founding Sparklers who lived in the Birmingham area. She was forty-eight years old and divorced, worked as a cashier in a local pharmacy and lived in a walk-up apartment on Southside with a cat named Sparks. The first time she ever saw the real Sparks in concert was on 1987's "Agitator" tour. It was love at first sight. When Sparks moved back to Birmingham four years ago, she couldn't believe her good fortune. As the president of his fan club, she had been in contact with him by e-mail for some time, but now their close proximity allowed her to meet him in person on at least two occasions. Life was great. Grace learned all this in the first five minutes of their first conversation. BJ was a talker.

Grace looked up the number in her dying phone and dialed it in Nick's. She padded barefoot to the back door. She would sit on the deck and listen to the birds as she broke the bad news. The thermometer by the door read ninety-four. She changed her mind, leaned her head against the sliding glass doors, and opted for air conditioning.

Three rings. She watched two squirrels chasing each other around the trunk of an oak tree.

Four rings. She watched her dog, Ricky, do his best to climb the tree, barking in a ferocity reserved exclusively for squirrels.

Five rings. She really needed to clean the glass on these doors.

Six rings. Her spirits rose a little, thinking maybe BJ wasn't home. Then they fell when she remembered she couldn't leave this news as a message.

"Hello." BJ's voice was a little breathless, as if she had run to catch the phone.

"Oh, hi. This is Grace Howard. I hope I'm not disturbing you." Her chipper tone sounded hollow to her own ears.

"What a nice surprise, Grace. No worries. I was just coming back in. I've been out putting flyers up in the neighborhood. My cat got out a few days ago—I still don't know how—and I haven't seen him since." Her words tumbled over one another like water rushing over Noccalula Falls. "What can I do for you?"

Grace closed her eyes. She felt like she was about to swat a butterfly. "Maybe you'd better sit down, BJ."

She told her everything. How she let herself in. How she found Sparks and how still he was. How she called the police and how the dog tried to bite everyone. She was talking as fast and free-flowing as BJ, but it felt good, cathartic, to put it all into words.

When she finished, there was silence on the other end of the line.

"BJ, are you still there?"

"Are you playing a trick on me? Is this some kind of sick joke?"

"Huh?"

"There have been death rumors before about him, you know. Back in '94, they said he drowned in a hotel pool in Japan. And in '97 it was a helicopter crash in New Zealand. It's not a joke, is it? Because it wasn't funny then and it isn't funny now."

Kelly Adamson

Grace spared a moment to be offended that this woman would think she would lie about something so serious, but in truth, she was just relieved that BJ wasn't crying. Grace was very uncomfortable around crying people.

"I'm sorry, BJ, but it's true. I saw him with my own two eyes."

More silence.

"They don't know what happened yet. A heart attack, most likely. Hard to believe, considering the shape he was in." Grace couldn't help picturing a flash of him standing naked and glorious in his tub the week before. "But stranger things have happened, I guess."

Grace could hear the sniffling now, the beginning of a real teeth gnasher coming on. She just wanted to get off the phone. "Well, I should go now. Will you be okay?" She crossed her fingers.

"Yeah, I'll be fine. I'll call Cassie and Vicki." Her voice squeaked with the strain of holding back the tears. "I just can't believe it. Everything was going so well for him. And he was so looking forward to working on his memoirs. We did a whole piece about it on the website. His fans were so excited." Her voice was deteriorating fast.

"Well, I've got to go," Grace said again, cursing herself for being a chicken. Then she stopped. "Hey, BJ, you probably know more about Sparks than just about anyone. Do you think he backslid on occasion, you know, took a drink now and then when no one was looking?"

BJ sniffed and gulped and sounded indignant. "Absolutely not. Sparks was proud of his sobriety. He thought of it as a tangible thing, his red badge of courage. He said in an interview one time that it was the hardest thing he ever did, getting sober and staying sober, but it was the thing he was the most proud of."

"You don't think he ever cheated?"

"On his wife, yes. On his taxes, maybe. On his sobriety, no."

With that dreaded task over with, Grace found a leash and took Karishma out into the front yard. She didn't want to risk a dog fight by letting her in the back yard with her own brood, Lucy, Ricky and Ernie. They would have to sleep outside tonight. She felt a little guilty about that, bringing a mean little stranger into their home and then making them sleep outside because of her.

She saw Nick peeking through the front window. He was worried about her, but she was fine. She waved and tried to smile.

She took Karishma back inside and fed her, while Nick rounded up a dog bed for her to sleep in. Ernie would have a field day smelling it the next time he was in. She added the gray drawstring bag that smelled like Sparks, and Karishma was content.

Then, even though it wasn't dark yet, Grace showered and crawled into bed, exhausted. Nick stood in the doorway, watching her like she was a pot about to boil. "I'm going to take a shower. Are you going to be all right till I get out?"

"I'm fine. Quit worrying about me." She tried for a lighthearted laugh, but it fell flat. "Really. Go take a shower. I appreciate your concern, but I'm fine. I promise."

She reached for the remote and turned on the TV. Her pacifier. But it let her down. One hundred and fifty channels and nothing on. A horror movie. A tear jerker. A commercial for burial insurance. Someone running for senate in an "I approved this ad" commercial. He looked like a crook to her. Shifty eyes.

She buried her face in her pillow and sobbed.

She sobbed until her pillow was wet and she had a raging headache. She sobbed until Nick was finished with his shower. He didn't say a word, just sat down on the bed beside her and pulled her into his arms.

When she finally dried her eyes, it was dark outside. Nick went down the hall to turn off all the lights she had turned on earlier. He brought her a box of tissues and some naproxen for her head. His cell phone rang as he climbed into bed.

"It says it's Shipps. I don't remember giving him my number."

"He's a cop. I'm sure he can get a phone number if he wants it."

He leaned back on the pillows and put the phone up to his ear. "Hey, man, what's up?"

Grace could only hear Nick's side of the conversation and just a mumble of noise that was Shipps.

"Oh, really? Already? Well, good. Whose are they?"

Nick sat up straight. "Who? Are you sure there's no mistake? Okay, thanks for letting us know."

He hung up and looked at Grace.

"What?"

"They got the fingerprints from the bottle at Sparks's house. There was only one set of prints on there. Only one person had touched the bottle."

"Okay. Who?"

"Bonnie Jo Knox."

BJ.

Chapter 5 — Sparklers

Grace slept very little that night, alternating between tossing and turning and staring at the darkened ceiling. As the sun came up, she listened to Nick's slow and steady breathing, annoyed that he could sleep so peacefully, annoyed that he had refused to call Shipps back and tell him there had been some mistake about BJ.

But of course, Nick was right. Opinions were not admissible in court. Fingerprints were. But that didn't make her any less annoyed.

She slipped out of bed and headed down the hall to make coffee, with a pit stop by the bathroom. Her reflection in the medicine cabinet mirror was ghastly. The dark circles under her eyes would be hard to hide even with makeup, which she seldom wore.

She peeked around the corner at Karishma while the coffee brewed. The dog was still asleep in her bed. Poor thing. She was exhausted. Her vigil with Sparks had really taken its toll. She might not have understood the concept of death, but she definitely knew something was wrong.

Grace filled the largest coffee cup she owned and headed for the deck. It was still early and only seventy-six degrees. She ignored her cell phone, still on the charger, and picked up her tablet instead. She wasn't ready for phone messages just yet.

Their dogs were delighted to see her. After much petting and ear scratching, Lucy and Ricky went back to running up and down the fence with the neighbor's dog, while Ernie stretched out in the early morning sun on the steps.

Kelly Adamson

Grace sat sideways in the swing, pulled her feet up and then stretched the nightshirt over her knees. She listened to the birds for a few minutes while she drank her coffee. Then she powered up her tablet and pulled up the website for the Sparklers.

The home page was a black-and-white photo taken during the 1992 "Accelerator" tour. Sparks was caught in action on stage, head thrown back, eyes closed, microphone in hand, wearing only black leather pants and a matching vest. He had a bulky ring on every finger. One was a skull just like the ones ringing the walnut desk in his office. His design. Made just for him by some master jeweler, no doubt. The world had been his oyster. And he was surrounded by pearls.

There was nothing on the home page about his death. BJ probably didn't have time to make any changes before the police came knocking on her door. Grace shook that image out of her head and made herself concentrate on the lead article. The headline read, *"The Secret Keeper* speaks. Will Sparks's memoirs be the juicy tell-all we've all been waiting for?"

The Secret Keeper was the name of Sparks's 1994 live double album, the last one released on vinyl. During her second week on the job, when Sparks personally performed all the band's songs for her, he told her that album was named for him.

It was an accepted fact that, while his band mates and hangers-on during the '80s and '90s stayed stoned to a man—cocaine, acid, heroin, you name it—Sparks's drug of choice was Tennessee whiskey. His friends were drug addicts, he explained, whereas he was a functioning alcoholic. He told her that, once he got to that point, he drank to maintain, not to get drunk. Getting drunk was an effort for someone like him. He may have looked wasted, understandably, since he always had a bottle in his hand, but getting knee-walking required too much work by then. Most of the time, he simply drank to keep the pink elephants at bay.

Because of this, his memory of all the stupid things everyone did was actually quite good. In a time before Google glasses and YouTube, even before cell phone video cameras, Sparks Westergard remembered all the good stories.

Grace made a face at the screen. This would have been a great book. And it would have been the start of something wonderful for her. She could have been the memoir queen, sought after by every celeb with a juicy story or two to tell. She could have been rich. Or even better, she could have been famous.

She clicked on "Discography" and looked at *The Secret Keeper* album. On the cover was a photo of Sparks in a dark alleyway, bathed in blue light, his finger to his pursed lips. The back was the same scene, but photographed from the rear, a view of Sparks's back with the fingers of his left hand crossed behind him. Facing him, unseen on the front cover, was a crowd of people stretching back into the darkness of the alleyway. Front and center was a buxom, fresh-faced girl in pigtails and denim, a battered suitcase in one hand. Track one of the album was called *Iowa Farm Girls*. Other people portraying songs crowded behind her in the narrow space. A Formula One racecar driver symbolized *Faster* and a man covered in tattoos was *Imprint*. Beside him was a guy dressed in a trench coat, his bare legs giving you the idea that was all he was wearing. He grinned lasciviously at the girl in pigtails, his hands holding his coat like he was getting ready to flash her. His hair was long and stringy and his skin looked sweaty. He was the *Creep* from track six.

Grace had forgotten how fun this album cover was. Every song had a representative. Albums were hard to find in 1994, with CDs already ruling the market. But this one was art. It was interactive and fun and challenging. She remembered what BJ said about the death rumors in '94. Part of that was thanks to this album. Just like *Abbey Road* had done for Paul McCartney, *The Secret Keeper* provided fans with plenty of clues that there was some terrible conspiracy going on and their beloved blond idol had gone to rock and roll heaven.

She couldn't remember them all, but knew for sure that the Japanese woman in a bikini, still wet from the pool, was supposed to be a sure sign that Sparks drowned in a swanky Tokyo hotel. People see what they want to see.

A few minutes later, Nick joined Grace on the swing with his own cup of coffee. He peeked at the tablet screen she had propped on her knees.

"BJ's website?"

"Yeah. Vicki and Cassie contribute, too, but BJ does ninety percent of it. It's a labor of love for her."

He watched as she clicked through the tabs: *Biography, Discography, News,* and *Photo Archives.*

The photo archives section was huge, hundreds upon hundreds of photos, most of them divided into folders with catchy names that corresponded to albums or tours. The first one was called, "In the Beginning." She opened it and was immediately sorry. Grinning up at her was a blond-haired boy strumming a battered guitar that was almost as big as he was. "Sparks at age five," the caption read. "A star is born." He wore red-white-and-blue cowboy boots and a tee shirt with Rocky and Bullwinkle on it. He was missing a tooth. His whole life was ahead of him.

She flipped the cover of the tablet closed.

Without looking at Nick, she said, "BJ could have given him the bottle as a gift."

Nick didn't answer, just continued to sip his coffee.

"Just because her fingerprints were on it, that doesn't mean anything," she said. "Just because he died of a heart attack while he was drinking from a bottle she gave him, doesn't mean she did anything wrong. It's not a crime to give someone a gift. It could have been just a coincidence."

Nick said nothing, but turned to her with his eyebrows raised and his head tilted to one side.

"Don't look at me with that tone of voice," she said.

"Grace," he began.

"Don't. I don't want to hear it. I know what you're going to say. You're going to say, 'If he was by himself, his fingerprints would have been on the bottle. And if BJ was there with him, why didn't she tell me so on the phone. And if he had a heart attack while she was there, why didn't she call 911.' Well, I don't know the answer to all that, but I know BJ would never have given Sparks alcohol. She loved him. What could possibly be her motive?"

"I don't know," Nick mumbled into his cup. "Crazy people do crazy things."

"BJ is not crazy!"

"How do you know that? Sure, you e-mail back and forth. You've talked to her on the phone. But what do you really know about her? She's a middle-aged woman with a cat and a part-time job in a drugstore. She probably owns every album Sparks ever sang a note on. She probably owns a lock of his hair and sleeps with a Sparks doll, if there is such a thing. Hell, maybe she made her own—a giant ragdoll with long, yellow yarn hair and leather pants."

"Stop talking about her like that. You don't know her."

"Neither do you, Grace. Not really. That's my point. You're too trusting."

She picked up her tablet and her empty cup and went back inside.

"Ah, don't be mad at me," he called after her. "I'm just trying to look out for you."

His cell phone started ringing as she stomped back to the kitchen. Good, maybe he would stop and talk to whoever it was instead of following her inside. She needed some alone time. She knew he was right—she didn't know

BJ, not really. One thing she did know was that she had an obsessive personality, at least where Sparks was concerned. She probably did have a lock of his hair and God knew what else, and that wasn't exactly a glowing recommendation of someone's mental state.

Grace herself had always been a little star-struck. She had become friends with movie star Killian Ross last fall in Las Vegas. Of course, she had almost gotten him killed as well, but that was another story. The point was that she understood the difference between appreciation and obsession.

The glass door slid open and closed. Nick walked up close behind her, only inches away. She knew he was going to put his arms around her, but he didn't.

"Truce?"

She nodded.

"I don't want to argue. You look so sad. Let's get out of here. Let's turn off our cell phones and go do something. Catch a matinee or go to the zoo or whatever you want. Anything just to take our minds off this for a while."

They were standing at the gates of the zoo when it opened. At lunchtime, they toyed with driving across to English Village and eating in one of the high-end cafes with white tablecloths, but were both more at home with corndogs and chicken fingers, so they ate at the zoo, overlooking the elephants. They didn't mention Sparks or BJ all day.

It was almost six by the time they got home that evening. Karishma was happy to see Grace, although she hadn't warmed up to Nick yet. Grace took her out and let her walk around the front yard, not trusting her off the leash.

When they went back in a few minutes later, Nick met her at the door with his cell phone in his hand. He'd been checking the messages that had come in while it was turned off. His face seemed a little whiter than usual. He motioned for her to sit down.

"What is it?"

"I had a message from Shipps. He said they rushed the autopsy considering the circumstances. He said Sparks died of a heart attack, brought on by something called Digoxin. They found it in the bottle, enough to kill a race horse, according to Shipps. Sparks was poisoned." Nick paused and cleared his throat. "They've arrested BJ."

Chapter 6 — Iowa Farm Girls

"I love those California girls,
With their skin all nice and tan.
Those New York City girls
All say 'Catch me if you can!'

But the prettiest girls
in the whole round world
Are those heartland hotties,
Those Iowa farm girls."

—Iowa Farm Girls (1994)

To his credit, Nick didn't say, "I told you so." He didn't say anything at all. He looked almost embarrassed, like he was sorry he was right.

Hands shaking, Grace busied herself with cleaning the kitchen. She fumbled one of the coffee cups. It bounced, surprisingly unbroken, off the tile floor, but the remnants of the cold coffee splashed all the way to the far wall.

"I'll get it," Nick said. "Go sit down. Take a deep breath." He took the other cup from her hand and guided her toward the living room.

She nodded, feeling a little numb. She sat on the couch and Karishma jumped in her lap. One hand scratched the dog's head and the other reached for the TV remote without even thinking. Autopilot. Habit.

The somber news anchor's voice said, "…found dead in his home in Mountain Brook." Her head snapped up in time to see a photo of Sparks, smiling and holding an award. It looked like a Grammy, although she didn't remember him winning one. She would ask BJ. BJ would know. Her throat constricted when she realized she might never get to talk to BJ again, not about carefree things like Grammy awards.

The picture of Sparks became a little blurry, but she could still hear the anchor. Thankfully, he didn't say anything about the cause of death, but instead made a big deal about Sparks being a native of the Birmingham area and a graduate of Homewood High School. A local boy made good. The press is much kinder to the newly dead. Sparks would have gotten a kick out of it.

The anchor ended by saying that Sparks was survived by his wife, Dana.

Grace felt a little sorry for Dana. She should call her. After all, Grace was the one who found Sparks. Surely Dana would have some questions.

She got up slowly, feeling much older than her thirty-four years. Nick was mopping when she passed the kitchen door on the way to get her cell phone from her purse. She wanted to say something nice to him, but couldn't. She was still a little hurt about what he said and more hurt that he was right. That part wasn't his fault, but she only grabbed her purse and returned to the couch.

The crinkling sound of the package of turkey jerky in Grace's purse made Karishma's ears perk up. She gave the dog a bite while her phone powered up.

Only one message. Not bad. There would be more now that the news was out.

She half expected the message to be from BJ. Instead, the recorded voice was unfamiliar.

"Hello, Grace. This is Vicki Deason. I know we've never formally met, but BJ speaks of you often and fondly. Any friend of hers is a friend of mine. You may or may not know that BJ has been arrested, charged with the murder of Sparks Westergard. Of course, that is utterly ludicrous, and I plan to do everything in my power to correct this injustice immediately."

Grace didn't know a lot about BJ, but it was clear she knew even less about her fellow Sparklers, Cassie Wynn and Vicki Deason. Vicki explained that she was a criminal attorney at a medium-sized firm in Austin, Texas. She was in the middle of an important case at the moment or she would have dropped everything when her old pal BJ reached out with her one phone call. She was, however, calling in a favor from an old law school buddy who practiced in Birmingham. Mild-mannered BJ was lawyering up, whether she knew it or not.

The phone rang while Grace was still holding it. An unknown number. Any other time, she would have ignored it, but something made her answer.

"Oh, Grace, I'm so glad I got you." The voice belonged to Dana Westergard. "The police took Sparks's phone so at first I wondered how I would find your number, but then I remembered his address book. Sweet, old-fashioned coot, I mean, who in the world keeps an address book anymore?" She laughed, but it sounded like she was trying very hard not to cry. "I couldn't remember your last name, but it didn't matter because he had you listed under "G" for Grace. Silly boy. Oh, Grace, I'm going to miss him." Her voice cracked and trembled, but she recovered herself with a couple of deep breaths. "I swear I didn't call to cry on your shoulder. I'm so sorry. It's just that the cops said you found him and I just…I don't know…I guess I just wanted to hear the story from you. Would you tell me?"

Grace went through it all again, a story she'd told five times now. Dana was sniffing, trying to maintain control of herself and Grace couldn't help but feel a little newly forged warmth toward her. They had never really had a conversation before. She had the feeling Dana thought of her as she would the gardener or the maid. She wasn't rude, but she wasn't going to take Grace shoe shopping, either. Still, Dana deserved a little respect for not acting like the pampered diva she had always imagined her to be.

"So, you have Karishma?" Dana asked after a pause.

"Yes. I'm sorry. I just hated to leave her there with all the cops coming in and out. She didn't want them touching Sparks and didn't want them touching her. She bit one of them before I could stop her. She just looked so miserable. You know how she is."

"Yes, I definitely know how she is."

"I'll bring her back, of course. Right now, if you like. I can be there in twenty minutes."

"Oh, God, no." Dana laughed again, another uncomfortable cross between laughing and crying. "She's an adorable little dog, but she was Sparks's dog, through and through. She's always hated me. I've had my ankles nipped by that crazy mop more times than I care to remember. Please, give her away if you can find someone who can handle her, or keep her yourself. But, whatever you do, don't bring her back here."

Grace promised to take care of Karishma and Dana thanked her, then thanked her for what she'd done for Sparks.

"To be honest, Dana, I really hadn't done anything yet. He just gave me the first batch of tapes the other day. I'd barely touched them."

"Oh, you had done more for him than you know. This book was giving him a new purpose. He'd been so bored lately, really feeling his age since he turned fifty. Since he started working with you, he had his old glow back, his old spark, if you will." She laughed sadly at her pun.

"I appreciate you telling me that," Grace said. "I enjoyed my time with him, too. You've got to know I've been a fan since I was a kid. And I hate that I won't ever get to finish the book. I was sure looking forward to it."

"Oh, but you have to finish it," Dana said. "That's one of the reasons I called. Sparks would never forgive me if I didn't see the book finished. I talked to him on the phone Saturday night and he'd already filled up all the tapes you gave him and had to go out and buy more. Said he ended up going to the thrift store before he found any. No stores sell tapes anymore. I had to poke a little fun at him for that.

"Anyway, I don't know how many that makes, but it should be a good start. And you can have access to any of his stuff over here. You know he had a whole room full of memorabilia. Trunks of stuff. I don't think he ever threw anything away. Like a hoarder. You can look through it all and see if it helps, you know, inspire you."

Grace took a deep breath and tried to sound respectful and dignified when she responded. The book was going to happen after all. "That's very kind of you, Dana. I'd be honored."

That settled, Dana presented the other reason she had called. She wanted Grace to help plan Sparks's wake. Not only had Grace never planned a wake, but she'd never even attended a wake. Still, she would have said yes to almost anything after Dana's generous offer. They agreed to start work at nine the next morning, and after they hung up, Grace did what she always did when she needed to learn about something quickly. She Googled it.

A modern wake wasn't that far removed from a viewing at a funeral home. The main difference was that a wake was generally held at the house of the deceased. What used to mean guarding the dead had evolved into a party to celebrate their life. Just what Sparks would have wanted.

Early the next morning, Grace swung by Daylight Donuts and picked up three apple fritters. Since working for Sparks, it had become her Wednesday routine and was turning out to be a hard habit to break. Even though Sparks wouldn't be waiting for his, strong black coffee in hand, she knew she wouldn't be eating alone.

The third party in their "Fritter-Fest" was Cindy, a middle-aged, country-music-loving tornado of cleanliness who had worked for Sparks since long before he met Dana. She only came in twice a week now, and they spent at least half an hour of each visit having a coffee break together. When she first started working for Sparks, Cindy was with a maid service in L.A., and none of the other maids could put up with his wild ways. It was like cleaning up after a frat party that never ended. One morning, one of the guests, who happened to be the drummer for Hard Target, got handsy with Cindy. She threw him in the pool. Sparks was delighted and hired her away from the maid service on the spot. That was sixteen years ago.

Mississippi-born and raised, Cindy had followed her husband to the west coast to convert the heathens in the mid-eighties. But when Sparks decided to move back to Alabama permanently, he didn't want to leave without Cindy. When he offered to pay her moving expenses, she jumped at the chance to move closer to home. Her husband was fine with that, as there were plenty of heathens in Birmingham to convert, after all.

Grace took the fritters to the front door of Sparks's house. The thought of using her usual entrance made a lump form in her stomach. Cindy opened the door and immediately turned away, bringing a wad of tissues up to her face to hide her red nose and eyes.

"Aw, damn it," she growled. "It's just you."

"I'm happy to see you, too," Grace said.

"It's not that. I just thought you might be that reporter who's been calling all morning. He's driving me crazy. I finally took the phone off the hook. I thought he might have shown up in person and I was looking forward to kicking his ass back down the steps."

"What reporter?"

"He said he was from one of them rock magazines. I don't remember the name. You know me, I'm a country girl. If it ain't got Toby Keith or Rooster Hathcock on it, I don't care about it."

Grace grinned at the thought of Rooster Hathcock. She'd met the country music superstar in Las Vegas last fall, where he'd helped her out of a jam with the Russian mob.

Rooster owned a ranch in Mississippi where he was building an Egyptian-style pyramid. He was also an unlikely friend of Sparks Westergard and the reason Grace got this job. She hoped he would come to the wake.

Sparks and Cindy usually discussed religion or cars while the three of them ate their fritters and drank their coffee poolside. Cindy's husband was a mechanic who built engines for race cars. He was also a Baptist preacher. Cindy could quote the Old Testament and was pretty quick off the line in a drag car.

Grace mostly just listened and watched the birds while she ate. But today, the two women steered clear of the pool, gravitating without discussion to the patio off the main kitchen.

Cindy chose a chair in the sun while Grace took one in the shade of the brightly colored umbrella that covered the table. The older woman kicked off her Crocs and wriggled her toes.

"My dogs are sure barking. Guess they needed a rest. I've been mopping up that danged blue gravel dust for the last two hours. All those people in and out the other day, and I'll bet not a one of them wiped their feet. They act like they was raised in a barn." She shook her head and scowled, like the real tragedy here was the dirty floor. But Grace could see her puffy, red-rimmed eyes and knew better.

They ate in silence for a few minutes, until Cindy said, "Shame about that girl from the fan club. How does that old song go?" She sang, a little off-key, "You always hurt the one you love."

"I have a hard time believing she did it," Grace said. "She seemed so nice."

"Yeah, well, they all seem nice. I've been with Sparks a long time and I've seen some seemingly nice people do some pretty crazy things. Once, not long after I started, a girl from New York mailed herself to him, next day air. No telling how much that cost. She probably put it on her daddy's credit card anyway. She sure was surprised when I opened the crate instead of Sparks. There she was in her little black nightie." Cindy laughed so hard at the memory that she had to wipe her eyes again.

When she recovered, Grace pushed the doughnut bag across the table. "You know, I ordered three out of habit this morning and I think, well, I think Sparks would want you to have his fritter."

Cindy's face clouded again as she reached for the bag. "He would. I know he would." She nodded solemnly, took a bite, and closed her eyes, enjoying the sugar and grease as much as humanly possible.

"That reminds me," she said with a mouthful, "I found something he'd want you to have. Hang on a minute." She hopped up and hurried inside, barefoot and carrying the fritter. She returned in a minute with a plastic Publix bag. She held it out to Grace with a grin. "It was under his bed," Cindy said. "Guess nobody ever looks there but me."

Inside the bag were twenty-four microcassettes, all labeled in Sparks's hand, all recorded in Sparks's voice. "You better get busy."

Chapter 7 — The Vault

I watch you leaving,

A silhouette in the morning light.

I blow a kiss and you wave goodbye.

I say I'll call and you say you'll write.

But, I really want to say,

(Hold me) when the night is dark.

(Hold me) You'll always have my heart.

(Hold me) when the cold winds blow.

(Hold me) Never let me go.

—Hold Me (1989)

Dana stepped out onto the patio behind Cindy. She was dressed in pink sleep shorts and a tank top with Hello Kitty on the front. Her long hair tousled from sleep, she stretched her arms above her head and yawned. A tall, blonde cat.

Whatever warm feelings of sisterhood Grace felt the day before began to cool in that instant. She assumed that most new widows might have a tough time in an empty bed for a while, but not Sleeping Beauty here. She looked for all the world like she was waking from the most restful sleep of her life.

Cindy disappeared back into the house without a word. Dana sure knew how to clear a room. Or a patio, in this case.

Grace reached for the empty Daylight Donuts bag, trying to clear it away before Dana and her washboard abs had a chance to give it a contemptuous look. Dana's breakfast probably consisted of organic celery juice and half an almond. She stuffed the trash in her purse and pulled out a notebook and a pencil.

Dana appeared startled by the sound and turned to focus on her guest. "Oh, Grace, I didn't see you there. My, you're certainly the early bird. As for me, I just can't function without my beauty sleep."

Grace plastered on a smile and tried to focus on the room full of memorabilia Dana was going to allow her access to.

"Morning, Dana. Hope I didn't disturb you."

Dana didn't reply, but stepped to the center of the deck and began a series of stretches and poses that lasted for at least ten minutes. It looked like a cross between yoga and tai chi, but since Grace was far from an expert on either, she really had no idea. Maybe it was something Dana's personal trainer, Raul, made up just for her. Something to keep her limber when they weren't doing their own little private workout.

Regardless, Grace didn't feel like being the audience for the adult Hello Kitty show. She turned her attention to her notebook, where she scribbled things like, "Invitations to wake—how? E-mail? Food? Entertainment?" She scratched out the last word. It seemed irreverent. It was clear she didn't know what she was doing. She put down the pencil and turned her chair so her view was of the yard instead of Dana.

Wide stone steps descended on either side of the patio, creating a sheltered, sunny semi-circle that Sparks had claimed as his own. Dana had a blueprint for the rest of the landscaping, but this thirty-foot radius was off limits to her and her gardeners. Inside it, Sparks had a concrete birdbath, two different kinds of feeders, a red birdhouse with "See Rock City" painted on the roof, and one chaise longue with a pattern of white skulls woven into the black fabric. Plants of all kinds grew in the small space, things that were special to

Kelly Adamson

Sparks. A peach-colored Freddy Mercury rose was in full bloom, along with a tiger lily given to Sparks by Hard Target's front man, James "Tiger" Scott.

Tiny yellow butterflies fluttered around a wall of Mexican petunias that nearly surrounded the area. "Yellow Sulfurs," Sparks said they were called. An ugly name for such pretty, little creatures.

Dana finished up her routine and brought the attention back around to her. "Thanks for letting me get that out of the way, Gracie. I always feel so much better if I start the day out right."

Grace knew then that she must've seen the doughnut bag after all. She forced another smile and said, "It's Grace, not Gracie."

"What?"

"My name. It's just Grace."

Dana stuck out her bottom lip in an exaggerated pout. "Oh, what a shame. I do so like the name Gracie."

Grace stood and gathered her things before her hostess could say another word. If the woman had the nerve to ask if she could call her Gracie, she was going to scream. Dana Westergard was used to getting what she wanted. Maybe "Hello Kitty" really meant "Spoiled Brat" in Japanese.

"It's hot as Hades out here and it's only nine o'clock," Grace said. "I hope you don't mind if we work inside."

At the mention of the word "work," Dana made another face, but seemed willing enough to lead the way back into the air-conditioned house. As they walked, she chattered on about how much more energy she had since she started working out with a personal trainer.

Grace gritted her teeth and tried to tune the woman out, focusing instead on the arrangements of fresh flowers that seemed to cover every flat surface. Flowers sent to cheer the grieving widow, no doubt. They passed the door to the back kitchen. Grace tried to keep her eyes down, but found herself looking anyway. The light reflected off the pool outside still danced on the wall behind the bar, just as it had on Monday morning. In her mind, Grace could still see "the body" lying there. Sparks, her friend, who was always in motion, now way too still.

The flowers sent by the Sparklers were still there on the walnut desk in Sparks's office, in full bloom now. Flowers of congratulations, not condolence like the others in the house.

In the center of the desk was a book covered in olive drab fabric. The spine was cracked and broken and the whole thing was held together by two rubber bands. Dana picked up the book with both hands like the fragile thing it was and held it out to Grace.

"I can't tell you how happy I am, how relieved, that you agreed to help with the wake," Dana said. "I'm no good at that sort of thing, no good at all."

Grace looked down at the book she held. Across the lower half of the cover, written in a careful, juvenile hand, it read, "Property of Sparks Westergard." The blue ink was faded, smeared in places. She'd seen enough of Sparks's handwriting to know it was his, yet it was different somehow.

"That's his address book," Dana said. "The one where I found you listed in the G's. I went through there last night after we talked and put a little star by all the people I want to invite. I put two stars by the people who absolutely, positively have to be there. You'll have to call them first, you know, check their schedules before we pinpoint a date."

"A date? It'll have to be in the next week or so, won't it? Whenever the funeral is."

Dana waved her hand like she was shooing a gnat. "No funeral. I'm just having him cremated as soon as they release his body. That's what he would've wanted. Besides, that way we can have the wake whenever we want it."

Grace squeezed the book and fought to keep her mouth shut.

Kelly Adamson

"Call Darlene at Sparks's restaurant, Stella D'oro, about the food once you get a date. Ooh, and tell her to bring those tarts with the goat cheese and blueberries. I love those. We can set up the bar on the patio where we were earlier, with hors d'oeuvres by the pool. Tell her I want them passed. I don't want them just sitting on a table. I want at least two servers, plus a bartender." Dana paused and looked at Grace. "Aren't you gonna write any of this down?"

Grace pulled out her notebook again and began scribbling furiously, careful to avoid looking directly at Dana, afraid of turning into a pillar of salt.

"Ideally, I'd get Nancy to help," Dana continued, "but the Slain Dragons are keeping her so busy right now. They're in Europe or somewhere promoting their new album. They say it's going to be the biggest hit of the year. Have you heard it?"

Grace shook her head, teeth clenched. She knew Nancy Johnson-Fleming had been Sparks's manager since the beginning. He was her first major act. He was her golden goose. It hurt to think the women in his life had already moved on.

After an hour or so, when Grace had seven pages of notes on the minutiae of party planning, Dana seemed satisfied. She hopped up out of Sparks's leather desk chair and gestured for her guest to follow. "And now for my end of the bargain," she said.

They stepped down into the dark music room, and Dana flipped a switch that illuminated dozens of guitars, all lined up on their stands against the wall. The DW drum kit sat silent at the far end of the space. There were no windows in the room. It would've messed up the acoustics, Sparks had explained.

A framed concert poster hung on the wall just inside the door. It announced The Who headlining at Boston Garden in 1973. The red, white, and blue Bull's Eye and Arrow logo dominated the poster. General admission was six dollars. It was autographed by all four original members, "to Dean," whoever that was. Sparks got the three surviving members to sign it again during their 1996 tour. That time, they signed it "to Sparks. Rock on."

Dana lifted the poster off the wall and set it aside. A digital lock was recessed into the sheetrock behind it. "This was built as a safe room or a panic room, whatever you want to call it. But Sparks called it the vault."

Grace had never noticed the outline of a door there, but hadn't been looking, either. The sound of the heavy lock springing open made her jump. There was no handle or visible hardware, but the heavy door swung open on its own and the lights inside came on automatically. It was larger than she thought, at least half the size of the music room, with boxes and cases piled on heavy metal racks that extended to the ceiling, a storage room for a rock god. A brown vinyl sofa crouched against the far wall, worn and battered, with a bit of stuffing sticking out a hole in one arm. It was the only visible concession to its possible use as a safe room.

Several of the larger trunks were on casters and had Sparks's name stenciled on the side. Dana hopped up on one of them and swung her feet back and forth like an overgrown kid. "So, what do you think? I told you he never threw anything away, didn't I?"

Everything on the longest wall was devoted to touring and seemed to be in chronological order. Sparks's public face. Tee-shirts from every tour, posters, pins, costumes, makeup, shoes. Everything was there, all the way back to some black-and-white handbills from the days when he had worked for beer and gas money. He had been his own roadie back then and done his own promotion, stapling sheets just like these to telephone poles around college campuses.

The room was a time capsule, as if the tours had just ended and he simply wheeled the boxes in and closed the door.

A gold mine.

Most of the boxes on the metal shelves were labeled in Sparks's handwriting, but the labels didn't make much sense to Grace. Inside jokes, maybe, or some of those "you had to be there" moments. One box was stuffed with old fan letters and labeled, "Sally Field." One with newspaper clippings inside was labeled "Deep Throat."

Grace sat on the floor and pulled a box into her lap. It was labeled "Shakespeare" and it contained a stack of lyrics, hand written on everything from toilet paper to part of a pizza box. The one on top was 1989's "Hold Me," easily Sparks's greatest hit. It had sent many a Spandex-clad teenager into a screaming, moon-eyed frenzy, including Grace. She could still remember every frame of the video, though she hadn't seen it in years. A shirtless Sparks, his blond hair teased out around him like a lion's mane, sang about love as he strolled down a seemingly endless hallway lit only by candles.

"Hello, beautiful." A man's voice interrupted Grace's internal MTV and she found herself blushing. She scrambled to her feet to find that she surprised Raul almost as much as he surprised her. He had only seen Dana. Of course, he had only been looking for Dana.

The new widow hopped off a storage trunk from the "Good Intentions" tour and glided over to take her personal trainer by his muscled arm. "I totally forgot we were going to work out this morning. Abs, right? Just let me get changed. Won't take a sec."

She turned back to her guest, who still clutched the box of lyrics to her chest like a baby. "Sorry, Gracie—I mean, Grace—but I've got to run. Just make yourself at home. And if you need to take anything with you—photos or whatever—you have my permission. Just, you know, bring it back when you're done." She scampered out the door and called over her shoulder, "Sparks trusted you and that's good enough for me."

Grace felt a knot forming in her stomach. Without realizing it, Dana had stuck a pin in Grace's ego. She thought Sparks had trusted her, but she was beginning to have her doubts. He'd never said a word to her about this room. His grief-stricken widow seemed to trust her more than he had.

She put the lyrics on the couch and went back to the shelves. There were hundreds, maybe thousands, of photos in dozens of boxes. They all had crazy names.

A box on the top shelf caught her eye. Its label read, "Blackmail Photos."

In the time it took her to push one of the rolling trunks close enough to the shelf to climb on, Grace ran through the scenario in her mind. Breathless, she saw herself lifting the lid off the box to see photos of Sparks's killer, maybe even some sort of note that would explain it all.

By the time she reached the box, she was laughing at herself. The labels had no rhyme or reason. She had to admit that. Blackmail photos could be anything from compromising photos of groupies to photos of Sparks with short hair and braces. No rhyme or reason at all.

The box was feather light compared to the others. It felt empty. Grace sat on top of the trunk and lifted the lid off the box. Inside was a single, bright pink index card. It read, "BJ has these."

Chapter 8 — Stella D'oro

Grace made the twenty-minute drive home in an hour and a half. She wound through parts of Mountain Brook she'd never seen, not caring that she was lost. She couldn't go home yet. She had to think, to try and wrap her head around all this. She'd been positive BJ was innocent, that this was all a big mistake somehow. But, finding that card, knowing BJ was in possession of something Sparks had labeled "Blackmail Photos," made her question her own judgement. Maybe Nick was right. Maybe she was too trusting.

She stopped at a place called Magic Beans and tried to order coffee. But, all they had were designer frappes and espressos with names like Java Jet and Black Hole.

She just wanted coffee. A little sugar. A little cream. The place made her feel old. The clientele were college kids. The barista called her ma'am. It made her think of Sparks. This must have been how he felt when she presented him with a digital voice recorder. He liked his hair long, his music loud, and he saw no reason to fix what wasn't broken.

Grace bought a bottle of water and got back in the car.

As she drove, she thought of the box in Sparks's vault. All it contained was a card saying BJ had the pictures. It didn't make any sense. If it really was what it looked like, why didn't BJ take the whole box? Maybe she left it as a warning for Sparks, so that every time he saw it, he would be reminded of the chubby drugstore clerk who held his fate in her hands.

The more she thought about it, the more absurd it sounded. By the time she got home, she'd convinced herself to forget about the box, at least for the time being, and concentrate on the wake. There was a lot of work to do. She settled in at the dining room table with her notebook, her phone, and Sparks's address book.

It looked even more fragile upon closer inspection. The gold star on the cover was faded and the spine was broken. She pulled off the rubber bands and found they were all that was holding the book together. It fell into three sections in her hands.

As promised, Dana had made little stars beside the names she wanted to invite, in lavender ink, the only ink in the book. Everything else was in pencil.

Grace never pegged Sparks as a man who would use anything that had an eraser. He was a "damn the torpedoes" type of guy. Again, she wondered how little she really knew about him.

The book held a lifetime of names and numbers. Almost every page was filled, the names at the top clearly written by a child. Seeing the progression of the writing was like watching time lapse photography.

She found the first double-starred name in the A's. It belonged to Sparks's old band mate, rock royalty David Hamilton Royce, better known as "Ax." He was with Sparks during the glory days, into the mid-nineties when everything they touched turned to gold. He'd gone on to play with three other bands since then, all big names, but none as big as Sparks had been.

Ax was the dark-haired prankster, always smiling and cracking jokes. Grace had read that he once managed to get a motorcycle inside the old Gold Nugget Casino in Las Vegas. They said he drove it between the rows of slot machines for a good sixty seconds before the security guards tackled him. On the Accelerator tour, he had thrown a naked mannequin from the balcony of his London hotel room. From the twelfth floor. Several passersby called the authorities to report a jumper. The hotel's management was not amused.

The phone rang five times before Ax's answering machine picked up. Grace left him a message. "Sparks is dead. You are invited to the wake. Please call with availability." Of course, the actual message wasn't that blunt, but it seemed like it to her. She felt herself tearing up again. This was going to be harder than she thought.

She took a deep breath, squared her shoulders, and called the next double-starred name.

Nathan "Honeybear" Ray wept like a child when Grace told him why she was calling.

"I heard it on the news, but I just couldn't make myself believe it," the big man said when he regained control of himself. "We've known each other for so long. We were just kids starting out, still wet behind the ears."

Honeybear was part of the original lineup, playing unpaid gigs on Southside with Sparks and Ax while the three were still in high school. He was one of the guys who helped staple those old black-and-white handbills to telephone poles.

"Sparks was always the front man. The girls went crazy over him, even then. He was our bait, you know. We were fishing for girls and he was our bait." He laughed a little and blew his nose and continued. "That's what it's all about, right? Sex, drugs, and rock and roll. Of course, if you know Sparks, you know it was sex, booze, and rock and roll for him. Hell, that bastard could drink more than anyone I've seen before or since, but never touched the chemicals. But, hey, I heard he stayed sober since he met that blonde. Is that true?"

Grace couldn't keep the surprise out of her voice. "You haven't talked to him since he sobered up? That's seven years now."

Honeybear made a groaning sound. "Another regret to add to my list. I should never have let that woman keep us apart. I know that now."

"What woman?"

"The blonde chick. The stripper. She took him away from all of us. But he was drowning in whiskey when he met her and she fished him out. So we had to let him go, you know. He would've died otherwise. And then they got married. Hard to believe."

"You mean Dana? She's not a stripper."

Honeybear snorted. "Exotic dancer, then. Whatever. Anyway, not anymore, she's not. She's got Sparks's money now. Ah, don't get me started on her. Guess she was good for him after all. Better than we were, anyway."

He promised he would be at the wake "come hell or high water," regardless of the date. He'd bought a small farm in Blount County when he retired from rock and roll. It was just fifty miles north of Mountain Brook, and he made the drive down often to give drum lessons to rich kids and rock and roll fantasy camp wannabe's.

By the time Nick got home that evening, Grace had made it through the whole book and called every name with two stars beside it. Thirteen names in all. She talked to twelve answering machines and one live person.

She saved one call in particular for last, country singer Rooster Hathcock. The last time she saw him, he'd helped her and Nick out of some very dire straits. He'd claimed them as friends then, and Rooster was the kind of person who took that seriously.

She hoped to speak with him personally, but had to settle for his voicemail. Hearing his boisterous, Mississippi twang was like a breath of fresh air blown in from an offshore hurricane.

It was thanks to the charming good ol' boy that Grace had her current job. His old pal, Sparks, needed someone to write his life story, and Rooster knew just the person, star-struck Alabamian Grace Howard, unhappy with her job as a secretary and itching to write full-time.

That first meeting with Sparks would be forever etched in her memory. Grace was sure she was the least qualified person who applied for the job, having published little more than her company newsletter, but she wasn't about to pass up the chance to meet her most beloved rock idol.

She hoped to get an autograph that day when she rolled up to the prearranged meeting spot, a trendy Italian restaurant on Birmingham's Southside called Stella D'oro. The sign on the door said it didn't open until six p.m., so she sat in the car hoping she hadn't written the time wrong.

It wasn't long before a short, round man wearing an apron over his baggy pants and tee shirt unlocked the door and waved her inside. The squat man didn't bother with a light switch, and by the time Grace's eyes adjusted to the darkened interior, the man had vanished back into the kitchen.

The building had a polished concrete floor and interior walls of reclaimed brick. Every table in the place was in deep shadow except the ones against the rear wall, lit by adjustable track lights that hung from the ceiling.

Sparks's blond hair seemed to glow in the artificial light and she stopped short when she saw him, eating a grilled artisan pizza with his hands, just like a real person.

She wasn't sure what she'd expected, but it wasn't the sincere smile and the warm handshake, his fingers slick with olive oil from the pizza.

He insisted she have a slice while it was still hot—good thing she liked spinach and goat cheese—and they talked for an hour without a lull in the conversation.

He had three questions for her, he'd said. They had no right answers, but they definitely had wrong answers, and some could be more right than others.

First, he asked if she was happily married, indicating her wedding ring. She said yes, with just enough force and indignation to make him smile. Apparently, that was a right answer.

Then he asked if she liked doughnuts, specifically apple fritters. Another yes, rewarded with another smile.

Last, he asked her favorite Sparks song of all time, and why.

She hesitated, wondering what his idea of a wrong answer would be. She decided to go with the truth. "Revved Up, because it reminds me of being fifteen, and of the first car my best friend owned, a three-cylinder junker that used a quart of oil a week, didn't lock and didn't have an air conditioner. But, it had a kick-ass stereo and we played that cassette all summer long. That was a great summer."

There was a gleam in Sparks's blue eyes as he listened to her answer. Then he slammed his open palm on the table, making Grace and the silverware jump.

"Man, I can't tell you how glad I am you said that. You're the first person who didn't name a power ballad, one of those Top 40 things that come up first when you Google me."

He laughed and held up his water glass in a salute. "But, Revved Up, that's digging deep. That's downright obscure. That would've been a B-side, back when there still were such things. And your story was good, too. I had a piece of shit like that myself once. Had to put a block of wood behind the tire when I parked it to keep it from rolling away. I had a lot of fun in that car."

He downed his water and then leaned back to stare at her. She felt thoroughly inspected.

"I've got a lot of secrets, Grace Howard," he said with a wicked grin. "Will you help me tell them?"

"Yes," she said, without hesitation.

"Okay, write this down."

She hurried to pull her pen and notebook from her purse, ready for secrets. Instead, he rattled off his address in the wooded hills of Mountain Brook.

"Be there at nine on Monday morning."

He looked at his watch, an overdone platinum monstrosity with a see-through face. It was probably worth more than Grace's current car. She

Kelly Adamson

grabbed her things and stood, recognizing the "watch peek" and not wanting to wear out her welcome.

He stood when she did, and yelled thanks and good-bye to the man in the kitchen. Sparks owned the restaurant, he'd explained at some point during the past hour, and he liked to check it out on occasion.

He held the door for her and they shook hands again on the sidewalk. He waited until she got into her car, then rounded the side of the building into the alleyway. He'd parked in back.

She watched him go with a thrill. She'd hoped for an autograph, but got a job, maybe the job of her life. Her big break. Her game changer. It didn't taste as sweet now. Would people think she was taking advantage of the situation, taking advantage of a dead man?

Grace laid her head on the table, her nose just inches from Sparks's tattered phonebook. It smelled faintly of pencil lead and flowers. The lavender ink was scented.

The back door opened and the familiar sound of Nick's footsteps came nearer. He touched her back tentatively, and when she didn't move, he started to rub her shoulders.

"I'm sorry about what I said earlier," he said.

She shrugged her shoulders as if to say it didn't matter, her head still on the table, but he misunderstood and pulled his hands back. Before she could say anything, Nick's phone rang.

He looked at the display and groaned. "It's Shipps. He keeps finding some flimsy excuse to call me so he can ask me about Leah. I've already told him I'm not playing matchmaker." His footsteps receded down the hallway as he answered the call.

Grace's stomach growled and she realized she hadn't eaten anything since the fritter that morning. It probably wasn't helping her headache either.

She stood up and stretched, momentarily visualizing Dana and her weird yoga mash-up.

She shuffled into the kitchen and opened the refrigerator. Paper containers of Chinese takeout and leftover pizza in foil wedges greeted her. She was sure Dana was having a baby carrot for dinner. Or maybe the grieving widow was splurging and having a regular-sized carrot.

Nick still had the phone in his hand, staring at it like it was a meteorite, when he stepped back into the kitchen. "They let BJ go," he said.

Grace shut the refrigerator door and stepped back, certain she had misheard.

"Shipps said she had an airtight alibi. She was Skyping with some fan club members at the time, one of whom is a lawyer. Turns out, all they had to do was check the computer records."

Grace didn't respond. She thought instead of the empty box at Sparks's house.

"Grace, did you hear me? BJ's innocent."

"BJ's innocent," she echoed.

"I thought you'd be happy."

"Oh, I am." Her voice sounded defensive, even to her own ears. "It's just, well, if she didn't do it, I'm just wondering who did. Did Shipps say if they had any other leads?"

"I didn't ask him."

"Why not?"

Nick held his hands up in surrender. "Okay, I guess I should've asked, but the truth is, I didn't want to owe him. I'm sorry he even has my number. I haven't heard from him in fifteen years and all of a sudden we're BFFs? No thanks. When he gives me information, I feel like he just wants me to be in his debt. And I know what he wants. He wants my sister's number."

Before long, Grace realized he'd stopped talking and was leaning against the doorframe with his arms crossed. She could feel him staring at her. He'd always been able to read her, to see right through her. She avoided his gaze and stepped back into the dining room. She gathered up the pieces of the address book and carefully slipped the rubber bands back in place.

Nick followed her and leaned in the same position, just a different doorway.

She stopped and put her hands on her hips. Nick called it her exasperated pose. "What?"

"I was about to ask the same of you," he said. "What's going on, poker face?"

She waved her hands in the air as if shooing imaginary gnats. "It's nothing, really." She forced a laugh. "It's silly."

Nick stood, not saying a word, until she finally gave in and told him about the box that had once possibly contained blackmail photos.

"And you think she left a note saying she had them?"

"I know. I know. I told you it was crazy."

"Did you ask Dana about them?"

"No, she was already gone with her Latin Lover by the time I found the box."

Nick shook his head. "Classy. Do you think Sparks knew about their little…extracurricular activities?"

Grace shrugged. "I guess we'll never know now. That's just one of the million things I'd like to ask him, but I'm too late."

Nick pushed off from the door frame and disappeared down the hall. He returned a minute later holding a gray felt bag dappled with long silky dog hair. Karishma followed close at his heels, a low growl forming in her throat.

"If only we knew somewhere he may have recorded some secrets," he said. "Maybe even—dare I say it—some memoirs?"

Grace took the offered bag and emptied the contents on the table. She tossed it back to Karishma, who immediately began rubbing her face on it, trying to remove the scent of anyone who wasn't her master.

Twenty-four microcassettes lay scattered on the table, all labeled in Sparks's hand. Twenty-four hours of secrets.

Chapter 9 — The Gallery

Testing. One, two, three. All right. I think I'm getting the hang of this thing now. Can you hear me, Grace?

Okay. I want to talk about my fan club, the Sparklers, and the three amigos—or amigas, I guess—who run it. First of all—and this is important, Grace, write this down —any performer without a fan base might as well be making fart noises in his hall closet. And any rock musician who tells you he plays for the art of it, well, he's lying. He's a big, fat-ass liar. It's all about the applause. It's ten thousand screaming fans working themselves into a frenzy over your sorry ass. Where else are you gonna get that? You think doctors get that? No way. You think doctors have groupies? Well, maybe they do. How should I know? But they have to go to school for a hell of a long time.

Okay, I'm getting off topic. The Sparklers. The fan club itself has been around since Cut to the Chase, *since before Nancy became my manager. Since before I met Dana. BJ started it and the other two girls joined on after* Back Talk. *They helped me keep my fan base in between albums and tours. And better than that, they helped me connect with a whole new generation of fans— ones who've never seen an album outside of a museum. I'm an old fart. I don't know anything about tweets and chats and blogs. But BJ and Vicki and Cassie did all that for me. They're my "on-line presence." At least, I think that's the phrase.*

I remember the first time I saw the website. I was in Natallia Gallego's office at SPF Records, before the live album, Secret Keeper, *whatever year that was. She was telling me how much she liked the site, you know, complimenting me on it, and hell, I didn't even know it existed. Nancy didn't know about it either. Can you believe it? BJ just did it. That sweet little Hobbit. She just did it, didn't even say a word. And damn, it looked good. She saved my ass that day. I was in a real slump, hadn't written a song in a year. I went in there with the mother of all hangovers, expecting Gallego to drop me, to tell me she didn't have room for dinosaurs like me. I was gonna be a has-been without a label and I didn't know if I even deserved one anymore. I thought it was over. And instead she showed me the number at the bottom of the screen that counted how many people had visited the site. My website. I'd never seen Natallia Gallego smile before. I owe that to BJ. She saved me.*

—Sparks Tape Name: Three Amigas

The tapes weren't numbered. They weren't in any order Grace could make out. Some were labeled with letters, some symbols, some seemingly random words and phrases.

The first one she popped into the tape player was labeled, "Speed Buggy," and contained the story of each and every car he owned, ad nauseam. The second tape was labeled, "Three Amigas." When she was through with it, she felt even worse for having doubted BJ. In Sparks's mind, his fan club's leader was a saint.

It made no mention of any blackmail photos.

The clock on the computer read 10:30 p.m. Nick was dozing on the couch, the History Channel providing a low drone in the background. She wished she could sleep too, but her mind was racing. She wanted to see BJ and didn't want to wait until morning. She wanted to ask her about the photos, but also wanted to make amends somehow for doubting her. Of course, BJ didn't know there was anything to make amends for. They were strictly one-sided.

Grace picked up her phone and tiptoed down the hall. She closed the door to the bedroom and called BJ.

A few minutes later, she scrawled a hurried note for Nick in case he woke while she was gone. She had the urge to take BJ something. Flowers? Candy? No. Flowers and candy paled in comparison to the pages she'd just transcribed. Sparks's words, unedited, in praise of a fan who had become a savior. The noise of the printer would surely wake Nick, so she ejected the USB drive she used for storage and slipped it in her pocket.

Headlights off as she backed down the driveway, Grace felt like a teenager sneaking out of the house. But, if Nick heard her, he would tell her she was crazy going downtown by herself at night. Maybe he was right, but it didn't matter. Impetuous or not, she needed answers more than sleep.

The directions put her at BJ's doorstep before eleven. Just on the outskirts of the UAB campus, the neighborhood that had once been posh was now home to students and fraternity houses. The Craftsman-style behemoths that towered above the tree-lined streets had largely been split into duplexes or quadplexes.

BJ's apartment was right behind the Payless Drugstore, on the second story of a cedar shake monstrosity that had been divided into six individual apartments. Grace took the wooden steps that led to the rear of the house, onto a wide balcony that BJ shared with two other apartments. The door stood open a few inches and music from Sparks's live album came blasting out from inside.

She knocked, but got no answer. She pushed the door open and looked inside.

BJ's apartment was surprising. Grace half expected it to look like the vault, filled with all things Sparks Westergard.

Instead, it looked like a little old lady lived there, or at least a big Jane Austen fan. What little furniture there was looked antique and fragile. Every flat surface was covered with a crocheted doily and porcelain teacups decorated with tiny flowers.

The whole place smelled of lemons. For a moment, Grace hoped it was lemon squares or some other baked good, but when BJ emerged from the hallway wearing pink dish gloves, she realized it was lemon scented cleanser. BJ had been using it to clean up after the fingerprint techs.

She looked a little frazzled, with tendrils of her curly brown hair clinging to her damp forehead. But she was delighted to see Grace, as if she had been on death row for years and was saved from the electric chair at the final hour. Grace might have laughed had it not been a possibility. If BJ had been found guilty of Sparks's murder, she could have faced the death penalty or at least life in prison.

Grace pushed the front door shut behind her, but BJ stopped her.

"I leave that open this time of night in case my cat comes back. This was his usual feeding time."

A stack of color flyers sat on the table by the door. A fat orange tabby stared into the camera. The caption read, "Have you seen me?" followed by BJ's phone number.

Her smile disappeared, and Grace changed the subject.

"Hey, I brought you something." She produced the USB from her jeans pocket with a hopeful smile. "Where's your computer?"

"I haven't gotten it back yet."

"Back?"

"From the police, you know." She looked away and Grace felt like an idiot.

"I'm so sorry. I didn't even think.... Well, look, I can paraphrase. I'll just tell you."

BJ pulled off the dish gloves and turned the music down. She got each of them a Coke from her apartment-sized fridge.

The two women sat on a well-upholstered Victorian sofa, the only seating in the room, while Grace tried to remember everything Sparks had said about his fan club and its leader.

When she was through, BJ excused herself and disappeared down the hallway. Grace could hear her blowing her nose and splashing water on her face.

She came back in a bit, composed, but with a red nose and puffy eyelids. She stopped in the arched doorway and beckoned Grace to follow her.

"I want to show you something."

The hallway was narrow, with a tiny bathroom on the left and a single bedroom at the end. It was huge by modern-day bedroom standards and probably started out its life as something other than a bedroom when this had been a single-family dwelling. The landlord hadn't bothered to lower the nine-foot high ceilings or add closets. That may have been a bad thing if you were trying to pay the heating bill, but it did wonders for the aesthetics of the old place.

Grace smiled. Here, finally, were the posters, tee-shirts, albums, flags and every other bit of Sparks memorabilia she'd expected to see all along.

Black metal clips looped over the picture molding at the top of the walls. Thin black chains hung from the clips and the most highly valued mementos were tastefully framed and hanging from the chains. Otherwise, the matte black plaster walls would have surely crumbled under the countless nail holes. Directional lighting ran along the ceiling on slim, aluminum tracks and spotlighted BJ's most prized pieces. The effect was dazzling.

If Sparks's room was the vault, then this was the gallery.

When Grace didn't speak, BJ said, "If I keep it all confined to one room, I don't feel like such a kook—or so I tell myself."

Grace laughed and shook her head. "Don't apologize to me. I think it's beautiful. And, if I'm being honest, I'm more comfortable in here than I was in your living room. All those antiques just brought out my inner klutz. I kept thinking I was going to break a saucer or something. This is more my speed."

BJ made a pained face. "I wish the cops felt that way. They acted like I had severed heads in here or something. You should've seen them."

Grace pointed to a framed pair of leather pants, prominently displayed on the far wall. "They just don't know fine art when they see it."

BJ laughed. She crossed to the bed and sat on the zebra-striped comforter. She waited patiently, uncharacteristically quiet, while Grace took everything in, frame by frame. She paused a few times to ask a question, or just to marvel at the depth of the collection or the expert framing. It must've cost a fortune. No wonder BJ lived in a low-rent neighborhood. It was clear where her money went.

A framed bandana from the *Secret Keeper* tour hung above the bed. "Sparks Out" was printed in bold yellow letters on black cotton. Sparks's signature sign-off at the end of every concert. After the encore, of course. "Good night! We love you! Sparks out, Birmingham!" Or Cleveland, or Dallas, or Tokyo.

A computer printer occupied a desk near the room's solitary, arched-casement window. Two thick stacks of photographs sat beside a blank space where a laptop computer had obviously been. Many of the photos were small, 4 X 6 or less, taken with personal cameras in the pre-digital era. On the top of one stack was a dark, blurry image of what could only be Sparks and his band back in the days when they played small clubs and were paid largely in beer.

The other stack of photos was face down, as if BJ had been going through them all, cataloguing them, perhaps, and this is where she stopped when the police took her laptop. Grace felt a flutter of excitement. This was why she was here. Blackmail photos.

Grace leaned over to examine a framed row of guitar picks and cleared her throat. "So, what happened, BJ? I just got bits and pieces of the story. Why did they suspect you to begin with?" She knew that part, but wanted to hear it from the source.

BJ took a deep breath and blew it out like she was blowing out a candle. "Well, when the cops came to arrest me, I was scared to death, you know. I cried in the car all the way to the jail. And I couldn't even wipe my nose because of the handcuffs. Can you believe they put me in handcuffs?"

Grace shook her head no. BJ stood five feet tall on tiptoes, a little soft around the middle, with a round face and soft brown curls kept short. She looked like a middle-aged cherub, not a killer.

"A detective named Morton told me that my fingerprints were on the bottle of bourbon that had poisoned Sparks. He said they knew I had access to Digoxin since I work at a pharmacy. He said they were going to ask for the death penalty, but I might only get twenty years or so if I cooperated and told him why I did it."

BJ dabbed at her eyes with a wadded tissue. "I told him I would never hurt Sparks. I'm his biggest fan. He told me Mark David Chapman was a fan of John Lennon, too. Can you believe he said that to me?"

Grace was uncomfortable around crying people. She crossed to the bed and thought about sitting down, but didn't. Instead, she reached out and patted BJ awkwardly on the shoulder. "There, there," she said. She'd heard people say that in movies when consoling someone, but wasn't really sure what it meant. It seemed to work, though, because BJ sniffed and straightened up and gave her a watery little smile.

"I called Vicki because she was the only lawyer I knew. She has a friend here in Birmingham who's a lawyer too. He came and met with me and once Vicki found out about the…time of death…she knew we'd been skyping then, with Cassie. We do it every other month at the same time. Anyway, all they had to do was check my computer records. And of course there were two credible witnesses to my whereabouts."

"What about the fingerprints on the bottle? How did they explain that?"

"It turns out, the bottle was mine. That's why my fingerprints were on it. It was in front of my door one night when I got home from work, just a couple of weeks ago. It was in a fancy bag, all decorated in black and white ribbon. It was so pretty, I put the whole thing up on the mantle so I could look at it. I'm not much of a drinker, so I just left the bottle in the bag."

"Who was it from?"

"It had a card that said it was from my secret admirer. I don't know much about bourbon, but I could tell it was expensive, even though it had a funny name, something like Rip Van Winkle. At the time, I thought it was from this guy, Grant, who comes in the pharmacy a lot. He drives a Cadillac so I thought he might be able to afford a bottle like that. He's always so nice to me, so I thought maybe. But, the next time I saw him, it was raining really hard and he said there were a lot of wrecks on the road and for me to be careful if I had a long drive home. Well, since the store's right there," she waved her hand at the far end of the apartment, "it was obvious he didn't know where I lived. It couldn't be him.

"Anyway, the first thing I did when I got home—when they let me go—was to get the bag down to look at the bottle. But it was gone."

"What do you mean, gone?"

"Gone. The bag was empty. Detective Morton had told me to call him if I could think of anything he needed to know, and I thought he needed to know that for sure. So, long story short, that's why they've been here fingerprinting this afternoon. They took my pretty bag, too."

Grace started to ask another question, but BJ had already gathered another breath and was continuing her "short" story.

"I talked to Vicki and she said it sounded like someone was trying to frame me for Sparks's murder. She said it sounded like they broke in and stole the bottle, and then put poison in it and took it to Sparks's house. That's crazy." She laughed, a little, nervous sound. "Doesn't it sound crazy to you, Grace? It's crazy, right? That's spy novel stuff."

"Crazy, yes," Grace said. "But that doesn't mean it's not true."

"But, I haven't had any broken windows or jimmied locks. I haven't noticed anything strange and I can't find where anything else is missing."

"If this is all true, these weren't robbers. They were only after one thing—the bottle. They're probably the ones who sent it to you in the first place."

As if in slow motion, BJ's face contorted and she began to wail. "My cat! That's how he got out. Someone broke in and scared Sparksy and he ran. My poor baby!"

Grace wasn't sure "There, there," would work here, so she tried, "No, no, no. Don't cry," which appeared to be much less effective.

"Come on, let's go back in the kitchen and have a nice cup of tea. You must like tea. You have all those pretty cups."

"I don't like t...tea," BJ stammered. "Just like the cups."

"Okay, okay." Grace whirled around, looking for something to help change the subject, to draw BJ's attention away from her missing cat. She grabbed a stack of photos from the desk and held them up in front of the weeping woman. "How about these, BJ? Tell me about these pictures."

She started flipping through them, laying them out on the zebra-striped bed. The photos ranged from racy to ridiculous to humiliating. Most featured men and women in various states of undress, under the influence of myriad substances. Most were blurry and overexposed.

It took longer this time, but BJ finally managed to pull herself together enough to look at the photos.

"Those belong to Sparks, his private collection," she muttered.

"Yes? Tell me about them. Who's the guy on the tricycle?"

That got a half-hearted smile. "That's not a tricycle. It's a micro-bike, a real motorcycle. The guy's name is Chico."

"Chico? I don't remember him. What did he play?"

"Play? No, he wasn't in the band. He was…well, I guess they would say he was part of the entourage nowadays, but they used to call them hangers-on. People who weren't in the band, you know, but were just there for the party. Sparks had a lot of them."

"So, all these people I don't recognize, they were hangers-on?" Grace picked up a photo of a pair of topless women, smiling and waving at the camera.

"Or groupies. Plenty of those, too. I know the names of some of the regulars, but a lot went by nicknames, and some I don't know at all. They called those two the Tiger Twins. I think they were Auburn students."

Grace picked up another one, an out-of-focus shot of Sparks and Ax holding up a seemingly unconscious man between them.

"That's Tommy Redfoot," BJ said, "the first bass player."

Sparks and Ax were holding Tommy under the arms while his head lolled to one side. Sparks was grinning and Ax seemed to be laughing out loud, his mouth open and his head thrown back. Someone had drawn a handlebar moustache and a goatee on Tommy with a blue marker.

"None of these look like something you'd want on the website," Grace said. "So, what are you doing with them?"

BJ took a fresh tissue from a box on the nightstand and blew her nose noisily.

"Sparks asked me to try and catalogue them," she said. "He wanted to identify as many of the people as he could. He knew they weren't publishable. He made me promise not to use any of them on the site. But he just wanted them for himself, to jog his memory, you know, for his memoirs."

Grace picked up a 3 X 5 of a stick-thin guy with long, bushy brown hair. In his outstretched hands were six small, white bundles, the size of marbles, each wrapped tight in clear plastic and tied with twist ties. Cocaine, she assumed. The man looked somehow familiar, though she was sure she didn't know him. Another hanger-on.

BJ made a funny, half-laughing, half-crying sound as she waved a groupie picture in the air. "Crazy, huh? He had these in a box marked 'Blackmail Photos.' He was joking, of course, but I guess it doesn't matter now."

She began picking them up, in some order only she understood, carefully, like they were lost sketches by Van Gogh. She stopped at one of a very intoxicated Sparks urinating on a potted palm in a hotel lobby. "He said these were his blotto years. It's easy to see why."

"Why in the world did he keep them? They're so embarrassing. Why didn't he take a match and set fire to the lot of them?" Her gaze stopped on an underexposed shot of Ax with someone in a headlock. Hard to say who, but it wasn't Sparks. Not blond enough.

"I asked him that myself. He said pretending something never happened doesn't make it go away. He didn't want to be one of those people who forget their history and are doomed to repeat it. He wanted to remember what it was really like then—what *he* was really like—because he never wanted to go back there." She put the photo on the top of the stack and stared at it. "He was so proud of his sobriety. That's why I just can't believe he fell off the wagon the night he died. It just doesn't make sense."

The last photo on the bed was of someone, Honeybear maybe, asleep, or passed out, face down on a lumpy beige sofa. Which would have been fine except he was wearing no pants. The blue marker bandit had struck again, this time drawing two large eyes and a wide grin across Honeybear's butt.

The photo made Grace remember Nick, asleep on their own sofa. She wondered if he'd woken and found the note yet. She was honestly surprised he hadn't texted her. She patted her pockets, looking for her phone and let out a groan. She was in such a hurry to slip out of the house unnoticed, that she'd left her phone and her purse. She'd come out with nothing but her keys.

It was close to midnight, and even though she felt guilty for leaving BJ in such a funk, she really hoped she could get back home before Nick woke up. He was always telling her to be more situationally aware. He said she was too trusting, and it was going to bite her in the butt one day. She really didn't want to prove him right. So, she made her apologies and said her good-byes, and promised to call BJ in the next couple of days.

BJ followed her to the door with a plastic Wal-Mart bag. "Please take these. A kid came to the door this afternoon selling them and I bought four dozen. I don't know what I was thinking—comfort food, I guess. Jail food wasn't that great. But, I'll never eat four dozen. Please take a box with you."

Grace peeked in the bag and saw the Krispy Kreme symbol smiling up at her. Her stomach growled.

She hugged BJ and thanked her for the Coke, the doughnuts and the tour of the gallery. Then she left through the slightly open front door and headed down the side stairs.

An oak tree as old as the house stood in the shallow front yard, plunging the entire property into complete darkness. That's why Grace didn't notice the two people loitering there until they materialized out of the shadows. A black man, dressed head-to-toe in black, leaned against the trunk of the tree. A woman with stringy brown hair and dingy clothes that hung loose on her rail-thin frame left the man's side when she saw Grace.

"You got a quarter?" the woman called.

"Sorry, no purse," Grace said, never breaking her stride.

The woman hurried to get in front of Grace, doing an awkward backwards trot so she could face her. "How about a cigarette? You got one of those?"

"I don't smoke."

Grace was no stranger to being approached for spare change. But something about this didn't feel right. She thought for a second about turning around and heading back to BJ's until the pair cleared off, but her car was in sight now, much closer than going back. She picked up the pace, keys at the ready.

"How about that bag? What's in there?" The skeletal woman abruptly stopped her backwards scuttle and Grace had to do a quick sidestep to avoid running right into her. "Maybe I'll just take that."

Grace felt him before she heard him. One quick shove and she was down. He must have put his foot out when he pushed her, because she didn't stumble, just fell like a tree. The dirt and gravel of the tiny front yard rose up to meet her. She managed to put her hands out to catch her fall, saving her from a broken nose, but the impact left her breathless and drove her car keys into her right palm.

She rolled over and sat up in the sparse weeds, glad she hadn't hit the sidewalk instead. She squinted up the dimly lit street, away from the rear of the drugstore, but the couple was long gone. She checked herself for damage. Her elbow was a little sore, the same one she'd fallen on in Las Vegas, but nothing was broken or bleeding that she could tell. She pushed herself to her feet and hurried the final twenty yards to her car, fumbling with the keys so much that she dropped them in the floor board once she was locked inside.

She grabbed the steering wheel and winced. Her hands would be tender for a few days. She turned her palms to inspect them in the light coming in from the street lamp. They were shaking so bad, she couldn't focus on them.

BJ and her open door came back to her suddenly. She should call her and tell her to lock it. Heck, dead bolt it and push that frilly sofa in front of it. She reached for her cell phone and cursed herself again for leaving it at home. Only then did she realize that the man in black had taken her doughnuts when he pushed her down.

Kelly Adamson

Chapter 10 — Preoccupied

The sun was high when Grace awoke the next morning. Nick's side of the bed was cold and the house was quiet. She felt a little stab when she realized he hadn't kissed her goodbye.

She got up and stretched, wincing from the pain in her elbow, stiff from her tumble the night before. Her palms were a little sore, but not as bad as she'd feared.

Karishma was waiting for her, so she pulled on some shorts and took her out for a quick walk. The little dog still wouldn't have anything to do with Nick, or anyone else for that matter. That included Grace's other dogs, which not only meant she couldn't just let her out in the fenced back yard to do her business, but she also had to keep Karishma closed up in the guest room when Lucy, Ricky and Ernie came inside. At least Karishma didn't seem to mind the solitary confinement—she liked her own company best of all.

Finally, Grace sat down in front of the computer with her phone, her notes on the wake, and a cup of coffee. All in all, she'd received five voicemail messages and three text responses from the first-tier invitation list, the ones Dana had marked with two stars in Sparks's address book. Nine out of the thirteen she'd called, in less than twenty-four hours. Most of the people said they'd make it no matter when the wake was. He'd obviously been very well liked.

The first message she listened to was from the one person she thought was going to prove the biggest scheduling challenge, Sparks's former lead guitarist, Ax Royce. It was no secret that Ax's current band, The End, was in the middle of a world tour and such commitments were not easily rearranged, not even for the death of a friend.

As luck—or lack thereof—would have it, Ax and his band were in the middle of a three-week hiatus before the kickoff of the European leg of their tour. Ax could make it any time in the next week and a half. After that, it would be three months before he saw the States again.

"If there's anything I can do, anything you need, you just leave a message on this number," Ax said. "Sparks was the genuine article. The real deal, you know."

This kicked the wake planning into turbo mode. Next Saturday would give Grace nine days. Setting up a party by then would be fine, easy peasy, but would the medical examiner even release Sparks's body by then? After all, it was the subject of an active murder investigation.

Then Grace remembered that wasn't actually an issue here. He wasn't going to be lying in state at his house. Dana was having him cremated.

Dana. Grace almost forgot about Dana. She'd have to run the date by her for final approval. She dialed her cell number and waited. Four rings before it went to voicemail.

"Hi, this is Dana's phone," said the chipper, recorded message. "Can't talk now. Busy living the dream. But, leave me a mes —"

Grace stabbed the disconnect button on the phone and laid it on the table. A major drawback of cell phones was that you no longer got the satisfaction of slamming down the receiver in annoyance. Well, you could, but you'd probably go through a lot of phones that way.

She wasn't quite sure why the message infuriated her so. It wasn't as if Dana had recorded it that morning. She'd probably had the same message as long as she'd had the phone.

No, it was her most recent memory of Dana that did it. Scurrying out of Sparks's memorabilia vault arm-in-arm with Raul, her blonde ponytail swinging behind her. Like Scarlet O'Hara dancing in her black mourning dress.

Okay, if Dana couldn't take time out of her busy Pilates schedule to help plan her late husband's memorial service, fine. Grace worked better on her own, anyway. She sent Dana a quick text message with the particulars. "Wake this Sat at 6 pm confirmed. Grace." She read it back. The insensitivity made her cringe. Then she hit "send."

The number for Stella D'oro was in her notebook along with Dana's special requests. Tarts with goat cheese and blueberries. Bar on the patio. Hors d'oeuvres by the pool. Two servers and a bartender. Expected head count of one hundred. Done.

Next, Grace left a message for Little Tater and Truckstop 119—another special request of Dana's. Considering the music twanging on Little Tater's outgoing message, Grace doubted they'd ever played a wake before, or anywhere that didn't have straw on the floor. She also doubted Sparks had ever heard of them and didn't expect a return call.

Two hours and thirty-two phone calls later, Grace had ordered flowers, rented a projector and returned all the calls and texts from the A-listers. Then she'd carefully reopened Sparks's ancient address book and called everyone Dana had marked with one star—her B-list of invitees.

She had a late lunch of a cupcake, followed by a handful of grapes to make it seem healthier. It was almost three in the afternoon and her cell phone was back on the charger. She was glad she had unlimited minutes. Wake-planning was turning out to require a lot more phone calls than planning the invasion of Normandy.

Her eyes went again to the tapes. They'd been tempting her all day from the far corner of the dining room table, all snug in their cookie tin. It had originally housed some German gingerbread cookies someone had given her for Christmas. The lid showed a Bavarian castle beneath a starry sky. She'd saved it with the intention of filling it with more cookies, but never quite got around to the baking part. It made a better tape case anyway.

Nick wasn't due home from work for another couple of hours, and Grace could transcribe a whole tape, maybe more, before then. Powering up her ancient laptop, she realized with a start that the USB drive she used for storage was still in the pocket of the jeans she'd worn to BJ's the night before. If she'd been a more conscientious housekeeper, those jeans would be in the washing machine right now. She always knew housework was overrated. She dashed out to the laundry room and dug around until she found the little orange stick in the hamper, then brought it back and snapped it into the laptop. The poor old thing was still booting up. It was eight years old, at least. Maybe ten. Ancient in computer years. It had crashed three times in the last six months. It still worked, but she no longer stored documents on it, for fear of the final blue screen of death.

A new computer was definitely on Grace's wish list, but she'd been out of work for two months when she got the writing gig with Sparks. That hadn't done her finances any favors. So, for now at least, her USB drive was her storage. But she needed a backup in case something unforeseen happened— like the rinse cycle. Making a mental note to get some sort of chain so she could wear the USB like a necklace, she dug around in the laptop's carry bag until she found a single, rewritable CD with no case. Old school backup.

She wasn't even sure the CD drive still worked, but the computer whirred and blinked obediently when she slid the disk in. While the file copied, she retrieved a CD jewel case, Sparks's *Secret Keeper*, to house the newly minted backup. It felt very appropriate.

She ran her finger across the photo on the cover. Sparks in the alleyway with his finger to his lips. And on the back, the crazy menagerie of hangers-on. Not so easy to see in this smaller format. There was the Japanese

Kelly Adamson

girl in the blue bikini. The creep in the trench coat. Where were all these people now? Did they know about Sparks's death? Could any of them be a killer? She squinted at the tiny faces. Under the right circumstances, she guessed anyone could be a killer.

The sound of the side door opening made Grace jump. Nick was home early and she hadn't even heard his truck pull up. Chiding herself for her lack of situational awareness, she took a deep breath. The smell of fresh cut lumber met her nose as he rounded the corner into the dining room. Fine remnants of sawdust peppered his shoulders and his dark hair, cut shorter than usual for summer. Grace had to admit she liked it better in the winter, when it curled up over his collar and down over his forehead.

"You're home early." She gave him a quick peck on the cheek, careful not to disturb the sawdust and create a need to vacuum. "To what do I owe this pleasure?"

"Saw broke," he grumbled. "Chinese piece of crap."

Oh, great. She'd hoped he'd be in a good mood for the favor she'd planned to ask him. Guess not.

"Sorry about that," she said, then echoed what she'd heard him say many times before. "They just don't make them like they used to."

He grunted in agreement and headed down the hall to the shower.

Grace followed him. "Have you heard from Shipps today?"

"Shipps? Why would I hear from Shipps?"

"I don't know. I thought he might have called you with an update or something."

Nick shook his head. "I haven't seen the guy in years, haven't even thought about him since high school. The only reason he talked to me the other day was to find out if I could set him up with Leah. But I think he finally got the message that I wasn't going to help, so I don't think I'll be hearing from him again."

"What? Why would you do that?" Grace stammered. "Leah might like him. Have you even asked her? She's always been partial to men in uniform. It might be a match made in heaven."

Nick gave her a suspicious look. "What are you up to?"

"Nothing at all." Grace raised her hands in innocence. "I'm just looking out for my sister-in-law's love life. That's all."

"Well don't. I fixed up Leah one time and it was a disaster. I swore I'd never do it again and I haven't. I thought I told you that story."

"No. What happened?"

Nick blew out a deep breath. "She was a sophomore at UAB. The guy I fixed her up with was a friend of a friend, or so I thought. I'd seen him at the range for months, seemed like a straight-up guy. Always said the right things. He really had me fooled."

Grace stood in the doorway of the bathroom and waited while he stripped off his work clothes, turning them inside out as he went, trying to contain the sawdust.

"They went on one date and the bastard..." Nick tossed the ball of clothes in the hamper with more force than was necessary. "Well, her roommate came home and walked in on them struggling on the sofa. Turns out this asshole didn't like it when girls told him no. He'd even ripped her shirt trying to get it off her."

"Oh, my God."

"Her roommate went after him with a can of bug spray that just happened to be sitting there. Thank God for ants, right? So, anyway, the two of them managed to get rid of him, and I never saw him again. And believe me, I looked."

Grace knew by the nerve pulsing in Nick's jaw that it was a good thing he hadn't found the guy.

"I'm just glad he didn't have a gun on him that night. He was a terrible shot, but at point blank range, it wouldn't have mattered. Anyway, I haven't fixed anyone up since then, especially not Leah. And I don't think Shipps will call me again. I think I made it pretty clear to him."

Now that he was wearing nothing else, Grace noticed a bandage on Nick's left hand.

"You cut yourself?" She reached for it, but he moved his hand away. Grace stepped back, hurt. He reached in the shower and turned on the water.

"What's wrong?" she said.

"Nothing. Guess I was just preoccupied."

"Preoccupied?"

He straightened and met her eyes without a hint of his usual easy smile. "Yes, with the fact that my wife snuck out of the house last night to go to Southside, without her purse, or her phone, or her pistol. You could've woken me up. I would've gone with you."

Here it was.

"No, you wouldn't have," she said, suddenly defensive. "You would've just told me to wait until morning. And I didn't want to wait until morning. I appreciate your concern—I really do—but I'm a grown woman."

"—who leaves without her ID and phone," Nick said.

"I never said I was perfect. Let's be honest. This would never have been an issue before Las Vegas. But that was a fluke, you have to admit. What are the odds of me getting kidnapped by a crazy mobster twice?" She laughed, but Nick didn't.

"I know you worry about me, but I promise I don't need a body guard. Give me some breathing room. You've got to relax."

She saw the muscle pulse in Nick's jaw again and thought she could hear his teeth grinding.

"I'll make a deal with you," he said. "I'll try to cut you some slack if you'll stop overlooking one very crucial fact."

"What's that?" She was ready to be defiant, hands on hips and chin up.

"There's a killer on the loose." Then Nick stepped in the shower and closed the curtain, ending the conversation.

Grace couldn't really argue with that logic, even though she was sure Sparks's murder had nothing to do with her. She thought about the guy who stole her doughnuts. Nick didn't need to know about that. He'd blow that way out of proportion.

She made her way back down the hall and plopped down in front of the computer. She looked at the picture on the CD cover again. Sparks with his "up-to-something" grin, his finger at his lips.

He had no enemies, his wife said. Everyone Grace had spoken to agreed he was a prince among men.

And yet, someone had cut him down. Cold, premeditated murder. And that someone was still out there.

She could hear the shower running. Nick had put his phone on the charger beside hers. She picked up his and scrolled through until she found the number she wanted. She entered it in her own phone, put his back and stepped out onto the deck.

Officer Loose Lips Shipps answered after one ring.

Chapter 11 — NO

> *"Agitator, agitator.*
> *You love to kick the hornet's nest.*
> *Rabble rouser, trouble maker,*
> *Never gonna give it a rest."*
> — *Agitator (1987)*

The next morning, a bird chirped in the crape myrtle outside the bedroom window, and Grace was awake when Nick came to kiss her goodbye.

They'd made up the night before. She'd promised to be more careful, and he'd promised to relax a little. At least to try. No winners and no losers. Compromise. Afterward, they'd curled up under the ceiling fan and fallen asleep in each other's arms.

After Nick left for work, Grace made a cup of coffee and took Karishma for a walk. It wasn't even eight a.m., and it was already 83 degrees. She contemplated why her day couldn't start without a cup of coffee, even on a steamy morning like this one. She sipped the sweet, hot liquid and checked her phone to see if Shipps had called. Instead, there was a text from Dana that had been sent around midnight. It said she wanted to come up with some sort of printed program for the wake. Something to give out to the mourners. Something glossy.

Grace gritted her teeth, a reaction Dana almost always brought out in her. Working on Sparks's memoirs now had blossomed into working as Dana's personal secretary. Fine. She wanted glossy. Grace would give her glossy. She thought of the stacks of promo material in Sparks's vault. Maybe Dana would like tour shirts made, too. Sparks's final appearance. Maybe she could sell tickets.

Grace's plan had been to spend the day transcribing Sparks's tapes, but it looked like that was going to have to go on the back burner again. Dana was proving to be just as needy as Grace always imagined her to be.

Back in the house, Grace added cream to her second cup of coffee and booted up the old laptop. She gave it an encouraging pat. "Sweet computer. Pretty computer. Please don't crash on me today," she whispered.

She stole another glance at the phone, willing Shipps to call her. When they'd spoken the night before, he'd hesitated when she'd asked how things were going. Apparently, Shipps's lips weren't as loose as they'd been in high school. It wasn't until she mentioned Leah's name that the poor guy began to warm to her. Still, there was nothing to tell, he'd assured her, but he'd keep her posted if he could. And please tell Leah hello for him. Grace promised, feeling more than a little guilty when he hung up. Still, it appeared Nick's sister was the only ammunition she had and it wasn't hurting anyone. That's what she told herself.

It only took a couple of hours to finish the program, an eight-page layout with one hundred percent of the photos and seventy-five percent of the copy lifted directly from the Sparklers' website. A blurb on the back page gave the three superfans credit for it all.

Although it pained her to do so, she e-mailed a PDF of the finished product to Dana for approval. The layout hadn't taken nearly as long as she'd thought, so she rewarded herself with a popsicle and retrieved the cookie tin that housed the microcassettes.

She reached in and pulled one out, like pulling a name from a hat. The label read *NO*. It was no use trying to figure out Sparks's labeling system. She opened a Word document on her flash drive, titled it *NO*, and popped the tape in the transcriber.

Even over such a tiny speaker, Sparks's voice filled the room. It was a voice made for rock and roll, like sandpaper covered in honey and bourbon.

"What's shakin', Grace! It's your friendly neighborhood rock god here, coming to you from beautiful Mountain Brook, where the Alabama sun is burning everything to a crisp and it's a glorious day to be me. Well, all days are glorious days to be me, but you already knew that.

"So, hey, I found something this morning and I said to myself, 'Self, you've got to tell Grace about this.' It all started back on the Accelerator Tour, '92, I think it was. We played two shows at Lakefront Arena in New Orleans. They love us down there. We stayed on a couple more days after, a little thank-you from us to the crew.

"Well, the first night off, it's about midnight, and it's me and Honeybear, Redfoot and Ax and a couple more, Detroit, Witty, Santa and some girls they'd picked up. About ten of us in all, I guess. One of the chicks sees this fortune teller's sign, big neon hand, and we all go in. It's this crazy place with stuff hanging in the front window, dried herbs and chicken feet and God knows what all. It was wild. So, we all squeeze in and it smells like incense and there's this tiny little woman sitting at a table. There's a crystal ball in front of her, just like in the movies, and she's wearing her weight in gold chains.

"We walk in and she puts her hand up in front of her eyes, like she can't look at us. She starts making this crazy noise like she's in pain or something.

"Then she says, 'Of your number, three will die young, and two will die soon, but only one will be responsible.' Those exact words, just like that. I'll never forget it.

"So man, we were hooked. This chick was the best theater we'd seen in a long time. And we were all 'live fast and die young' and too stupid to worry about it. So, we're firing questions at her, all at once, you know. Who's gonna die? What do you see? But she never even looks at us. She just gets up and

leaves, goes through this back door and this big dude comes out. He says 'Madam isn't feeling well. You gotta go.'

"Ax tries to pay the guy, but he won't take it. He dodges the money like it's on fire. He keeps saying 'Go. Go.' He starts trying to shoo us out like we're stray dogs chewing on his chicken feet.

"We all get outside and the guy locks the door behind us and turns off the neon hand sign.

"Damn! I'd been thrown out of better places, but never like that. But, you know, we didn't think much about it, other than a good laugh. We just walked on, found some Irish pub that was really rocking and forgot all about it."

The tape ran in silence for several seconds and Grace wondered if that was end of the side. Then Sparks cleared his throat and said, *"It was just three months later, right after the tour wrapped up, that Redfoot died. Accidental OD. That still hurts, even now. I'd known him since the seventh grade. Redfoot was....He was a gentle soul.*

"Now, I don't believe in hocus pocus. It's not like I thought this little woman could predict the future. But it did make me think about my own mortality for the first time. And during some self-pitying bender, I wrote down what I wanted done with my ashes upon my untimely demise. That's what I found this morning. It's a short list. My whole life down to three bullet points on one sheet of wrinkled notebook paper. You can put it in the book if you want.

"First and foremost, I want someone to sprinkle some of me at The Nick. I know, I know, it's a hole in the wall, but it's a Birmingham legend. It's where we played our first real gig and a hundred more after that. I think there were seven people in the audience at that first show, man. The Nick was good to us, always had something for us, no matter what.

Kelly Adamson

"Second. On December 3, 1983, we played the Whiskey A Go Go on Sunset Strip. We weren't the headliners. Hell, we weren't even on the sign, but we played. And I knew at that moment that I belonged there. That world was mine for the taking. We were artists there. We were invincible. Assuming the Whiskey is still standing when I'm ashes, I want some of me to go there.

"I'm going to have to change the third one. It says 'Mom's house,' but you know my mom passed away in 2012. I've given it some thought and I think if someone could sprinkle a little of me on her grave at Elmwood, that would be great.

"That's it. But, I want to add a fourth place now that my life is way different than it was back when I wrote this. I've got a little spot here in the back yard where me and Karishma like to lie in the sun and watch the birds. I've got a rose bush there named after the lead singer of Queen. That man had the best range in rock and roll. I could be good fertilizer.

"After that, I don't care. It's up to Dana, I guess." Sparks laughed. *"My little darlin' can can do whatever she wants with me, just like always. Sparks out."*

—Sparks Tape Name: NO

Grace's fingers faltered on the keyboard. It seemed like everything she heard about Dana made her like the woman even less. *"Do whatever she wants with me, just like always."* Grace shook her head, trying to clear away the image of Sparks as a shaggy, blond puppy and Dana smacking him on the nose with a rolled up copy of *Cosmopolitan.*

Her brain and her fingers needed a rest. She made another cup of coffee and a peanut butter sandwich and sat in front of the TV. It was too hot to eat outside and her dogs would've gotten it all anyway. Karishma didn't beg. One of her few endearing traits.

Midday, nothing on but judge shows and soap operas. The local news was showing coverage of the senate race. It was down to two, both running nasty smear campaigns and neither showing any substance of their own.

Grace muted the TV and picked up her tablet instead. She had an e-mail from Dana, approving the glossy wake program with only one change. She wanted to add a photo and had attached it to the e-mail. Grace clicked on the icon to see a happy couple, posing in front of the Eiffel Tower. Dana wore miniscule denim shorts and a tee-shirt cut off high enough to show her tanned midsection. Sparks beamed beside her in basic rocker black. Probably the first time Dana had ever been out of Alabama.

Grace made the change grudgingly and e-mailed the order to Kinko's.

When the telephone rang, Grace jumped. The screen showed the time as 2:32. She'd been asleep for almost two hours. She rubbed her eyes and answered the call.

"Mrs. Howard? This is Officer Louis Shipps."

A rush went through her. Something had happened. She sat up straight on the couch. "Please, call me Grace."

Karishma snorted, the sudden commotion rousing her from her sleeping spot behind Grace's knees.

"Are you feeling okay? You sound kind of…"

"No, no. I'm fine. I'm glad you called." She tried to sound casual. "Do you have news for me?"

"News?"

"Yeah, do you have any new leads? Have you arrested anyone?"

"Now, Mrs. Howard, we talked about this."

"Grace."

"Grace, you know even if I heard any new information, I'm not supposed to tell anyone. That's an ongoing investigation and you're a civilian. You understand that, right?"

"Oh, sure. I just thought…well, if it was something that wasn't a secret." She made a face at the phone. She cursed herself for appearing too eager. She'd have to back off, put on kid gloves if she expected to get anything out of Shipps.

"What can I do for you, Officer Shipps?"

"When you called last night, you asked if I knew anyone who would be willing to do a little private security work at the Westergard wake."

"Yes."

"I've given it some thought, and I'd like to take the job myself, if you don't mind."

"Oh? Well, that would be great." Grace kept her voice even, trying not to show her hand this time. "The florists and caterers and all won't start arriving until about 4:30, so if you could be there by then, that would be perfect."

"Will do."

"It's not that I'm expecting trouble or anything, but you never know."

"Mrs. Howard, until we apprehend the killer, it's perfectly right to take precautions. As a matter of fact, I'm sure Detective Morton will have someone in the area, maybe even parked out front. Come to think of it, if you called him, he'd probably provide someone to be stationed inside the party."

"No, no. You'll do just fine. I don't want to make a circus out of this." Dana would probably do that all on her own. "And please, call me Grace."

Chapter 12 — Inglenook House

The next night, Nick surprised Grace with dinner reservations at Vinnie's, their favorite Italian restaurant.

She was skeptical of his motives at first and suspected she was going to get another lecture on personal safety and situational awareness. But it soon became clear that he just wanted ravioli. Nick had always been better at letting things drop than she was. An annoyingly enviable trait.

They ate and drank and enjoyed each other's company. The marinara was even better than at Stella D'oro, and a lot less expensive. Dean Martin sang "That's Amore" in the background, and she could feel herself relaxing. She'd needed this. They'd both needed this.

Over dessert, Nick asked how the memoirs were coming along. Grace told him about the New Orleans fortune teller and the ashes.

"Have you told Dana?" he asked.

"About what?"

"The ashes, of course. She'll have to make arrangements to have him scattered." He paused and studied her over his fork full of ravioli. "That's a strange thing to say—have him scattered—but that's what it is. And she might want some help with it. Maybe one of his old bandmates could do the Whiskey a Go Go thing."

Grace nodded, her mouth too full of cannoli to reply. She hadn't given it much thought, but now realized that someone would have the unsavory task of divvying up Sparks's remains into separate portions. She'd call Dana, but not tonight and not tomorrow. She needed a break from Dana.

She pushed the dessert plate away. She seemed to have lost her appetite.

Grace thought her part of the wake arrangements were done. Her plans for the week ahead were devoted to transcription.

Then Dana called and it went right to the back burner. Again.

The message was left on Grace's phone at 1:34 a.m. on Monday morning. She was beginning to think Dana had some sort of disease where she never slept. Or maybe she was just a cyborg. Either way, Grace didn't listen to the message until 8:45 a.m., when actual human beings were awake.

"Hi, Grace, it's me. I just had a few more teensy-weensy things that need to be taken care of before Saturday." Dana's voice sounded like her usual chipper self, in spite of the time. "First of all, there are just so many people calling and wanting to know what charity they can donate to in Sparks's memory. Well, I just don't know much about that sort of thing. I was hoping you could choose one and set that up and, you know, get the word out. Make it something Sparks would have liked. Whatever." Grace could almost see Dana waving her manicured hands dismissively as she spoke. It seemed nothing was near and dear to Mrs. Westergard's heart except her own implants.

Grace wrote the rest of the requests in her notebook, wondering just how long a voicemail message could be before it cut the caller off.

"I can't tell you how great it is to have you helping me with all of this, Grace. You've just been the absolute best. I'm so glad Sparks hired you and, who knows, maybe I'll get you to do my memoirs after you finish with his."

Grace took a deep breath, unclenched her teeth, and tried to put the phone down gently. She began to count to ten, got to five and called BJ.

Monday was BJ's usual day off work, and she sounded genuinely excited when Grace asked for help.

"I know just the place," BJ said. "The absolute, perfect place. Sparks would love it and they really need the help. Wayne's one of our customers. He's a great guy, and always asking me to come by for a tour. Let me call him, and we can go over there this morning. Come pick me up. I'll be ready to go by the time you get here."

Grace didn't ask. She didn't even try to get a word in. She just picked up her keys, her purse, and her phone, and headed to BJ's apartment.

BJ was waiting on the curb when Grace pulled up to her building. She jumped in the car like a kid heading to Disneyworld. Wayne had been delighted to hear from her. Grace thought she detected a blush in BJ's round cheeks as she rattled off the directions. They were heading for the Inglenook House, a local program for recovering alcoholics, and Wayne was the director.

"Oh, yeah, I've heard of them," Grace said. "That's a wonderful idea, BJ. Sparks would love it. I knew I asked the right person."

BJ blushed even redder and, for once, had nothing to say.

Housed in a building on First Avenue North, Inglenook House was in one of the oldest parts of downtown Birmingham. The cornerstone on the building read 1890, and it might have been a historic landmark if it hadn't been built as a warehouse. No gargoyles. No fountains. No Greco-Roman friezes. It was a building built for a purpose, next to the train tracks that had delivered its cargo for almost a hundred years.

Now its sturdy block walls housed an interfaith ministry and a twenty-bed facility for recovering alcoholics. They also operated a soup kitchen that was open to anyone in need.

A shiny, black, Lincoln town car was parked at the curb at the front door, a new, silver Ford SUV right behind it.

Kelly Adamson

Grace pulled into the vacant spot behind the Ford and let the car idle. "Do you think we're interrupting something? I doubt that your friend Wayne owns that Lincoln."

BJ shook her head. "He didn't say anything about it when I talked to him on the phone. He said he'd be expecting us."

The women got out and made their way up the cracked sidewalk past the two expensive vehicles, like new pennies in a sack of old coins.

The entrance was recessed into the front of the building, a heavy wooden door with the Inglenook House logo painted on it. Grace reached for the long, metal handle just as it swung outward. She lurched sideways as it hit her on the shoulder, knocking her off balance and back into the sidewalk.

A man grabbed her arm just before she collided with the Lincoln.

"Oh, please forgive me. I'm terribly sorry, miss." He carried a hard-sided case, like a professional photographer might use.

She rubbed her arm and tried to smile. "No, no. My middle name is Klutz. No worries."

Satisfied, the man made his way to the SUV and drove off.

Behind him, four more men filed out of the building, the first two in identical black suits. Both were medium height, wiry and even moved the same. They could've been twins, except one was black and the other white. One held the door while the other continued on to the driver's side of the Lincoln.

After them, a taller, thin man, impeccably dressed in a dove gray suit and an easy smile, sauntered out, his hand clapping the shoulder of the fourth man. This one was much shorter and much more casually dressed in cargo shorts and a tee shirt. Wayne, presumably.

The taller man said, "I can't thank you enough for accommodating us on such short notice."

"Nonsense," Wayne said. "I always have time for a new donor."

The man's smile widened as he shook Wayne's hand. "Well, that's fine, and I hope I can count on your support, come September."

Wayne laughed, a noncommittal sound, not a yes and not a no.

The man stepped to the town car, where the white twin waited with the rear door held open. At the last moment, he noticed Grace and BJ. He inclined his head and said, "Ladies," just before the man in black shut the door.

He wore a smile, but there was something in his eyes that didn't seem quite friendly. It was incredibly, uncomfortably familiar.

Wayne spotted them and seemed more than just professionally happy to see BJ. He gave her a clumsy hug, and she blushed scarlet.

"BJ! I was so happy to get your phone call. A very pleasant surprise. And this must be the friend you mentioned." He took Grace's hand in both of his and shook it warmly, ushering them inside out of the heat.

The lobby was large and inviting, with mixed furniture that looked worn, but comfortable. A radio played somewhere in the distance.

Before Wayne could say anything else, Grace said, "I have to ask, who is that man who just left? I know I've seen him somewhere."

"Oh, I'm sure you have," Wayne said, gesturing for them to follow him. "He's running for senate. You've probably seen his ads on TV."

Grace nodded, then remembered the man's eyes. She hadn't liked them on the commercials either. Maybe it was a hazard of being a politician. Shifty eyes.

Wayne, on the other hand, had beautiful eyes, sparkling and crystal blue.

"He stopped by with a donation," Wayne patted the pocket of his cargo shorts, "and asked if he could take a few photos—good-will stuff, you know."

BJ, for once, was completely silent. Her eyes never left Wayne as he showed them around the facility, pointing out the dining hall and chapel. There

Kelly Adamson

was even a sparse gym at the rear of the building, in an open area that still held heavy metal racks along the wall from its warehouse days.

Wayne was in his mid-fifties, short and stocky, with light brown hair and a full beard. His teeth were crooked, but his smile was genuine. Grace was beginning to understand what BJ saw in him.

"I used to know Sparks a little, back in the day," he said. "I played bass in the early 80's in a punk band called Downward Spiral."

"I never knew punk was popular in Birmingham."

"It wasn't. And we were no exception. Prophetic, huh? Sparks and his crew were younger, just starting out, but we all knew they were going places, you know. Even then. You either have it or you don't, and they had it."

He waved them forward into an old freight elevator and he pulled the top half of the door downward. The bottom half rose to meet it. He propped a booted foot on it to keep it closed and pushed a metal button that must have, long ago, had an arrow painted on it. The cage rose, slowly and noisily.

"I know what it's like," Wayne continued. "The rock and roll life. I drank, did drugs, whatever anybody had. I might say it was fun, but there were a couple of years there where I don't remember much at all." He tugged at the collar of his tee-shirt as he spoke, and Grace wondered if not remembering was worse than remembering.

He took his finger off the button and the cage stopped with a jerk, almost even with the second floor. The door parted as soon as Wayne took his foot away and the trio stepped out. Doors lined both sides of the hallway, most of them open, showing a setup like a dorm room with two beds in each. Double rooms, Wayne explained as they walked, were better here than singles, and kept the men from being alone. Solitude was the enemy of the recovering alcoholic.

A large, sunny day room ran the length of the building at the end of the hall. Two men sat on a couch playing a video game on an old console TV.

One had his leg in a cast and the other was pale and emaciated, and not much older than a teenager. The older man grinned and waved his game controller at Wayne as a greeting. The younger man didn't seem to notice them.

Wayne waved back but didn't disturb them.

"Where is everybody?" Grace asked as they headed back to the elevator.

"Most of them are at work. That's one of the things we stress here. We help them find jobs. We have a lot of good partners around the city who'll hire our guys. It gives them something to do as well as make their own money and get back a sense of pride."

They loaded into the old elevator again and Grace watched with a smile as BJ and Wayne stole glances at each other on the ride down.

"It's hard to believe you were ever an addict," Grace said. "You seem so squeaky clean."

Wayne chuckled. "Oh yeah, I knew all the dealers in the area. I even knew the bootleggers if we happened to be traveling through a dry county. Some of the dealers have moved on, turned their lives around, tried to make amends in their own way. Some are respectable now, important people. But some weren't so fortunate."

"What made you change?" It was the first thing BJ had said since they got there.

"Well, I've told this story a lot of times," Wayne said, "but it's one of my favorites. You see, one morning, I woke up to one of Birmingham's finest rousting me. Not the first time I'd passed out on the steps of the Methodist church there in Five Points, at the fountain. You know the place?"

The women nodded. Everyone in Birmingham knew the beautiful, landmark church on Southside, with its terra cotta roof, octagonal bell tower, and the Storyteller Fountain that stood in front of it.

"But what made that morning different from the others, I don't know. The bells started ringing, calling everyone in to worship and I found myself going in, too. Now, I can't say my turnaround was immediate—no bolt of lightning, no hand reaching down out of the clouds for old Wayne. But I started going back there, every Sunday, and every Sunday I got a little stronger. Then, one day, I realized I hadn't had a drink in a week. It was then I knew my chains were broken. I was lost, but now I'm found. It's not that easy for most people, I know. And I feel like that's why I was spared. I've been put here to help them. I want them to know they're not alone."

Grace and BJ left Inglenook House and headed over Red Mountain. Passing by the statue of Vulcan that towered over Birmingham, they headed back down into Homewood and stopped at Crape Myrtle Café for lunch.

The waitress brought them creamy chicken and rice soup and corn bread. They ate in silence for a few minutes, enjoying the food and the easy background drone of the other diners.

"Oh, before I forget," Grace said, "Dana wants a slideshow projected on the rear of the house once the sun goes down. Pictures of Sparks. And I was wondering if you would mind putting that together. You've got more pictures of him than anyone I know."

BJ looked up from her soup and cocked her head, clearly puzzled.

"At the wake, I mean."

"Oh, the wake. Of course." BJ nodded and looked away, busying herself with refolding her paper napkin on the table. Grace felt a jolt, as if someone had touched her with a low voltage taser.

"Oh, dammit. I haven't formally invited you, have I? Is that it?"

BJ shrugged off the slight and gave a weak smile.

"Don't be ridiculous," Grace said. "You know you don't need an invitation. Don't think for a second that you're not wanted there. You and

Cassie and Vicki—all three of you. Sparks would want you to be there. No, Sparks would *insist* that you be there."

BJ nodded, but still didn't meet Grace's eye. "Aw, I know you would invite me, but what about Dana? The only time I met her, she looked at me like I had two heads or something. I guess I don't look like *her kind of people.*" She held up her hands to do air quotes over the last four words.

"It probably just slipped her mind," Grace said, knowing that was a lie. "She knows how important you were to her husband."

To be honest, there were probably a lot of people Dana should have included on that list, but didn't, like a representative from Sparks's record company. Grace had remembered that one on her own. Whether Dana had left them off on purpose was another matter, one Grace didn't want to think about. She had confronted the grieving widow about why none of Sparks's family was starred in his address book, but the answer made her feel even worse. She resolved not to ask Dana anything else.

Sparks was an only child, Dana had informed her. His father died in Vietnam without ever getting to play a single game of catch with his baby boy. His mother married and divorced four times in the years following his death, never able to find anyone to replace the man she loved and lost. Sparks wasn't close to any of his stepfathers, all of whom were around for a year or less. His mother succumbed to lung cancer in 2012. That left Sparks with one great-uncle as his only living relative. Grace tracked him to a nursing home in north Georgia. Possibly the unkindest cut of all, Great-uncle James was suffering from Alzheimer's and didn't remember having a great-nephew.

So, that was that. Dana was all Sparks had in the way of family. No wonder he'd turned a blind eye to her dalliances.

"The truth is, I'd love to make the slideshow," BJ said. "Truly. But I don't have my computer back from the police yet."

Grace groaned, feeling stupid all over again. "Let me pull my big foot out of my mouth and start again. Do you think Cassie or Vicki would be able to put it together? All I could do would just be to take pictures off the Internet. That's not what I want."

In truth, she knew she could go back to the vault at Sparks's house and get all kinds of never-before-seen shots, but she needed to involve the Sparklers. Especially since she'd somehow forgotten to invite them.

BJ said the other ladies would be honored to help. She would call them as soon as she got home.

"Too bad you can't use those stacks of hard copies you have at your house," Grace said, trying not to sound too interested. "What did you say he called them? Blackmail photos?"

BJ nodded. "Yeah, too bad. But those are awful. And very few are actually of Sparks, anyway."

"I've been thinking. You said he was teasing when he called them that—blackmail photos, I mean—but maybe there's some truth to it. You've seen them all. Do you think any of those pictures could have gotten him killed?"

BJ's eyes widened, but she quickly dismissed the idea. "I don't see how. No one even knew they existed except Sparks. He told me he had them in a locked room at his house. Besides, other than a few naked people or some obvious drug use, there wasn't much to see. Lot of people passed out, of course. That seemed to be a popular subject. But nothing that would have surprised anyone, considering that crowd. Everyone knew they were wild."

"That's kind of proving my point, though," Grace said with an encouraging nod. "If there was really nothing to them, why was Sparks so intent on protecting them? Why did he make you promise not to publish any of them? Surely some of them were publishable, out of that whole box. There must have been at least a hundred pictures."

BJ nodded, nibbling slowly on the last piece of cornbread. "One hundred and sixty-one. And yes, some of them were good. But he must've had his reasons. I guess that's one more question we'll never get to ask him."

Grace cleared her throat, plunging ahead into the question she'd been working up her courage to ask. "Would you mind very much, I mean, would you, by any chance, let me borrow those photos?"

BJ gave her a startled look, as if she'd just asked to borrow her underwear.

"Just for a few days," Grace continued hurriedly. "I only want to take another look at them. I'll give them back to you." She held up her right hand as if about to testify in court. "I, Grace Howard, do solemnly swear that I will protect those photos with my life."

BJ's face softened and she nodded, the tight brown curls springing gently around her head. "It's okay," she said. "You can borrow them. I guess part of me was just thinking that the last thing Sparks ever said to me was when he told me to guard those pictures and not let anyone else have them." She sniffed a little and squared her shoulders, but this time there were no tears. "If Sparks trusted you with his deepest, darkest secrets, then I trust you, too." Grace felt that pin prick again, uncomfortable in the knowledge that he must not have trusted her after all.

Both women had ordered pie for dessert, and they ate in silence a few more minutes before Grace said, "Did that man in the suit at Inglenook House look familiar to you?"

BJ grinned and blushed a deep scarlet. "I guess I didn't notice."

Grace laughed, genuinely relieved to have a new and much more enjoyable topic of conversation. "Oh, right. You only had eyes for Wayne. So, what's up with that?"

"We're just friends. That's all." BJ giggled and waved her hands in the air as if shooing the notion aside.

Kelly Adamson

"Yeah, that hug he gave you when we first got there sure looked friendly."

That drew more embarrassed giggles from BJ, and Grace breathed an audible sigh of relief. She hadn't meant to leave the woman out and she certainly wasn't trying to alienate the Sparklers, especially now that she would need them more than ever.

The oak tree in front of BJ's apartment building was massive. It hadn't had to compete for sunlight or rain for the past one hundred years and its canopy easily shaded several thousand square feet. Two people wouldn't be able to link arms around its trunk.

Grace craned up at its gently rustling leaves as she passed underneath, a Wal-Mart bag full of blackmail photos hugged tightly to her chest. The crack head and her ninja friend were nowhere in sight, but she wasn't taking any chances this time. They weren't going to steal this bag. Pepper spray in hand, she hurried back to her car and headed home.

Chapter 13 — Cindy

Bag of fritters in hand, Grace kept her usual Wednesday morning with Cindy on the patio of Sparks's house. Dana was mercifully still asleep, so Cindy kicked off her Crocs and put her feet up. The patio furniture was top quality, imported wood from a rain forest, or some such. Something Dana chose because it was the most expensive offering from the decorator, no doubt. It made Grace smile when the housekeeper put her size nines up on the seat of one of the chairs.

Grace was tempted to kick off her sandals as well and make use of the fourth chair as a footstool when she remembered the photos. She pulled the Wal-Mart bag out of her purse.

"How long did you say you've known Sparks?"

"Since before he moved back to Birmingham full time," Cindy said. "Almost sixteen years."

"Maybe you can identify some of these people for me, if you don't mind. They were all in a box marked 'Blackmail Photos.' I'm trying to see if there's anything in here that Sparks would think was worth hiding."

Cindy grinned with a mouthful of fritter. "You trying to be Nancy Drew or something? A little amateur sleuth? That's okay. I read those, too. Always wanted to drive a roadster when I grew up, just like Nancy."

Grace grinned back, not sure how to respond to that. She pulled the stack of photos from the bag and held them out to Cindy. The woman waved them away with sugar-covered hands and a shake of her head. "Spread 'em out on the table," she said, "or they'll be stuck to me."

Grace obliged, and Cindy leaned low over the pictures, examining them, studying them, her nose almost touching a few. "Man, these are ancient. Gotta get in my way-back machine for these."

The yellow sulfur butterflies flitted around Sparks's little circle of garden below and Grace watched them while she waited. It was quiet in this secluded part of Birmingham, so close as the crow flies to downtown, yet sheltered somehow, by terrain, winding roads, and the unspoken camaraderie shared by the old-money families in any big city. The only sounds were birds and the summer breeze blowing through the vast screens of southern trees. No traffic, no barking dogs, no sirens. Only the occasional sound of a "Hmph" or "Uh-huh" from Cindy.

Out of the one hundred and sixty-one photos in the bag, Cindy was able to positively identify the subjects of only thirty of them. "Most of these are so old, way before my time with him. But I recognize a few, at least by nicknames. But nothing fishy. No bad blood that I know of."

Cindy tapped one of the 4 X 6's with her fingernail. "This guy, Mr. Eight-Ball here, he looks familiar. But I can't place him. And I can't put a name to him." The face of the skinny man with the frizzy brown hair stared up at them, outstretched hands frozen in time with the tiny bundles of drugs. "Of course, guys like him were a dime a dozen back in the day. But the good ones knew enough to stay under the radar or they wouldn't be around for long, you know."

"Makes sense." Grace nodded absently. "I don't imagine Sparks himself would have had much to do with drug dealers, though. It's not as if he owed one money he never paid, or anything."

"You should bring all these to the wake," Cindy said. "Ask Ax or Honeybear to ID them. They were with him in the beginning. They might remember." She shrugged. "Or they might not. Won't hurt to ask."

"You don't think that would be inappropriate? At the wake, I mean?"

"Inappropriate? This crowd doesn't know the meaning of the word. Trust me." Cindy snorted. "Speaking of inappropriate, have you shown these to the widow Westergard?" Her tone did nothing to hide her disdain for her new employer.

A chuckle escaped from Grace before she could stop it. She glanced back into the house for signs of said widow, but saw none. "No, she's only known him seven years, and these pictures are much older than that. You said so yourself."

Cindy grunted in agreement and started on her second fritter.

A jolt of deja-vu hit Grace as she watched the older woman. "I hope you're planning on coming to the wake Saturday, and not waiting on a formal invitation."

The piercing gray eyes looked up from the pastry, and for a second Grace could see the woman who'd thrown a drunken musician in the pool for getting fresh. "Humph. Who's gonna keep me away?" she mumbled.

Kelly Adamson

Chapter 14 — Sophia and the Stones

Yellow roses and huge white spider mums decorated every imaginable surface in Sparks's house. There was nowhere left for the caterers to put the food, and that left Grace clumsily lugging an overloaded vase of flowers from the dining room down the marble hallway in search of a new home.

Every open room she passed was already decorated. She panted a little, struggling with the three foot-wide bouquet until she finally reached the end of the hall. It was the bathroom, Sparks's bathroom, the one where she'd walked in on him, dripping wet and singing, looking every inch the rock god he was. Was that only two weeks ago? He'd been glowing that morning, golden, resplendent. Now, leaning back, Grace caught sight of the vaulted skylight over the tub and smiled. Sparks would've been resplendent in the dark.

She sat on the edge of the tub and slowly lowered the vase onto the floor in front of her. The tallest bit of greenery was even with the top of her head. Of course, Dana had chosen the flowers. Heavy handed, as usual. Her only contribution to the wake planning.

And now it was finally time. The week had gone by in a blur of last-minute details and 2:00 a.m. texts from Dana. Grace finally began muting her phone at night on Tuesday.

The flurry of activity had only allowed enough time to transcribe two tapes during the week. On the first one, Sparks had talked about the loss of his mother to cancer. It took Grace half a day and half a box of Kleenex to get through it.

The second tape told the story of the original lineup of the band, with Ax, Honeybear, and Redfoot. Sparks told of how they met, of practicing in

Honeybear's barn until his dad unceremoniously unplugged them and told them they were drying up the cows. Their loud music was apparently distressing to the barn's true occupants and was keeping the brown-eyed bovines from producing any milk.

The first of many disapproving audiences, Sparks promised.

In spite of the solemn occasion, Grace was looking forward to meeting Ax and Honeybear with a fangirl glee that paled only to the thrill she'd felt when first meeting Sparks.

They would all be arriving in a few short hours and, so far at least, everything was on schedule. The florists had been early, in fact, and were there when Grace arrived at noon. She'd watched as the lighting guys unspooled cable and the caterers unloaded boxes and chafing dishes from a white van.

Officer Loose Lips Shipps met each of them at the gate, inspecting the deliveries. He was in civvies, a dark suit and tie, though he'd shrugged out of the jacket almost immediately, and hung it for safekeeping on the back of Sparks's desk chair. The inspections seemed a little like overkill, but Grace was glad he was there, even if she had chosen him for selfish reasons. She planned to corner him before everyone else arrived—including Nick—and get as much information out of him as she could about the investigation. Maybe now was a good time for that.

Grace nudged the big vase into the approximate center of the front of the tub with her foot—close enough—and headed back out to find Shipps.

There were two closed doors on the right side of the hall that Grace knew led to guest rooms. Passing the first one, she distinctly heard the sound of a dog coming from inside. Full of indignation—after all, this was Karishma's house, and the little fur ball would never allow some other dog in her domain—Grace backed up and opened the door, not pausing to knock.

What she saw surprised her even more than a puppy would have. A little girl, five or six years old, sat cross legged in the middle of the bed. She

Kelly Adamson

seemed a little startled at the door opening, but smiled when she saw Grace. The smile lit up the room. She must have passed the little girl's friend-or-foe meter. Her little hands pressed a button on the controller she held and the video game paused, the animated puppies stopping in midair as they chased soap bubbles.

The girl had a round face, big, dark eyes and shiny black hair pulled back in a purple sequined scrunchy. "Hi," she said, "I'm Sophia. Who are you?"

"Um, I'm Grace. It's nice to meet you, Sophia."

Looking around the room, it was clear to see the girl had made herself at home. There was a plastic suitcase with a cartoon princess on front in one of the chairs, and on the bed, a baby doll and a stuffed dog were arranged against the pillows so they could watch the progress of the video game. A small pair of tennis shoes lay discarded on the floor, along with a purple pair of socks with ruffles at the top.

"Are your mom and dad here tonight?"

The girl cocked her head to one side, as if that might be a trick question. "My mommy's in Heaven," she said matter-of-factly, "but my daddy's here. He's a friend of Ms. West-er-gard." She pronounced each syllable carefully.

Grace was thrown off balance by the little girl's answer. And then it hit her. "Is your daddy's name Raul?

Sophia nodded, her ponytail bouncing. The pair was silent for a few seconds and then the girl looked down at the controller in her hands. "Can I play my game now?" She was asking for Grace's permission. Raul, or someone, had taught her manners.

"Sure, sweetie. I've got work to do anyway. You keep playing."

The last part was unnecessary as the animated puppies resumed their antics before Grace backed out the door and closed it behind her. She wasn't quite sure what to make of that. She hadn't seen Raul anywhere. But she knew Dana had gone upstairs to shower and change, so that probably answered that.

It was almost five o'clock when Dana and Raul finally surfaced, slinking down the stairs arm in arm. The grieving widow and her spiritual counselor. Grace ducked into one of the half-baths and held her breath until they passed. She couldn't find it in herself to feel pity for a woman who was playing grab-ass at her own husband's wake. It didn't help that she was dressed in a tight, black satin sheath that looked more like something you would wear under your dress, not an actual dress itself.

Grace had arrived at noon, wearing a conservative black pantsuit over a pale grey silk blouse. Like Officer Shipps, she'd abandoned her jacket immediately. But that was five hours ago, most of which had been spent outside in the Birmingham heat, directing the AV guys, the tent guys, the bartender, and so on. Never mind that it was the pinnacle of inappropriateness to have a bar at the wake of a reformed alcoholic, but Dana was to thank for that little cherry. The last half-hour had been spent trying to cut Shipps away from the herd long enough to question him. Impossible, considering that every time he saw her, he jumped immediately into action, redoubling whatever efforts he was currently undertaking, as if he thought she was about to fire him for laziness.

At any rate, Grace was beginning to regret not bringing along fresh clothes, or at least some deodorant, some perfume, or maybe some wet wipes. The image staring back at her from the mirror above the bathroom's sink was frightful. Wisps of limp hair stuck to her face and neck while mascara—which she rarely wore—smudged under her eyes like the walking dead. The silk blouse showed circles of perspiration under her arms and there was surely a similar stripe down her back.

There was nothing in the opulent, but tiny, powder room to help. On a whim, she ducked out and headed back down the hallway to Sparks's marble bathroom.

She closed the door behind her and looked around for the first time. A linen closet larger than her clothes closet at home held all the necessities—French milled soaps, salon shampoos, Egyptian cotton towels. She wet a washcloth and washed her face and neck, then stripped off the grey silk blouse and made a more thorough job of it. The closet also yielded a brush, hairspray and deodorant—men's deodorant, of course, but she was in no position to be picky.

She picked up a bottle of cologne and sniffed. It sent a jolt straight through her to smell the scent of Sparks again. She hadn't even been certain she'd recognize it, but it was instant and absolute. Before she thought better of it, she splashed it on her neck.

After a few minutes, she felt more presentable, though now shirtless. The grey silk was spotted with water now, completely unwearable.

Across the room, the door to Sparks's bedroom stood open. Not the room he shared with Dana, but the one he used when she was gone, or he was working late, or just wanted to be alone. The one where his reading glasses sat beside the bed and his tee shirt with the Rolling Stones logo on front lay crumpled on the floor. Grace crossed the room as quietly as possible and felt for the light switch.

The room was spotless now, thanks to Cindy. No clothes on the floor, but there was a dresser. Grace opened drawers until she found it. Clean and folded neatly, on top of the stack. The gray material was soft as her silk blouse and a little thin and shrunken from a multitude of washings. The famous logo with the ruby red lips and tongue was still quite visible on its front, if a bit faded.

She picked it up, smelled it, hugged it to her chest. She held it in front of her and looked in the mirror. Growing chilly in her white lace bra, she only hesitated a second before slipping the tee-shirt over her head. Standing tall, she smiled at her reflection. Sparks would love it.

Kelly Adamson

Chapter 15 — Honeybear and Rooster

Grace scanned the room for a familiar face and saw quite a few. Familiar from album covers or MTV, but few she'd actually met.

BJ was there too, her tight brown curls bobbing up and down, deep in conversation with a middle-aged woman and a slightly younger man, both conspicuously dressed in designer suits. Sparks was a leather and denim kind of guy, and his mourners had all come dressed accordingly. The two suits must be the SPF Records representatives, Natalia Gallego plus one.

Grace took a step forward to introduce herself when Cindy's voice rose from behind a shaggy, blond hulk who looked very much like a World's Strongest Man competitor.

"Honeybear! You old so-and-so, come here and give little Cindy some sugar."

The big man obliged with a booming laugh, lifting Cindy off the floor as he did, a feat a lesser man would never even attempt.

"Why don't you ever come and see me, you big lug?" she demanded, batting him on the arm in mock reproach.

"Aw, you know the cows keep me busy now, Cindy," he drawled. "I still give lessons every now and then, if the price is right. But, it's gotta be pretty damn right to get me off my little patch of ground in Blount County."

"Ha! That little patch of ground covers about a thousand acres, I reckon. I don't blame you for not wanting to leave. But, I'm glad you came tonight."

Grace eyed the giant of a man, wondering what drum stool could possibly hold him. He hadn't looked that big back in their heyday, but then, he was generally at least partially hidden amidst the jungle of drums and cymbals that were one of the calling cards of rock musicians in the '80s and '90s. Not to mention the fact that heavy drug users didn't tend to be muscular. His size was largely a byproduct of his post-rock, Farmer Brown lifestyle.

Cindy saw her standing there with her mouth open, and reached out to grab her arm and pull her into the conversation. "Ah, Grace, there you are. I want you to meet somebody." Cindy took her by the shoulders and turned her around. That's how she found herself staring up into the face of one of the greatest rock drummers of his generation.

"Honeybear, this is Grace Howard. She's been working with Sparks on his book and she put this whole shindig together. Grace, this is Nathan Ray, but everyone knows him as Honeybear."

Grace had spoken to him on the phone, had heard him cry when he spoke of his old friend, and waited uncomfortably while he gathered his composure. She shouldn't have been feeling these butterflies. She should have been able to stay poised and professional, to say, "It's a pleasure to meet you, Mr. Ray. I'm sorry for your loss." But, instead, all she could do was grin, a big, idiotic grin.

Honeybear didn't seem to notice, but took her hand—which had been hanging limp at her side—and shook it firmly and reverently, like he was meeting the President, or John Bonham resurrected.

"Grace, I'm so glad to meet you," he said like he meant it. "Sparks called me a couple of months ago to tell me he was gonna write a book, and he wanted to know if he had my permission for a couple of the stories he wanted to tell. That's the kind of guy he was. Wanted my permission. He said he had a girl who was gonna help him write it. He'd just met you that day at his restaurant. He sounded so excited. Like the old Sparks was back."

His nose had turned red above his thick beard and his brown eyes were bright with tears. He straightened himself up and cleared his throat, grasping for composure.

"I just want you to know…" He laughed a little shakily, then took his massive hands away from Grace's and rubbed his face briskly.

Cindy rescued him, slapping him on the back with enough force to get his attention. "Aw, come on, Bear. She knows. She's got a couple dozen audio tapes Sparks made, all with embarrassing stories about you, I'm sure. Poor girl's gotta listen to them all and try to make heads or tails out of them. She might even be calling on you for help, if that's okay."

Honeybear nodded down at them, smiling again at last, even if it was a little watery. "You've got my number, Grace. You call me if you have any questions, I'll try to help if I can, but I'll admit some of that time was a little fuzzy around the edges."

"That's a good lad," Cindy said, taking him by the elbow and steering him toward the patio. "Now let's go get something to eat."

"I'll second that," said an oddly familiar voice coming from behind Grace. "My belly thinks my throat's been cut."

Grace whirled around, looking for the owner of that particular Southern drawl. A passing waitress, carrying a tray loaded with canapés, sidestepped quickly to avoid a head-on collision with her.

There he was, ten feet away in a crowded room, but with a voice that could be heard in the rear of a stadium. Rooster Hathcock.

She found her own voice finally—realizing vaguely that she hadn't spoken a single word to Honeybear—and called out to Rooster. The man at his side turned to her with a grin. It was her husband, though she hadn't recognized him, dressed all in black with his unruly hair combed down flat. Where had he gotten those clothes? It appeared he'd actually gone shopping.

Rooster saw her then and threw his tattooed arms open wide. The waitress with her tray ducked and hurried to a less crowded part of the house.

"Hot damn, if it ain't your better half, Nick. Come here darlin', and hug me like your husband ain't watching."

She hurried over and threw herself into the embrace of a man she'd met only once before. He laughed and kissed her on top of the head. Rooster had named them his friends when he met them in Las Vegas less than a year before. During that weekend, he'd been instrumental in keeping them alive. What were friends for?

"Just between you, me, and the fencepost, I gotta say I was surprised to get your call inviting me here," he said.

"Why is that?"

"Aw, there's no love lost between me and Dana Westergard, you know."

Grace smiled. "That seems a common theme. I guess if she only invited Sparks's friends who she actually got along with, it'd be a pretty empty house right now."

"Damn straight. But she knows I remember her when she was still on the pole—and I don't mean NASCAR."

"You knew her when she was a stripper?" Grace asked.

"Oh, yes. I'm not proud of it, but I've spent more than my fair share of time in some less than savory gentlemen's clubs."

"Are you blushing?" Grace gave him a friendly poke in the ribs and he grinned, turning even redder.

"I don't do it anymore, you understand. Me and Misty…. Well, I'm in a committed relationship now."

"In other words, Misty would kill you if she found you in a place like that."

Rooster slapped his thigh and laughed loud enough to turn heads in an already noisy crowd. "You got me there," he said. "But the fact is, I know what Dana was. She tried to look all innocent in those Daisy Dukes and pigtails, but she was a specialty girl."

"Specialty girl?" Nick said. "Is that what it sounds like?"

Rooster nodded and grabbed a few canapés from a passing tray. "You know it, brother. If you flashed enough cash, she'd bark like a dog for you. Whatever you wanted."

Dana's blonde head was visible at the other end of the room, where she greeted mourners at the front door, hugging them, accepting their words of comfort with an appropriate mix of gratitude and sadness.

"They said she quit all that the first night Sparks saw her dance. I guess she saw her ship coming in. You know what P.T. Barnum said, 'There's a sucker born every minute.' But, I couldn't blame the man—Sparks, I mean— she's got one hellacious body." He wriggled his eyebrows salaciously and laughed. "Anyway, Sparks said she made him happy and I guess that's so. He even quit drinking for her. And good God, that boy could drink. Still, I think everybody he knew had a piece of that before he did, and it just didn't seem right to me."

"How about you?" Grace asked. "Did you get a piece of that?"

"I don't kiss and tell."

"In other words, Misty would kill you if she found out," Nick said.

Rooster laughed again. "Oh, lord! Please don't tell her." He snagged two beers from a passing waiter and offered one to Grace. She shook her head. "No thanks. I'm technically working."

He turned up one bottle and held the other out to Nick, who took it with a nod.

"I assume Sparks knew all that about Dana," Grace said, "if he met her at the strip club."

Rooster gave a half shrug. "If he didn't, he was the only one. It sure wasn't a secret, not back then, anyway. She tries to act all respectable now, I know, like it never happened. That's why she's not a fan of yours truly. She knows I know what she really is. I'm not saying taking your clothes off for money makes you a bad person. I'm just saying I wouldn't trust her as far as I could throw her." He took another swallow of beer and continued. "As a matter of fact, my first thought when I heard Sparks was dead was that Blondie'd finally gone and done it. Before she met Sparks, she danced at this club down on the coast. They always said that if a guy didn't tip her well enough, she'd put a little Visine in his drink when he wasn't looking. Make you puke your nuts up, you know."

Grace almost choked on the bottled water she'd been drinking. Rooster pounded her unhelpfully on the back.

"You okay?" Nick asked, blotting the front of her Rolling Stones tee shirt with a paper napkin. He stopped and looked at the big red tongue, but didn't say anything.

She nodded, her eyes on Rooster. "Is that true? I mean, do you know that for a fact?"

Rooster gave a skeptical grunt as he chewed a mouthful of cheese and crackers. "No proof, of course. There were guys who got sick down there, more than their share, I reckon, but it could have been some bad oysters, not necessarily some crazy bitch dosing people with eye drops. I do know that's why she got fired. Too many complaints. Nobody in town would hire her. That's how she ended up at Peachy's."

His eyes narrowed as he looked past Grace toward their hostess, the one and only person in the receiving line, shaking hands and nodding solemnly, flaxen hair falling fetchingly about her shoulders. "All I know is, I wouldn't put anything past old Daisy Fay."

Chapter 16 — Moth to a Flame

"I try to cool my engines,
But you never let me go.
My friends think I should lose you
And they love to tell me so.

You're gonna be the death of me
Is what they always say.
But I can't outrun my feelings.
It's too late to walk away."
— *Cool My Engines (1996)*

It was 8:30 before the sun went down enough for the slide show to be seen properly on the rear wall of the house. The Sparklers had done a brilliant job putting it together and it was a shame that only BJ was there to see it. Vicki, a Dallas-based attorney, was in the middle of the biggest criminal case of her career, while Cassie, who lived near Seattle, was due to give birth to her fourth child in the next few days. On bed rest, she had been more than happy to do the lion's share of the work on the presentation. But travel was out of the question.

Grace stood at the top of the stone steps, looking down over the pool below, sparkling like a case in a jewelry store, the landscape lighting worth every penny of Sparks's money that Dana had spent on it. The ten-foot images of Sparks flashed across the back of the house, close to the spot where he and

Karishma had watched the birds, close to the Freddy Mercury rosebush, where some of his ashes would soon be sprinkled.

About half of the pictures were familiar to Grace—publicity shots, concert stills and the like—but the other half showed Sparks in a way most people had never seen, candid shots, playing with Karishma, composing in his music room, asleep on a plastic float in his pool. Some of the photos included guests who were present at the wake. There was one of a young Honeybear, fifty pounds of muscle thinner, along with the other original band members, Ax and Redfoot. It drew some cheers from the shadowy figures filling the yard below.

As Grace watched, eyes unfocused, the real Honeybear materialized, coming up the stone steps in front of her like a magician had conjured him and blocking her view of his younger, 2D self. He had in tow the real Ax, who was talking in a fake Scottish accent and flapping his arms like a huge bird, recounting some story that had Honeybear howling with laughter.

Ax's hair was cut to his shoulders now, a little thinner and laced with gray, but he was otherwise unchanged from the version projected on the wall behind him.

Grace was directly in their path, but couldn't bring herself to move. It didn't even occur to her as she watched the pair ascend.

Four steps away, Honeybear finally looked up. He grabbed Ax's outstretched arm and said, "There she is, man. It's Grace, the girl I was telling you about."

Grace's 17-year-old self would have swooned at this. Her grown-up self smiled graciously and offered her hand to the guitarist, determined to do more than stare open-mouthed as she had with Honeybear earlier.

"Finally," Ax said with an easy smile and twinkling gray eyes, "I get to meet the famous Grace, the girl with the golden pen."

She chuckled, realizing with a sudden rush that his charm was genuine. "I don't know where you get your information, but news of my fame has been greatly exaggerated. Yours, on the other hand…" She spread her hands, palms up, and inclined her head to both men as if to say, "Cute, but I saw your induction into the Rock and Roll Hall of Fame."

Tall aluminum bar tables had been set up around the patio and Honeybear motioned them to a vacant one in the back corner. Three chairs, two rock stars, and one flickering candle. Grace's teenaged dream fulfilled.

The nimble waiter from earlier appeared out of the shadows like a ninja, carrying a tray of wine glasses this time. Grace took one, determined to make it last the rest of the evening. The idea of drinking at Sparks's wake still made her feel uneasy, at the very least a little disrespectful, but she was definitely the only one.

"Honeybear told me you might want to ask us some questions, and I told him I'd do anything for a pretty girl," Ax said, tilting his wine glass toward Grace in a toast.

She held her own glass up to touch his and took a sip. It was sweet, Moscato maybe, although what she knew about wine wouldn't fill a shot glass.

Over Ax's shoulder, she could see the top corner of the slide show, eerie and disjointed from this angle. With a start, she remembered the blackmail photos, all 161 of which she had brought with her, safely stowed in her purse in the bottom drawer of Sparks's massive walnut desk.

She straightened up and looked at the men in a new light. "Well, actually, if you're serious about that offer, I have something inside I'd love for you to take a look at."

Ax hadn't brought his reading glasses to the wake and, as a result, was absolutely no help in identifying the people in the photos. Honeybear appeared to be warding off the middle-age presbyopia better than his erstwhile guitarist and recognized the very first picture he got his hands on. Of course, it was of his own posterior, with a smiley face drawn across it in blue marker.

"Your butt was a lot smaller back then, man," Ax said.

"I thought you couldn't see them," Honeybear said, pulling the photo back defensively.

"I can't, but I have a fine memory of your lily white ass, since you always seemed to be mooning somebody or other." Ax shook his head in mock disgust. "Like two aspirins kissing."

Honeybear had the good graces to at least pretend to be embarrassed. Or maybe it was genuine. After all, he was a farmer now, not a long-haired head banger. "Aw, man," was all he managed to say. If the light had been better, Grace was sure she could have seen him blush.

It took a while, considering the number of people who found them in their secluded corner and stopped by to say hello, but Honeybear knew about half of the people in the photos. Unfortunately, he knew the vast majority by nickname only.

"I would like to see some of these people again, actually," he said, running a long finger over the slightly blurred image of a pretty brunette in a jester's hat and Mardi Gras beads. "It's a shame I never knew their names. Didn't seem important at the time."

"Yeah, what was that chick's name who always wore all the bracelets and had the big hair?" Ax held his hands out from his head to emphasize the abundance of hair.

"You're describing every woman under the age of forty in 1990," Honeybear said.

"True, but this one drove a brown Firebird. And she had the biggest…" he held both hands in front of his chest like he was holding two cantaloupes. Then he glanced at Grace and said, "She had the biggest stereo in that car."

Grace rolled her eyes. "I know what this means." She mimicked the hand gesture and Ax grinned.

"You mean Birdie." Honeybear said. He shook his head, looking embarrassed again. Or at least apologetic. "We weren't very creative with our nicknames, were we?"

Ax held his hands out and started ticking off the names from memory, folding his fingers down as he went. "Cold Cut, Smokey, Witty, Chico, Sweet Pea, Alice. We thought we knew those people. They were always around, but we didn't even know their real names."

"Alice is a real name," Grace added unhelpfully.

"Yes, but it wasn't *his* name," Ax said. "He was just a big Alice Cooper fan."

"I remember him," Honeybear said. "His mascara was always running."

"Strange little guy. But most of them were. I mean, you'd have to be pretty strange to follow this bunch of hairy delinquents around the country just to get the scraps from our table."

Honeybear, who was still staring at the blurry brunette, said, "But we sure had some pretty nice scraps."

Ax plucked a can of Good People beer off a passing tray and continued with a nod to Grace. "For some of them, it was profitable, you understand. Like Smokey and Witty, our suppliers."

Honeybear gave a dispirited grunt. "Poor Smokey."

"Five or six years ago," Ax explained, "they found Smokey in his own car with a needle still stuck in his arm. He OD'd in his own driveway. Can you believe it?"

Grace shook her head to show that, no, she couldn't believe it, although, of course, she knew nothing of Smokey or his drug habits.

"And Witty just disappeared. Like a ghost," Honeybear said. "Not too long after Redfoot died."

Ax nodded. "We heard all kinds of stories about him. Heard he was doing time. Heard he was dead. Even heard he got a sex change operation in Brazil or somewhere and was living as a woman."

Honeybear laughed, spraying his mouthful of beer and narrowly missing the photos on the table. "God, but he'd make an ugly woman!" he sputtered.

The light from the lone candle reflected in the drops of beer in his beard and made them sparkle like diamonds.

"Not a pretty man, huh?" Grace said. "Did he at least have a good sense of humor, with a name like Witty?"

Honeybear wiped his face with his hand and a waitress appeared at his side with a stack of bar napkins, as if she'd been waiting on this cue. "Not that I recall. I don't think I ever saw him smile. Maybe it was ironic, like calling a guy my size 'Tiny.'"

"Mnn-mmn." Ax held up his hand like a stop sign while he swallowed another mouthful of beer. "Don't forget, he smiled at that girl, what's-her-name, Redfoot's girl."

"CC," Honeybear said.

"Yeah, CC. He had all kinds of smiles for her."

Honeybear stretched in the aluminum chair and sighed. Grace could see the tattoo of a drumstick on the inside of each of his forearms. She wondered what the cows thought of those.

"I don't know, man," he said. "That whole thing was one hot mess."

"I know. I know. You always felt sorry for him, but let's face it—the guy should've known better." To Grace, he added, "This girl was so far out of his league, it was like…" Ax closed his eyes and twirled one hand in the air, searching for the right analogy.

"Like a praying mantis trying to hook up with a butterfly," Honeybear said.

Ax slapped the table and nodded. "That's it, man. This guy had nothing to offer a woman like that. No personality. No looks, no money, no brains, at least none that I ever saw."

"Aw, he wasn't any worse that the others," Honeybear said, "and he always had the goods. Remember? He'd just show up. He didn't carry a pager like other dealers back then. He was just like the Great Pumpkin. You just had to believe and there he'd be."

"True. But that wasn't enough for a girl like her. She was too good for *us*, and we were rock stars. How did a greasy bag of farts like Witty expect to get anywhere with her?"

"Damn, she was fine," Honeybear muttered.

"But she was Tommy Redfoot's girl?" Grace asked, considering herself well and truly part of the conversation now.

"Oh, yeah," Ax said, "from the first time they laid eyes on each other. I was there. I remember. Redfoot was a good looking kid, mind you. All the girls wanted a piece of Tommy. And he had that little-boy-lost thing going on. You know what I mean?"

Grace did, and nodded.

"The women all ate that shit up. So, Redfoot was no stranger to pretty girls, because there were always a few more waiting in the wings for him. But, he saw this one and, bam!" He clapped his hands together and Grace jumped. "It was like he had no control. She was his new drug."

A moth buzzed and bumped around their tiny candle and Honeybear pointed at it. "Like that."

Ax made a deep noise of agreement and all three sipped their drinks for a minute and watched the moth.

"When Redfoot died, that girl was so broken up, they said she tried to kill herself," Honeybear said. "And the next thing we knew, she was gone. Moved to New York or something. Cold Cut said he heard she went into modeling up there."

"I remember that," Ax said. "I kept thinking I'd see her on TV or in some magazine ad, but I never did."

"What's her name?" Grace asked, adding quickly, "besides CC."

Both men shrugged. "Hell, I don't know," Ax said. "I was doing good to know my own name back then."

Grace noticed belatedly that her wine glass was empty. She decided to take advantage of the liquid courage to press her luck a little further and said, "So, what happened to Redfoot, exactly? I mean, I know he OD'd, but what's the real story?"

Ax stiffened, his schoolboy grin gone, replaced by a scowl.

"That's the official story, of course, and I guess it's true, but considering the sheer volume of drugs that boy could do and still play an entire concert," Honeybear shook his head slowly, "well, it was definitely a shock."

"There were no witnesses?" Grace prodded, careful to keep her voice neutral.

"Well, that's the real kicker, isn't it?" Honeybear said. He leaned back farther in the tall, narrow chair, as far as his bulk would allow, and crossed his ankles. "We were all living out in L.A. then, and that's where it happened. Redfoot had a little house in the hills, nothing fancy, but with a killer view of the city from the balcony. It was our usual hangout and we'd all been there that night. Same old, same old. Too much booze. Too many drugs. Too many girls."

Ax tilted his beer bottle in a mock salute and said, "Ah, those were the days."

"When they found him," Honeybear continued, "it was morning and most everyone had crawled back under their own respective rocks by then. There was only one other person still left at the house, but he'd passed out at some point in the night and didn't remember a thing. Just woke up and Tommy was dead. So, to answer your question, no, there were no witnesses."

He had put emphasis on the words "passed out" when he spoke, and Grace saw him make brief, furtive eye contact with Ax. She waited for a minute, but no name seemed to be forthcoming. She cleared her throat, a little dry now that her wineglass was empty, and said, "Who found him?"

The two men stared at each other openly now, and Grace thought maybe they were just waiting to see who would speak first.

Finally, Ax leaned forward and, with one quick motion, trapped the moth between his open palms. Then slowly, he squeezed his hands together and crushed it. He dropped the insect into the candle and the flame sputtered and popped. Without looking up, he said, "Sparks."

Chapter 17 — Ashes to Ashes

It was well after midnight before Grace found herself with a few minutes alone. Not that she was complaining, mind you. The roster of people she'd rubbed elbows with over the last five hours made her want to sneak into Sparks's garage and see if his DeLorean was really a time machine after all. The hair metal bands of the '80s and '90s were all converging on Mountain Brook, and it was bound to adversely affect the space-time continuum.

Nevertheless, when she could finally look left and right and see no one approaching with another half-remembered anecdote for Sparks's autobiography—what part of *autobiography* did they not understand?—she seized the opportunity with both hands, ducked down the hall into Sparks's big marble bathroom and closed the door behind her.

There was no seating in the room, even though there was plenty of space, so Grace leaned back against the door and slid down until she was sitting on the cold, stone floor. She blew out a deep breath and let herself go limp. It had been an exhausting night.

And to top it all off, she wasn't one bit closer to finding out who killed Sparks. The blackmail photos had been a sure thing, she thought, but instead of producing the answers she'd been counting on, they just brought up more questions. Now they seemed little more than ghosts, blurry mementos of a time long past. Dead ends.

Instead of following the leads she thought the photos would produce, her head was swimming with new information, and she didn't know what to make of it all.

Kelly Adamson

The story of Tommy Redfoot's untimely death left her with a slightly queasy feeling. She felt sorry for the little-boy-lost whom the girls adored, and the gentle soul Sparks had spoken of.

The photos all showed him smiling, straight black hair falling halfway down his back. Big, dark eyes framed in a bronze face. Grace thought of a tee-shirt she'd seen long ago. It read, "Die young and leave a pretty corpse." Tommy had done that.

But the looks Ax and Honeybear had exchanged as they told the story weren't mournful. They were angry and strained. The two men said that Sparks had been the only one present at the time of Redfoot's death, but that he'd been passed out at the time. From all Grace had heard of Sparks in his prime, there wasn't enough Scotch in all of Scotland to make him pass out. Did his old bandmates think he had lied? Did they think he'd witnessed something after all? If so, why would he hide it? By Sparks's own admission, Tommy had been his closest friend.

Grace pressed her palms against her temples and squeezed to ease her growing headache. Too late, she remembered Ax and the moth and pulled her hands away.

As if this wasn't enough to think about, she also had Rooster's revelation about Dana, the Visine Queen of the strip club. Rooster was suspicious of the new widow, but it seemed like a stretch to Grace. Dana might have been cruel enough to cause intense gastrointestinal distress to a bad tipper, but that didn't mean she was capable of murder. Plus, her tears for her late husband seemed genuine. Surely she wasn't that good an actress.

A vision swam before Grace's closed eyes, a vision of Dana and her personal trainer, Raul, locked in a passionate embrace in a darkened hallway. Grace had slunk away as quickly and quietly as possible from that scene, but part of her now wished they'd seen her. At least they might have the decency to look guilty when they saw her now, or even better, avoid her altogether.

On second thought, maybe Dana was a better actress than Grace gave her credit for.

If what Rooster said was true—and she had no reason to doubt him—Dana wouldn't be the first woman to marry a wealthy man for his money. She wanted out of the life she was leading and didn't want to spend the rest of her life on a stripper pole in the Appalachian foothills. So she hitched her wagon to Sparks's star and settled in for the sweet life of spray tans and housekeepers and pool boys. Fast forward a few years and in walks the swarthy Latin hunk of her dreams. She falls hard for the penniless personal trainer, but can't stand the thought of giving up her mansion and her Escalade for him. Dana might not miss Sparks, but she would sure as hell miss his money. And in the modern days of prenuptial agreements, Dana was bound to be back on the pole again if her adulterous ways were exposed, much less if she left her cash cow altogether.

Grace's opinion of the black widow was sinking again. Maybe she did kill Sparks after all. Sure, she was in Biloxi at the time, but she could have hired it done. There was almost nothing the right amount of money couldn't buy.

Someone knocked hard on the door above Grace's head and she gasped, scrambling to her feet with one hand over her hammering heart.

"Hey, Grace, you in there?" The voice belonged to Cindy, the housekeeper, who, Grace thought with a flash, seemed likely to share Rooster's estimation of Dana.

"Yes, I'm here." She stumbled back to a quasi-sitting position on the side of the overgrown tub. "Come in. It's open."

Cindy pushed the door a few inches and stuck her head in tentatively. "You okay?"

Grace nodded, still a little breathless, and waved her inside. Perhaps this was a good opportunity to ask Cindy what she really thought of Dana.

126   Kelly Adamson

While she pondered just how to word the inquiry, *Do you think your new boss murdered your old boss*, Cindy spoke again.

"Dana's looking for you. She says there's something she wants to give you."

Grace raised both eyebrows in a silent question, and Cindy shook her head in a silent answer. If she knew what it was, she wasn't saying. She turned to head back down the hall. Grace followed, noticing for the first time the black ribbon she'd tied in her neat, graying ponytail. She was dressed in black jeans and shirt, with tiny black crosses dangling from her earlobes when she walked. For the first time since Grace had met her, she wasn't wearing Crocs. Her feet looked tiny in the black satin ballet flats.

Cindy stepped aside at the back door and motioned for Grace to go through first. It seemed eerily quiet outside, with nothing but the hum of the mourners talking together in small groups by the pool. Little Tater and Truckstop 119 had been a no-show, much to Grace's relief, and BJ had simply loaded the house's sound system with Sparks's collected works. Now that was conspicuously absent from the background noise as Grace stepped onto the patio.

She stopped when she saw what was ahead of her and felt Cindy's hand in the middle of her back, urging her slowly forward.

Dana stood at the top of the stone steps that led down to the pool, bathed in the glow of one of the floodlights someone had re-aimed from the back of the house. That someone was most likely Dana.

The people on the steps, around the pool, and in the yard all seemed to be waiting for something, talking quietly over their drinks, with one eye on their hostess. She turned back to them and clapped her hands for their attention like a kindergarten teacher.

"My friends…" she began, and Grace gave a small snort of disgust that she then tried to cover up with a cough. The woman had some nerve calling these people her friends. Most of them couldn't care less about her, with the exception of Raul, who had at least had the good sense to make himself scarce when the guests began to arrive. Grace had seen him only twice since then, once carrying two large buckets of ice for the bartender, and again heading toward the room where his daughter now slept surrounded by stuffed animals.

Grace heard her own name and snapped to attention. Dana was motioning for Grace to join her at the top of the steps. She closed the distance with some apprehension, cursing herself for not listening to anything after "my friends."

Dana linked her arm in Grace's own and pulled her close. To anyone watching, they might have been best buds. Maybe they met for Sunday brunch and got pedicures together. Just a couple of gals. But while Dana's voice droned on about how Grace was keeping Sparks alive by penning his life story, Grace fought hard against the urge to pull her arm away. Dana's skin felt oddly chilled and her muscles seemed to ripple like a python.

There was polite applause from the crowd and Grace forced herself back to the moment. She gave Dana a tight-lipped smile and murmured thanks.

Dana unwound her arm and bent over a large, leather tote at her feet. She pulled out a smaller bag, one of several, and held it out to Grace. It was an inconspicuous black gift bag with ribbons for handles, but no tissue paper sticking out of it. Maybe it wasn't really meant to be a gift. Grace took it and peered inside. It held a red, plastic container with a screw-on lid, roughly the size of a can of Coca-Cola.

"I wanted Grace to be a part of this because I don't think she realizes what a treasure she has been to my husband, what the gift of her presence and her belief in him meant. You all know Sparks—you know how much he loved to tell a story, and he had a million of them. Once he made up his mind to write this book, and once he found someone he trusted to do it justice," she paused to smile beatifically at Grace, "I saw a change in him. It was like the sun coming out from behind a cloud. The last few months of his life were probably the happiest he ever had, and I owe that in part to this this woman, Grace Howard."

Dana's voice choked up just the right amount at the mention of her name. *And the Oscar goes to… Dana Westergard,* thought Grace.

Another smattering of applause and the diva turned to address her personally, although still loud enough for the people by the pool to hear.

"So, Grace, as you know, it was Sparks's wish that his ashes be divided and sprinkled at some of the places that meant the most to him. His mother's grave at Elmwood Cemetery was one of those places. It would mean a lot to me—to Sparks—if you'd do the honors there."

Grace blinked a few times in the bright spotlight and realized her mouth was hanging slightly open. Was she supposed to say something, make a speech, perhaps? It didn't matter, since she couldn't find her voice.

At last she managed a nod of acceptance, whereupon Dana embraced her, much as one might a cigar-store Indian, and she retreated from the patio to more applause, carrying her small bag of Sparks as if it were nitroglycerin.

She'd known this was coming, ash-wise. After all, she was the one who'd told Dana about it, having heard the tape. But she certainly hadn't expected to be charged with any of it herself.

Inside the house, her knees flatly refused to carry her further and she sank down into the soft leather sofa across from Sparks's desk. She set the bag on the cushion beside her and stared at it.

Moments later, Nick was there, his hand stroking her hair. He paused and knelt in front of her, apparently not wanting to move the bag in order to sit on the couch.

He made no sound as he waited, one hand on her arm. Grace finally took her eyes off the bag and looked at her husband. He was uncharacteristically clean shaven and wearing new clothes, but his hair, slicked back earlier in the evening, had returned to its natural state of randomness, a soft, dark shock that would curl if he let it grow long enough.

He would go with her to Elmwood whenever she decided. He would hold her hand. He would carry the ashes. He might even say a prayer for the immortal soul of Sparks Westergard. Whatever she needed from him, he would give. That much she knew, without him having to say a word.

She put her head on his shoulder and closed her eyes.

Kelly Adamson

Chapter 18 — Dana and the Check

"Get this party started.
Everybody raise your cup
Punch it into overdrive.
I wanna see you get revved up!"
— *Revved up (1989)*

The alarm clock came on four tiny paws the next morning in the form of Karishma. She yipped from the doorway of the bedroom until Grace finally threw a pillow at her. The dog dodged gracefully, then continued her yipping from atop the pillow.

Karishma still hated all other living creatures, including Nick, whose response to the noise was to pull the covers over his head. This meant the responsibility of walking the dog fell completely on Grace's shoulders.

She grumbled, bleary-eyed and cotton-mouthed, and thought momentarily of pushing Karishma and the pillow out into the hallway and closing the door. Only the knowledge that she would have to clean up dog pee later finally forced her feet to the floor.

The reflection in the mirror above the dresser was frightful. She'd fallen into bed without a shower a little before two a.m. and it showed. Her hair, stiff with hairspray, stuck up in every direction and what little makeup remained on her face was smeared in a vertical trail down her left cheek.

She cinched the flannel robe around her waist and attached the pink leash to the now prancing dog. "I liked you better when you hated me," she mumbled.

After slipping her feet in the only shoes in easy reach—the short, black boots she'd worn to the wake—she stumbled out the door and stood sourly in the middle of the front yard while Karishma went about her business at the other end of the leash.

Across the street, her neighbor backed out of her driveway and did a double take when she saw Grace. She pulled her little Fiat up and waved a bejeweled hand out the driver's window. The diminutive Mrs. Davenport was the only person Grace knew who could make a Fiat look big.

Grace tugged on the coffee-stained lapels of her robe, suddenly aware that one of the pockets was torn. Mrs. D. was perfectly put together as usual, but nice enough to pretend not to notice that Grace was anything but.

"Good morning, dear. Still got your little houseguest, I see."

Karishma growled and snapped at the woman as if she knew she were the topic of discussion. Grace gave the leash a quick tug and said, "Yep, and she's wearing out her welcome fast."

Mrs. D. chuckled. "The McKenzies have a new little dog that looks just like that, but not so temperamental, I don't think."

"I should hope not."

"And Sheila and Stan," she pointed down the street like a tour guide, "they had to have their little poodle put to sleep last week. Sweet little thing, seventeen years old if he was a day."

Self-proclaimed head of the unofficial neighborhood watch, Mrs. D. knew all the gossip that was worth knowing. She usually kept the scandalous bits to herself, unless you asked nicely. This morning, however, she was late for brunch with her book club and dashed off with a regal wave, while Grace headed back inside with Karishma, now lighter by a few ounces.

A muffled melody greeted her as she stepped back inside and kicked off her boots. Her cell phone rang from the depths of her purse, playing "Revved Up," one of Sparks's earliest rock anthems, and Grace's favorite.

Kelly Adamson

By the time she found it, the ringing had stopped. The phone was almost dead, but before putting it on the charger, she had to check and see if there was a message from Shipps. He hadn't spoken to her at all at the wake, although she'd seen him several times, always at a distance, blending in nicely in his civvies once he abandoned the jacket and tie. His eyes constantly scanned the crowd, on alert for anything out of the ordinary. By the time she left, she'd forgotten all about him, concentrating instead on the bag of Sparks on her passenger floorboard.

But now, she couldn't wait to hear his report. Maybe he'd noticed something. Maybe he'd seen something. And maybe, just maybe, Loose Lips Shipps would tell her about it.

Instead, she heard the voice of Dana Westergard. The call had come in at 3:45 a.m., and she was glad the phone had been in her purse and not by her sleeping head.

"Hey, Grace. I just wanted to tell you again how grateful I am for all your help with everything. I really can't thank you enough, and I think it all went really well.

"But the reason I'm calling is that the guy you hired for security, that policeman, he was great, but he never came back in to get the check. I have it right here if you want to deliver it to him since I know he's your friend and all. I'll leave it in the top drawer of Sparks's desk for you.

"The cleaners will be in and out all morning—some women Cindy knows—but I won't be here. I'm going to have a spa day. I really need a massage."

This was followed by a pause and a dramatic sigh. Dana was nothing if not dramatic.

"Tonight was so…hard. I guess that's the word I was looking for. Harder than I thought it would be. But everyone's gone now and this big, old house is so quiet when it's just me here. Maybe I should get a dog."

Grace's eyebrows shot up and her gaze turned toward Dana's dog, curled up and snoring lightly in her commandeered dog bed.

"Well, anyway, I think I've had a little too much to drink tonight. I really hate drinking, and I never did it around Sparks. I don't know what made me do it tonight, except maybe I thought it would help me...forget, you know. But it didn't. It doesn't."

The chipper voice cracked then, as Grace had known it would, but it didn't sound contrived this time, just melancholy. Or maybe, thought Grace, it was the sound of guilt.

Grace's mood lightened after she hung up the phone, when the realization hit that playing delivery girl for a check was the perfect excuse to see Shipps. She wasn't going to bother calling. He might tell her to mail it, and she wanted to speak to him in person. He'd said he had to be at work at three o'clock Sunday afternoon, so she planned to be in the precinct parking lot half an hour early, waiting for him. Was that considered stalking? She hoped the police wouldn't frown on it.

Strange bumping noises, followed by a loud thump, came from the front bedroom. She put the phone on the charger and went to investigate. Nick hopped on one foot in the middle of the room, holding the other in both hands and cursing through clenched teeth. What appeared to be the contents of the closet lay scattered around him.

"I was trying to get the suitcases out," he said, nodding toward the rubble. "And I think there was an earthquake or something. Did you feel that?"

"You know we don't have earthquakes in Alabama," Grace said.

"Tell my foot that," he said, "I think it's broken." He fell back on the bed and wriggled his bare toes in the air.

"I have a feeling if you can do that, it's not broken. Now, just why, pray tell, are you getting the suitcases?"

"The contractors' convention in Knoxville. Don't tell me you've forgotten." Nick sat up and shook his head, sore toes forgotten. "I've told you at least three times and it's circled on the calendar. In red."

"But it's not this month. Is it?"

She was close enough to the bed for Nick to easily grab her around the waist and pull her down on top of him. "You just don't want to see me go, do you?"

"No," she said with a grin, "but I love to watch you walk away."

"The feeling is mutual," he said, smacking her lightly on the bottom.

She tried to roll away, but he held her by a flannel-covered arm. "Hey, while I've got you here, there's something I want to tell you."

Grace stilled, surprised by his serious tone. His usually smiling face was strained, and lines showed above his brows that she'd never noticed before. She reached out to smooth his forehead, and he closed his eyes momentarily at her touch. Then he straightened and pulled her hand into his.

"I want you to do something for me while I'm gone."

"Okay."

"I don't want you to get mad at me for saying this, and I don't really know of a nice way to say it."

She narrowed her eyes, but stayed silent.

He took a deep breath. "I want you to stay out of Sparks's murder investigation while I'm gone. I know it's too much to ask you to stay out of it altogether, but at least stay out of it while I'm gone."

Grace pulled back and gave him her most indignant look. "What, exactly, do you think I'm doing? Running around all cowboy vigilante?"

"I have no idea what you're doing. All I know is that you've been showing some pictures around, trying to get them ID'd. Pictures Sparks had labeled 'blackmail photos.'"

"I'm writing a book, remember." She wriggled out of his grasp and stood with her hands on her hips, chin up. "That's what you do when you're writing a book. You look for information."

"Looking for information on his life is one thing. Looking for information on his *death* is another thing entirely."

"Well, what if there's something in those photos that could help find his killer? I can't just ignore that."

"If you think so, even for one instant, you should hand those photos over to the police, and you know it." He gave her an authoritarian glare and she threw back her head with an exaggerated groan. When she looked back down, his expression had softened, his shoulders relaxed, but his eyes were still on her.

"I can't help it if I worry about you," he said. He held up a hand to stop her objections. "I know. You can take care of yourself. You're a grown woman. You humored me at first with the gun safety and the target practice, but I'll admit you're a surprisingly good shot. That being said, you can also be…" he paused and closed his eyes, running a hand through his hair. "What's the word I'm looking for?" he said under his breath.

Grace crossed her arms and glowered at him through narrowed eyes. "You were going to say reckless, weren't you? Reckless and impatient and stubborn. Is that what you were going to say?

The corners of Nick's mouth twitched with the effort not to grin. "Of course not. Why should I say it when you've already said it so well for me?"

He dodged away from a playful swipe at his shoulder, grabbing her again around the waist and pulling her back down onto the bed. He pinned her beneath him in one quick move.

"I'm not going to ask you to promise me, because I'd just be wasting my breath. But please, please, be careful. I don't have to remind you there's still a killer on the loose."

She opened her mouth to protest, but he silenced her again, this time in her favorite way, with his mouth.

At noon, Nick left to get his truck serviced before his trip to Knoxville. Apparently, the contractors' convention really was that week. He'd be leaving on Tuesday and not getting back home until Sunday. With all the craziness going on lately, it had completely slipped Grace's mind.

Well, she could pass the time all right. She planned to stay in and transcribe tapes. The bulk of them would be done before he got back. She was going to do her level best to stay out of trouble, if for no other reason than avoiding Nick's "I told you so."

But he wasn't gone yet, and right now, she had a check to deliver.

She knocked on the French doors that led inside from Sparks's patio shortly after one o'clock. Cindy's head peered around the corner from the back kitchen and then an arm followed, waving Grace inside. A blast of arctic air came through the open door, the temperature turned low for the comfort of the team of cleaners who'd worked all morning to get the place back into *Southern Living* magazine style.

Grace found Cindy at the bar pouring two glasses of lemonade. "You waiting till all the heavy lifting was over?" Cindy said with a grin. "You did good if that was your aim."

"Finally. I hid around the corner for an hour. Thought they'd never get finished," said Grace with a theatrical roll of her eyes. "My doctor says I can't be that close to actual work. I'm allergic."

"Humph."

"I'm just here to pick up a check anyway. Dana left it for the guy who did security last night."

Cindy nodded.

"The truth is, I'm glad everyone else is gone, because I wanted to talk to you alone." She took the glass of lemonade and perched on a barstool.

"Oh, yeah?" Cindy hopped up on the counter with the grace of a ballet dancer, not a middle-aged maid. "I'm all ears."

Grace didn't know where to begin. It had seemed easier when she ran through it on the drive over. But now? She turned up her glass and drained half of it in two gulps. Her gaze fell to the floor where she'd found Sparks's body and a shiver ran through her. Whether it was the air conditioning, the cold drink, or the memory, she didn't know.

"You didn't come all this way to get my lemonade recipe," said Cindy. "Lemons, water, and sugar, by the way. What's on your mind?"

"I was just wondering," Grace said slowly, feeling as if she were about to poke a wasp's nest, "who you think killed Sparks."

She looked up from the floor long enough to see that Cindy was staring at her, head cocked to one side, mouth pressed into a tight line.

"That's a hell of a thing to ask, don't you think? The way you said that made it sound like you thought I had some kind of insider information. What are you accusing me of?"

"No, no, no," Grace protested, shaking her head like she was running from the wasps. "Please, I didn't mean it like that at all. I just meant…" She sighed, knowing she had to come out with it now. She made a pained face and looked squarely at Cindy, who sat, arms folded and back stiff, waiting for an answer.

"I just wondered if you thought anyone you know," she paused and waved one hand around, trying to encompass the house, trying to say *Dana* without saying *Dana*, "might have a motive. Anyone you're suspicious of, maybe. You saw a lot that went on around here that other people didn't see."

Cindy relaxed a little, unfolded her arms and took a sip of lemonade. She nodded slowly and eventually seemed to reach a decision.

"You're asking me do I think his wife killed him, the woman who swore to love, honor, and cherish him? The woman he quit drinking for?" She sucked in a deep breath and blew it out slowly before going on. "I want to say no. Every fiber of my Christian being wants to say no. But the truth is, I've seen a lot of bad things happen in my life. I've seen a lot of folks do a lot of terrible things to people they claimed to love.

"If you're asking me if I think she had motive, well, I guess to some, the thought of having to give all this up," she made a similar all-encompassing gesture like the one Grace made, "in order to live in an efficiency apartment over a gym and eat ramen noodles the rest of her life might be sufficient motive. But if you're asking me if I think she's a killer, I say anyone could be a killer given the proper motivation. That doesn't make it so in this case, but it doesn't make it not so either."

"Well, you're a lot of help," said Grace dryly. "A real oracle you are."

"What did you expect? You thought I had some video of the murder I'd been holding back for some reason?" Cindy scoffed and hopped down from the counter to refill her lemonade. "Sorry to disappoint. No videos." She held out the pitcher to Grace, who waved it away.

"But, on the other hand, if you're asking me if I think Dana Westergard is a no good, spoiled, heartless, selfish, conniving, two-timing, low-life bitch, who could kill her own husband and sleep like a baby that night, then I reckon I'd have to say yes."

Chapter 19 — Rain at the Station

Like everything in Mountain Brook, the building that housed its police department was well-equipped, well-appointed, and boasted tasteful architecture that didn't clash with or detract from its surroundings.

They gave out traffic tickets, arrested a few shoplifters, and investigated the occasional stolen BMW, but the men and women behind Mountain Brook's thin blue line weren't burdened with many murder cases. This was in direct contrast with their neighbors at the Birmingham precinct, who were as well versed in drive-by shootings and home invasions as any other major metropolitan city.

Grace circled the block and settled for a parking place facing the library. The station was directly behind her, flanked by the fire station to the left and a small patch of woods to the right. She carefully edged her ten-year-old Chevy in between a Range Rover and a Mercedes. A quick glance in the rearview mirror confirmed that she had a perfect view of the front door of the precinct house. She was forty minutes early and confident Shipps couldn't get inside without her seeing him. He wasn't getting away this time. A paycheck was the perfect enticement.

She buzzed down all four windows and prepared to wait. Her dashboard said it was 92 degrees, but her car was parked in the narrow shade the library and its ornamental row of crape myrtles could provide so early in the afternoon. In addition, the sun kept disappearing behind gray clouds, and a stiff breeze blew with the promise of a late afternoon shower.

Rummaging through her purse for the bottle of water she'd taken from the fridge at Sparks's house, her fingers closed first on the small, plastic tape recorder Cindy had given her before she left.

Sparks's Dictaphone, found underneath the bed in his downstairs bedroom, along with a tumbleweed of dog hair and one odd sock. The tape in it was half wound, but not labeled yet. Not that any of Sparks's markings had been much help. Mostly symbols or random words, they were a filing system only he understood.

Still, listening to the tape would give Grace something to do while she waited for Shipps. And hearing Sparks's powerful, larger-than-life baritone again would be a comfort to her. Something in the dark corners of her mind was telling her that she was becoming addicted to it, like a caffeine fix in the morning, or that endorphin high that runners claimed to chase. It had been several days since she'd listened to a tape, and she missed it. It wasn't the same as listening to one of Sparks's CDs. Anyone could do that. But hearing him talk, and knowing that it was directed at her alone, was something intensely personal. A one-sided conversation, to be sure, but a conversation nonetheless. His final words might be on this tape, and no one else had heard them yet.

A quick glance at the side mirror and she pressed the button to rewind the tape. Nothing happened. She flipped the battery compartment open and wriggled the AA's with her finger. She made sure they were facing the right direction. Still nothing. Grace dropped the Dictaphone back into her purse. It would have to wait until she could get fresh batteries.

A gust of wind blew in the driver's window and whipped Grace's shoulder-length hair in front of her face. The gray sky was growing darker by the second, and a low rumble in the distance could only be thunder. The temperature had fallen to 87, five degrees in the past ten minutes.

She was glad the weather had cooperated for Sparks's wake. It had been a perfect night, meteorologically. The patio and pool areas had glowed like giant fireflies. No Hollywood set designer could have asked for more.

Grace had stayed in the house after she got the ashes, not able to bring herself to mingle anymore, perfect weather be damned.

Cindy had watched the whole thing, though, and told her the other bags were presented with much ado and ever-increasing fanfare by Dana.

The second bag went to a stunned Rooster Hathcock with the instructions that it be taken to the Sunset Strip in Los Angeles and somehow—the somehow part was left entirely up to Rooster's discretion—sprinkled around and within the Whisky a Go Go.

The third bag went to Honeybear with the request that the contents be sprinkled in the parking lot of The Nick, one of the first clubs in Birmingham where Sparks and the boys were regular headliners, sometimes playing to a crowd of ten or fewer and receiving payment in draft beer.

According to Cindy, Honeybear had stood next to Dana while she talked, as still and imposing as a Buckingham Palace guard, with tears dripping from the end of his beard.

The fourth bag was presented to Ax Royce, who approached Dana as if she were a poisonous snake, coiled to strike. Dana appeared not to notice this, possibly chalking it up to the fact that she was about to hand him a bag containing ashes of one of his oldest friends. She said she knew Ax's band, The End, was in between legs of a world tour and she thought it would be a fitting tribute to her late husband if part of him could go on tour too. She asked Ax to sprinkle just a little at every gig.

"Man, you should have seen his face," Cindy said. "He was white as a sheet. I thought he was gonna be sick right there, but he didn't. He muscled through, took the bag and went back to his table in the corner with Honeybear."

"She wants him to take the ashes on tour?"

"Yep, take them in his carry-on, or whatever. Let Sparks visit all the big venues one last time."

Grace's eyes were wide with disbelief. "That's a little harsh, don't you think? She knows Ax can't refuse. She must really have it out for him. Making him drag his friend's ashes around the world. Open it up every night. Relive the whole thing just before every show." She shook her head. "That's cold."

"That's Dana," Cindy said. "After that, she asked if anyone had a Sparks memory they wanted to share. So people started coming up beside her, like it was center stage at the Grand Ole Opry, and telling their favorite Sparks stories to the crowd, most of them R-rated and at least half of them involving too much alcohol. Ax and Honeybear left then, sometime in the middle of the stories. I didn't see them leave, but I can't blame them. Poor kids. They were in most of those stories, too."

The next rumble of thunder was much closer than the first. The front must be a fast mover. A few oversized drops hit the windshield, mesmerizing as the first raindrops of a thunderstorm always are. Grace stared at them for a moment until lightning lit up the sky outside like the flash of paparazzi. The following thunder was almost immediate, so close it made her jump. Someone's oversensitive car alarm sounded around the corner.

She had just enough time to turn the key and roll up the windows before the downpour engulfed her car and obscured her view of anything except the brick wall of the library building in front of her. She looked in the rearview mirror and saw nothing but rain. The front door of the police department was less than a hundred yards away, but it may as well have been a hundred miles.

Twisting around, she got up on her knees so she could look back between the seats, hoping for a better view than in the mirror. She could make out the shapes of several police cars, parked in a neat row in front of the building, but little else. Movement to her left made her turn just as another flash of lightning lit the scene and a clap of thunder shook the car.

Rain blew across the street in sheets, but the figure in dark sweatpants and a tee shirt seemed almost oblivious to it as he made his way slowly down the sidewalk toward the station. His head was down and his back was toward her, his broad shoulders hunched against the rain. Still, something seemed familiar about the man, seemingly out for a leisurely walk in a storm.

When he reached the leeward side of the police station, he stopped and leaned against the brick. Wherever he was headed, he seemed content to wait there in the semi-shelter until the wind died down.

Grace fidgeted in her crouched position, hoping for a look at the drenched stranger's face. Her opportunity arose after several minutes of not-so-patient waiting.

The rain had slowed, coming straight down now instead of blowing across the parking lot like a mini-hurricane. Something caught the man's attention and he turned his head toward Grace. She ducked back in case he happened to see her staring, but not before she got a good look at him. Goosebumps stood out on her arms. What was he doing here, standing alone in a downpour outside the police station? Something was rotten in Mountain Brook, and Grace was going to find out what it was.

As she peeked around the headrest, the man pushed off from the wall and turned the corner, heading for the front door of the station. He paused in front of it, squared his shoulders and reach for the door.

Knuckles rapped sharply against Grace's driver's window. She jumped like a jack-in-the-box, hitting her head on the roof of the car and biting her tongue in the process. She fell sideways into the passenger seat and muttered a few choice expletives.

Her driver's window had begun to fog on the inside, but she could still make out the face of Louis Shipps, a mixture of concern and amusement

Kelly Adamson

turning up one corner of his mouth. His pale blond hair wasn't wet, meaning he must be carrying an umbrella. He motioned for her to roll down the window and she did, trying to remind herself this is why she was here in the first place.

"Everything okay, Mrs. Howard?"

Grace managed a shaky, self-deprecating laugh as she climbed back into the driver's seat. "Oh, sure. You just startled me, that's all. I was waiting for you, actually."

"Oh?"

"I have your check from last night."

"Oh. Well, great. I figured she'd mail it, but if you brought it, that's even better."

He held out his hand, open palm just across the threshold of the window. Grace looked at it, then back at him. "Um, I need to go to the bathroom. Can I use the one in the station?"

The bemused expression returned to Shipps's face, but he stepped back far enough for Grace to get out of the car and held the umbrella so it covered both of them.

"I shouldn't have had that third cup of coffee," she said, trying to hurry him across the street. They leapt over the flooded gutters and were jogging by the time they reached the front door. Grace didn't wait for Shipps to be a gentleman, but grabbed the door and hurried inside.

The man she was looking for was huddled in a straight chair beside the front desk directly across the lobby. His back was to her and he had a towel across his shoulders, supplied by the front desk officer, no doubt, to try and keep the man from dripping all over the station. There was already a puddle underneath his chair.

The detective Grace had met at Sparks's house came out of a side door and approached the man in the chair, oblivious to his audience.

"I think everything went really well last night…" Shipps began, but Grace shushed him with a wave of her hand. The main attraction was taking place about fifteen feet away.

"I'm Detective Morton. You wanted to see me?"

The man in the chair nodded slowly, water still dripping from his dark hair.

"Yes. My name is Raul Edgar Castellanos and I'm here to confess to the murder of Sparks Westergard."

Chapter 20 — Grace: The Secret Keeper

The words seemed to echo around the room, circling and repeating in Grace's head. *I'm here to confess to the murder of Sparks Westergard.*

So, the boyfriend did it.

Detective Morton looked up and scowled at her gaping at the unfolding scene. He said something that sounded like, "Step into my office," to Raul and gestured toward the door he had appeared in only moments earlier.

Raul stood up slowly, still dripping, and Morton followed him, closing the door behind them with a pointed glance over his shoulder at Shipps.

Grace felt Shipps straighten beside her, shifting into officer mode.

"Well, I guess I should be going," she said without looking at him. "I'm sure you have work to do."

"I thought you needed to use the bathroom." He'd taken a step back toward the door, effectively blocking Grace's exit.

"Oh, yeah, the bathroom. I guess the rain just made it seem worse than it actually was."

The ladies' room stood at one side of a short hallway, in the opposite direction from where Morton had taken Raul. Grace hurried to the door, leaving Shipps with his arms folded and his eyes narrowed, watching her down the length of his long nose.

Inside, Grace washed her hands and stared in the mirror at her wide-eyed, pasty, and slightly damp reflection.

The boyfriend did it? She never would have guessed. He definitely didn't seem like a criminal mastermind. He didn't seem like a mastermind of much of anything. But there was the old saying about books and their covers.

God, how she wished she could be in Morton's office right now, the proverbial fly on the wall. This would change everything. She couldn't wait to call BJ and tell her the news. And now Nick could lay off with his killer-on-the-loose warnings, and her life could get back to normal. She had to get out of here and make some calls.

With luck, Shipps had been called away while she was in the bathroom. She pushed the door open a few inches and peeked around the corner. No such luck. He was still there, waiting for her, a suspicious policeman look on his face. She took a deep breath and decided the best defense was a good offense.

"Say, if that guy just confessed to a murder, shouldn't he be in an interrogation room with one of those two-way mirrors?" Grace said, striding purposefully toward Shipps. "In handcuffs? A dangerous criminal should be in handcuffs."

"Depends," Shipps said.

"On what?"

"A lot of things," Shipps said. "Taking a confession is a delicate balance. If he's telling the truth, you don't want to scare him away by treating him like a criminal. You've got to reel him in. And on the other hand, if he's just a nut job, you want to figure that out quick before you get too far along in the process."

"A nut job? No way. He's the wife's boyfriend," Grace said. "He's crazy about her but she couldn't live without Sparks's money. He had access to the house, and Sparks knew him and would have let him in. Means, motive, and opportunity. Bam! There's your killer."

Shipps's eyes widened considerably at this and, too late, Grace bit her lip. She really needed to learn to shut up.

"You don't know he's the killer," Shipps said slowly. "And, more importantly, you can't go around telling people that. Understand?"

Grace's mouth fell open and she started to argue, but Shipps still blocked the exit, pale eyebrows raised and jaw firmly set.

"Until Detective Morton says otherwise, this is an ongoing murder investigation, and if you go around spreading gossip about it, you are effectively obstructing it. Got it?"

She made a face like she'd just sucked on a lemon.

"I'm gonna have to ask you to promise me that you won't tell anyone what you just heard. Not until he's either formally charged or released. Not your husband. Not your best friend. Not your cat. Don't post it. Don't text it. Don't tweet it."

She opened her mouth again and Shipps's eyebrows rose even higher. He was a much more imposing character than she'd originally thought, quelling her protests with a look. She could picture him as a young Viking. Draped in wolf pelts, bearded and hairy. It made a striking visual. Maybe she'd speak to Leah about him after all.

She nodded.

"Say it," he said.

"I promise I won't tell anyone until he's either charged or released." Her voice sounded like a six-year-old having to apologize for pulling her sister's hair.

Shipps nodded, but didn't move from the door. "I believe you," he said finally. "Now, maybe you'd like to tell me why it is that you just happened to be sitting outside the station in your vehicle at the exact same time this man decided to confess to the murder of your former boss?"

"That was just a coincidence," Grace said. "I didn't know he was going to be here."

"I don't believe in coincidences. As a matter fact, you were acting mighty peculiar in your car. Some might even say suspicious."

"That's absurd."

"Is it? When I knocked on the window, you jumped so high, you nearly gave yourself a concussion."

"You startled me."

"Were you following him?"

"I didn't even recognize him. I was just wondering what kind of idiot would stand outside in such a thunderstorm. I was just waiting for you so I could give you your check." Grace blinked, clamping her mouth shut. She straightened and smoothed her damp shirt.

Shipps held out a hand for the check.

Grace cleared her throat before replying. "It's in the car. We left in such a hurry."

Shipps grunted, but when Grace snuck a glance at him, it looked like he was trying to keep from grinning.

"All right," he said after a pause, "I'll make a deal with you. We both know that it's not against the law to overhear sensitive information by accident. But we also both know that it's not against the law for me to hold you here for questioning without charging you."

"What?" Her voice squeaked. "You wouldn't dare!"

"Only for forty-eight hours."

"I haven't done anything!"

"Mm-hmm. And I want to keep it that way." He nodded slowly, letting his words sink in, letting her squirm. "I'm gonna let you go, but I'm holding you at your word. If news of this gets out, I'm gonna know who told."

Grace nodded, not trusting herself to speak.

Shipps pushed open the door of the station with one long arm and stepped aside for her to go first. She hurried out with Shipps right behind her. On the sidewalk, in front of a bed of begonias beaten down by the rain, she stopped and whirled around.

"Why are you following me?"

One corner of his mouth turned up and he held out one open palm, empty where a check should be.

"Oh, crap," Grace muttered, and turned back toward her car.

Grace's fingers drummed against the steering wheel, her teeth clamped so tight, it made her jaws ache. She didn't want to go home, to a nice quiet house where her thoughts could run wild. But, she couldn't chance being around people, either. Nick had told her time and again that every thought she ever had was clear on her face. Anyone who knew her would have it out of her in a flash.

"Is something troubling you, Grace?"

"No, not at all. And I didn't just hear Dana's boyfriend confess to her husband's murder." As good as Sparks had reportedly been at keeping secrets, Grace was his polar opposite.

And now she'd been *asked*—under threat of an obstruction charge—to keep quiet about Raul's confession. The police had to cross all their T's and dot all their I's. They couldn't run the risk of anything messing up their case. It made sense, of course, but it didn't make it any easier to keep a secret.

There was only one place she could go where she could be alone without being alone, not risk running into anyone she knew, and vent her frustrations all at the same time. She put her car in gear and headed for the indoor shooting range.

She paused to unload her pistol before getting out of the car, embarrassed that she was so preoccupied she almost walked into the range office with a loaded gun. Rookie move. That wouldn't have won her any friends inside. She ejected the clip and pocketed it, then pulled the slide back and left it open, so it was obvious there wasn't a round in the chamber.

Once inside, cocooned in her own bay, she had plenty of time to think. Load, focus, breathe, fire, reload. Her groups got smaller and smaller. It was therapy, catharsis, and time for contemplation. An hour, a box of a hundred cartridges, and four bullet-riddled zombie silhouettes later, Grace felt renewed. And one hundred percent positive that Raul was nothing but a pawn in someone else's game.

As she climbed back into her sweltering car, the phone buzzed from somewhere in her purse. She fished it out and stared at it. Four text messages and five missed calls, all from BJ. The first text just read, "Call me." The last text read, "OMG! Where RU? Call me! URGENT!!" Everything was *urgent* to BJ. Maybe Wayne asked her out. Or she found her cat. Either way, hearing about it might take Grace's mind off of Raul and Dana, at least temporarily.

She cranked the car, aimed the air vents at her face and returned the call.

"Where have you been? Never mind. Just listen." Grace didn't have a chance to speak, even as BJ's agitated voice wound up for the giant run-on sentence that was about to come. "Wayne called and he said that some guy came in and told him that Sparks's killer turned himself in to the police. I asked him what guy, and he said he works for that big donor we saw at Inglenook House the other day. The guy had left his sunglasses—a really expensive pair—and came back to get them. I asked who the killer was, and he said...." She paused, apparently reading where she had scribbled the name. "Raul Castellanos. He was at the wake, wasn't he? That young, handsome guy with all the muscles and the nice smile?"

"That describes him pretty well."

"The guy told Wayne that Raul was having an affair with Sparks's wife." BJ whispered the last as if she hated to say it out loud. "He said it's all the talk down at campaign headquarters."

"What campaign headquarters?"

"Oh, that tall guy we saw get in the town car the other day is running for senate or something. That's why he was giving a big donation and wanted pictures. To make himself look all benevolent to the less fortunate. You know how it goes. It's all PR."

Grace adjusted one of the air vents and sat up straight, eyes wide. She had missed the larger point, which was that her secret wasn't a secret anymore. It must be common knowledge now, and even if it wasn't, at least BJ knew and Grace wasn't the one who told. She blew out a huge breath, as if she'd been holding it for the past two hours.

It all came tumbling out then, seeing Raul in the rain outside the police station, following him in just in time to hear his confession, and Shipps's admonition to her to keep her mouth firmly shut until charges were brought. Grace told it all, and felt ludicrously relieved at the telling. It was clear she would make a terrible spy.

"So, I guess he's been charged, then," BJ said.

"I guess so," Grace said, a little miffed that Shipps hadn't called her personally to relay the news. But, he did have work to do. And maybe he assumed she'd see it on the news. It would be a big story, after all.

"I can't believe you were right there and heard the whole thing," BJ said. "And I can't believe Raul was the killer all along. He seemed like such a nice guy at the wake last night. He fooled everyone. Poor Dana."

"Humph. Poor Dana," Grace muttered.

"What's that supposed to mean?"

"I don't know, BJ. It's just all so fishy, don't you think? If the guy's motive was to kill Sparks so that he and Dana could be together, why would he turn himself in just when all of his plans were working out? No one suspected him. He probably would've gotten away with it. It doesn't make sense."

"That's a good point. But, if you're saying he didn't do it, why would he take the blame for a crime he didn't commit? And, if he didn't do it, who did?"

Grace hesitated only for a second. "I'll tell you what I think, if you want to hear it. Keep in mind that I have zero proof of any of this. It's just a gut feeling."

"Oh, do tell. I love a crazy theory as well as the next guy."

"I think Dana's behind the whole thing. I think she's been using Raul all along. She wanted out of the marriage, but she didn't want to lose any of the money. Rooster Hathcock said she'd have to go back to being a stripper if it weren't for Sparks, and she's way too used to the good life now."

She heard BJ gasp on the other end of the line, but continued. "Dana put the poison in the bottle. She's probably the one who sent it to you to begin with. It was all part of the setup. She stole it back, or more likely, had Raul steal it back. Then she conveniently went to Biloxi for the weekend so that her alibi would be unshakable."

"But...but who was there with Sparks when he drank it?"

"Oh, she used her feminine wiles on Raul to convince him to go over and get Sparks to have a drink with him. Let's face it—Raul's no Einstein. But he probably follows orders very well, her orders, at least."

"Okay, stop right there," BJ said. "Why on earth would Sparks, who hadn't had a drink in seven years, break his sobriety to have a drink with the guy who was sleeping with his wife?"

"Stop shooting holes in my theory," Grace said through clenched teeth. "Do you want to hear this or not?"

"Go ahead."

"Where was I?" Grace cleared her throat. "Oh, yes. So, now that Raul is out of the picture, all of the money goes to the grieving widow and she's free as a bird—no husband twenty years her senior, no boyfriend with a five-year-old to take care of— just her and her double D's and her passport."

"Can I shoot another hole in your theory?"

Grace groaned theatrically. "I guess you're going to, anyway."

"I'll remind you of what you said earlier. Why would he turn himself in just when everything was coming together?"

"To save Dana. She convinced him to be her fall guy and convinced him she'd never make it in prison and he had to confess in order to save her."

"Save her from what? No one suspected her."

"Dana convinced Raul they did. She told him they were coming for her and he had to be her knight in shining armor."

BJ snorted. "With all due respect, that sounds like a dime-store romance novel."

"I wouldn't be too sure about that," Grace said. "People will do crazy things when they think someone they love's in danger."

The phone was quiet for a moment, so long that Grace thought the call had been dropped. Then BJ said, "Even if all this is true—and that's a mighty big *if*—you don't have a lick of proof."

"No. Not yet. But I don't intend to let her get away with murder."

Chapter 21 — Fortune Cookie

"I love you in leather
Or dressed up all in lace.
But I love you best in nothing at all,
With just a smile upon your face."

— *Love You in Leather (2007)*

It was after five by the time Grace got home. BJ had talked her into waiting until the next morning before going back to Dana's, undoubtedly hoping she'd cool off and change her mind overnight. But Grace was convinced that Raul hadn't acted alone. He might have been the bullet, but Dana's was the hand that pulled the trigger.

Nick was in the shower. Signs of his upcoming trip were everywhere. His one suit hung over the hall door, draped in dry cleaner's plastic. Two suitcases leaned against the end of the couch, a pair of tennis shoes and a bag of trail mix resting on top.

Outside, his truck was parked at the gate, ready to go early the next morning. Grace knew without looking that the gas tank was full and the tires were properly inflated. Inside were jumper cables, bottles of water, and road flares. Nick never left anything to chance. Unlike his irresponsible wife, she thought, who was planning to singled-handedly confront a murderer the next morning.

The sound of the shower stopped and Grace rapped lightly on the bathroom door.

"I'm home."

"Honey, is that you?" Nick's muffled voice called. "You'd better get out of here. My wife's due home any second now."

He opened the door to see her scowling, hands on hips, feet planted firmly apart.

"You're a real comedian, you know. You should start doing standup."

He feigned surprise at seeing her there and then flipped the end of the wet towel he was holding around her waist and used it to pull her towards him.

"I'll be here all week," he said, and gave her a quick kiss.

"Actually, you won't," she said, motioning to the suit hanging over the door.

He nodded. "In that case, tip your waitresses." He stepped back and retrieved his cell phone from the vanity. "Speaking of waitresses, I think I'll order some Chinese food."

Grace nodded her agreement and then stopped, straining her ears to hear the high-pitched, yet slightly muffled noise coming from the far end of the hall.

"What's that?"

"It's that annoying feather duster you call a dog. She growled at me one too many times, so I shut her in the spare room."

"You big bully," Grace said, without any heat. "Don't tell me you're afraid of a nine-pound puppy with painted toenails and a bow in her hair."

"I wasn't afraid of her. I was just afraid I might make an oven mitt out of her if she showed me her teeth one more time."

She tossed the wet towel back at him with a shake of her head and took the dog outside.

Mrs. Davenport was in her usual spot inside her front window. The two women waved at each other as Grace took a seat on the front steps. She wondered vaguely why she hadn't led with the headline about Raul the moment she saw Nick. It was huge news, after all. But the answer undoubtedly lay in the fact that she didn't believe the headline.

The driver from Chu's pulled up just as Grace reached for the door to head back inside. Less than fifteen minutes. Mondays were definitely not busy nights for Chinese delivery, but that was still some sort of record.

The boy stepped out of the car carrying two bags of food and, for a moment, Karishma was silent. She even gave a slight wag of her tail. Maybe, just maybe, there would be someone she didn't hate on sight. The driver's tip might be a terrier.

Grace held her breath, but the little dog stood patiently, waiting until the boy got closer. As he reached the foot of the steps, Karishma lunged at him, catching air off the porch and heading straight for the boy's chest.

Lucky for the driver, the dog was still attached to the leash and the leash was still attached to Grace. It pulled tight in her hand and the dog gave a little yelp of surprise when she reached the end. For a split second, she was suspended in midair, like Wyle E. Coyote stepping off a cliff. All that was missing was a sign that read, "Yikes!" The next second, Karishma was down in a heap of hair and claws. Then she scrambled back up the steps and growled at the boy—who clearly had some sort of superhuman powers—from behind Grace's legs.

Nick gave the driver an extra-large tip and carried the bags to the kitchen, where he continued to laugh the entire time he unloaded the bags and set the table.

"Did you hear the news?" Grace finally asked, spooning dog food into Karishma's personalized, porcelain dish.

Nick paused as he poured egg drop soup into two bowls. "What's that? Delivery driver eaten by rabid feather duster?"

"She's had her shots, thank you very much, and no, that's not the news." She put the dish on the floor and turned to face him. "I figured you hadn't heard or you would've said something."

"What?"

"Dana's boyfriend, Raul, turned himself in to the cops today. He says he killed Sparks."

Nick put the soup down and stared at her. "Seriously? I met him last night. He seemed like a nice guy."

"Yeah, that's what everyone says." Everyone being her and BJ.

"Well, in the words of the Shadow, *Who knows what evil lurks within the hearts of man?*"

"I don't think the Shadow said it. I think he just knew it."

"Whatever." Nick waved a paper carton of rice in the air dismissively. "I'm just glad it's over."

They were halfway through their Happy Family when Nick said, "So, are you going to tell me what's wrong, or are you going to make me guess?"

"What?"

He waited, staring at her over the rim of his water glass.

"How do you do that?" she asked. "Narrow your eyes and roll them at the same time. Very school-marmian of you."

He put down the glass, leaned back in his chair and crossed his arms, never taking his eyes off her.

She kept eating and tried to ignore him.

"I can do this all night," he said. "Can you sleep with me staring at you?" He leaned forward over the table, eyes wide. "Am I making you nervous?"

Without looking up, Grace picked up a fortune cookie and tossed it at him. He caught it one-handed.

"Nothing's wrong," she said, still not meeting his gaze. "I was just thinking about Sparks, I guess. Raul may have confessed, but that doesn't bring him back. It's just sad."

She didn't have to pretend to look upset then. She felt awful lying to Nick, even though it was only a little white lie, she reminded herself. And it was for his own good. She didn't want him to worry about her while he was out of town. It would ruin his trip.

Nick reached across the table and took her hand in his. He gave her fingers a squeeze and said no more about Sparks or Raul.

He talked instead of the convention in Knoxville and how much he would miss her while he was gone. Then, he opened the fortune cookie she'd thrown at him and grinned. "You know, someone told me that fortune cookies are a lot more entertaining if you put the words *in bed* at the end of each one."

Grace gave him a skeptical look and reached for her own cookie. "What are you talking about?"

He held the tiny slip of paper up and read, "Your greatest treasure is right in front of you…in bed."

She grinned and bit her cookie in half. She held up the paper, crunching, and read, "Always trust your instincts."

"In bed," Nick finished with a laugh. "Pretty good, huh?"

She nodded. "You know what my instincts are telling me right now?"

He raised one eyebrow in question. "I hope they're saying the same thing mine are."

"Are yours telling you to clean these dishes up later and go see what's happening in bed instead?"

"Close," he said, pushing back his chair, a wicked grin spreading across his face. "My instincts are just saying to hell with the dishes."

Nick left the next morning while it was still dark, headed for Knoxville. Grace walked him to the door and kissed him goodbye, the throw from the end of the bed draped around her shoulders. She waved at him as he pulled out of the driveway, watched until the tail lights of his truck disappeared up the street, and then went back to bed.

The phone rang at nine-fifteen, waking her from a dream that contained fortune cookies, an alligator, and a person dressed like a can of hairspray. The vision of it faded as she picked up the phone and heard the voice at the other end.

"Hey, I'm glad I caught you. Listen, you should look and see if you can find any evidence that she might be planning to leave soon. You know, suitcases out, maybe a passport or an airline ticket sitting around."

Grace rubbed a hand across her face and yawned. "Who is this?"

"It's BJ, of course. Who did you think it was?"

She looked at the clock with one eye and remembered.

"Dana. Right. That's a good idea." She cleared her throat. "But, why the sudden change of heart? You thought she was innocent yesterday."

"No, no. I was just playing devil's advocate. I've always thought she was shady."

"Shady?"

"Yes, and besides, I was watching that movie where the guy kills his wife and he makes it look like the handyman did it. And he would've gotten away with it, except somebody sees him putting his suitcase in the car. So they know he's getting ready to run. You know the movie I'm talking about, the one with that hot Scottish actor from the time-traveler show—what's his name?"

Grace ignored the last part. "Hold up. Are you saying that I should spy on Dana, maybe get some binoculars and hide in the bushes to watch what she puts in her car?"

BJ laughed, a high clear sound that matched the teacups and doilies in her living room. "Don't be silly. Of course not. I don't even think that's legal. Besides, she probably parks in the garage. I just think you should find an excuse to go back in her house and snoop around, that's all."

"Oh, that's much better," Grace said. "I'll be much less likely to be shot as a prowler."

"Exactly."

"You're not kidding."

"No, I'm not kidding. Can you think of a better plan?"

Grace couldn't, but that might have been just because she hadn't had any coffee yet. Either way, she had to admit she'd been thinking of taking photos of some of the things she'd seen in the vault. She needed to get back to writing his book, and without Sparks there for inspiration, his collection would have to do.

And Dana had extended an open invitation to her, after all. It wouldn't seem fishy if she showed up with a camera. Right?

It was Cindy who answered the door when Grace rang the bell an hour later. "Gee, if I'd known you were going to be here, I'd have brought apple fritters. You working Tuesdays now?"

Cindy didn't answer, but the dark look on her face was enough to make Grace pause, an odd feeling of dread growing in her stomach like a jagged ball of ice. "What is it? What's wrong?"

Cindy made a noise, half disgust and half dismissal, as she turned from the door, her Crocs quiet on the pale marble.

"Nothing's wrong," she said, "unless you count having to box up Sparks's stuff and hide it all away like it's garbage that's stinking up the house."

Grace followed her down the hall, taking a right at the main kitchen. This was part of the house she'd only seen once, touring it unwillingly with Detective Morton the day Sparks was killed.

"Nothing at all," Cindy continued, "if you're doing all of this while his wife runs around in hysterics until she hyperventilates." She stopped and turned so abruptly that Grace had to put up her hands to keep from bumping into Cindy. "And the crying isn't for her late husband, mind you," she said, "but for the man who murdered him."

"What?" The ball of ice in Grace's stomach splintered.

Cindy nodded. "Oh yes. Rest assured the water works didn't start until she got the call about Raul. She's lost her sugar daddy and her boy toy in the space of a few weeks. Serves her right. *Ye ask, and receive not, because ye ask amiss, that ye may consume upon your lusts.*" She nodded sagely, the preacher's wife in her briefly visible. "But I get stuck boxing up Sparks's clothes and stuff and moving it all to the vault while she locks herself in one of the guest rooms. She needn't flatter herself that I'd disturb her."

The women stepped into the master suite, a scene straight out of *Southern Living* magazine, if you ignored the plastic storage containers that lay open on the bed, half full of Sparks's clothes and personal effects. Dana was moving him out of her bedroom and out of her life.

Grace made a faint "oh" sound when she recognized some of the things from Sparks's personal bedroom in one of the tubs. His reading glasses—folded now—rested on top of the stack.

Cindy resumed packing, roughly tossing socks from a drawer into one of the plastic containers.

"How did she know?" Grace said. "About Raul, I mean. Who told her?"

"I don't know. I heard her phone ring and then she started yelling and crying. She didn't tell me who it was and I didn't ask." Cindy overshot the tub with a pair of socks and grunted as she bent to retrieve them.

"You wanna know what the real kicker is? Well, after she got off the phone, I asked her where Sophia was, since my first thought ran to her. You know, Raul's a single parent. The girl's mother's dead and he doesn't have any family around these parts. He used to bring her here with him a lot and the two of us would have tea parties and watch cartoons while Raul and Dana were *working out*." She held up her fingers in air quotes on the last two words.

"Sophia. Right. I met her at the wake. Cute kid," Grace said. "Where is she now that Raul's in jail?"

"That's what I wanted to know. I asked her where Sophia was and do you know what she had the nerve to say to me?"

Grace shook her head.

"She said, 'Who?'"

"Who?"

"Yes, sir. She said, 'who?' So, I said, 'Raul's *daughter*. She's been here dozens of times.' So, Dana says, 'She's at her house, I suppose. Why should I care?' So, I said, 'She's *five!*'" Cindy snorted in disgust. "Have you ever met a more self-centered person than Dana Westergard?"

"That is pretty bad." Grace made a face. "So, I guess the police have her, huh? I mean, I'm sure Raul told them he had a child."

"He may have been a sleaze ball, but he loved that little girl. His whole face lit up when he looked at her. I'm sure she's fine," Cindy said. "But Dana just makes me sick. I'm not working here anymore after today. I'm moving all this stuff just so she doesn't throw it all away. I'm doing it for Sparks, not her. And when I'm done, I'm outta here."

"I can't say I blame you," Grace said, as the older woman stuffed underwear into a plastic container. She started to tell her she'd miss her, but thought better of it. Cindy wouldn't appreciate the sentimentality. Instead, she pulled the camera out of her bag and held it up. "You said the vault was open. Mind if I take some pictures in there?"

"Take whatever you want. The grieving widow won't miss it."

Grace turned to go, but then remembered the real reason why she was there. "By the way, have you seen anything that might make you think Dana's planning a trip? She's not doing any packing of her own, is she?"

"No," Cindy said. "She's too busy wallowing in self-pity like a hog in mud." She raised her voice at the last, as if she hoped the sound would carry to the guest bedroom.

The door to the vault was propped open with a statuette on a wooden pedestal. Grace's breath caught when she saw it. A silver astronaut holding a flag shaped like the letter M. Damn, Cindy wasn't kidding. Dana was getting rid of everything with Sparks's name on it.

Inside, the room that once seemed so spacious was cramped now, with barely enough space to squeeze between the boxes. She made her way down the center aisle, snapping random photos, moving things around as best she could. Flash, flash, flash. But her mind kept returning to the moon man at the door.

The award was for the "Agitator" music video, filled with leather and flames and scantily clad women. Grace remembered watching the presentation with her friend Lee. The two girls sat cross-legged on the floor in front of the TV, eating popcorn and watching Sparks accept the award for best rock video of the year for 1989. His head was covered by a zebra-striped bandana, long blond hair glowing like strands of gold beneath it. She remembered seeing him raise the statuette over his head in triumph. The very same statuette that was now being used as a door stop.

The image on the camera's display grew fuzzy. No, that was her vision. She wiped her wet eyes with the back of her hand. The room seemed suddenly too warm and way too small. Like a tomb.

She turned and squeezed her way back out as fast as she could, past the posters and the albums and the sheet music, past the tour shirts and the costumes and the equipment. She tried not to look at the little silver astronaut on her way out the door.

Nick called late that afternoon to tell her he'd arrived in Knoxville safely. She was glad he hadn't called a couple of hours earlier, when she was curled up on the sofa, crying like she'd just lost her best friend.

In fairness, it had been more than twenty-five years ago. Lee had a brand new driver's license and a shiny, silver Firebird. She'd driven home that night after the awards show was over, a cassette tape of "Cut to the Chase" blaring through the car's speakers as it squealed out of Grace's parents' subdivision.

No one ever knew for sure what happened, but the first responders said Lee died on impact less than a mile from home, her Pontiac smashed against an enormous oak tree like a bug on a windshield.

It had been the end of something for Grace that night. The end of slumber parties and painting each other's fingernails and gossiping about boys until dawn. It was years before she let herself have another best friend and he was on the phone with her now.

Nick knew her well enough to know something was wrong, even over the phone, and it wasn't long before she was telling him the story of her morning.

"I'm sorry," he said after a minute, his voice soft and deep. "I'm sorry for the whole damned thing and I'm sorry I'm not there."

Kelly Adamson

"It's okay," Grace said, trying hard to sound convincing. "I'm fine, really. I just don't understand Dana, that's all. She's so ready to get rid of Sparks, so upset over Raul, and she didn't even know his little girl's name. I thought for sure she was behind it all, but why would she have Cindy over there packing up Sparks's stuff?"

"Maybe she just wanted a witness to see how distraught she was."

"Maybe, but Cindy said she just kept saying Raul didn't do it. Why would she say that if she was the one trying to frame him?"

"Beats me. I don't speak 'crazy.' But something doesn't sound right. She's definitely a narcissist, and maybe even a sociopath, but I can't help thinking that she would have made some contingency plan for the kid if she was guilty. After all that careful planning, leaving Sophia out would just be sloppy."

Grace sat very still for a minute, letting that sink in. There was something there she'd missed. Something else she should be focusing on. But what?

"Grace? You still there?"

"I'm here."

"Listen, if you want me to come home, just say the word," he said. "You know you're number one on my list. Hell, you're the whole list. You know I'd do anything for you."

She smiled. "I know you would. I know you have. But I promise I'm fine. I'll see you in a few days."

She told Nick she was going to transcribe a couple of tapes and turn in early. That was her plan for the evening. But, after they hung up, it was still gnawing at her, the feeling there was something very obvious she'd overlooked.

Chapter 22 — Daisy Fay

*Hello Grace, my little firecracker. It's three a.m. and all the normal
people in the world—like you—are snug in your bedsy wedsies, snoring
happily away. Not insinuating that you snore, of course. Not a lovely young
thing such as yourself. It's just that yours truly here has always been a night
owl. Works in my favor when I'm on tour, but the rest of the time...well, it's
usually just me and a bag of Fritos watching infomercials and ordering a
bunch of shit I don't need. Why do I need a Magic Genie Duster? When's the
last time I dusted anything?*

    *It could be worse, eh. It used to be me and a bottle of Pappy Van
Winkle, but that's all behind me now, thanks to that hot blonde I'm married to.
Man, it's hard to believe that used to be my life. I still remember the night
when everything changed. Guess I always will.*

    *Me and Ax and Honeybear had gotten together to do that reunion
project over near Anniston. There's this recording studio up there on the back
side of nowhere called Huey's. Been there forever. They've got state-of-the-art
equipment and great session musicians nearby if you need them. They've got
an engineer who's world famous. Got a wall of gold records and even a couple
of Grammys. We recorded some of our best stuff up there back in the day.*

    *Anyway, the only entertainment for miles around was this crummy little
one-stage strip joint called Peachy's. They sold greasy chicken wings and
lukewarm beer and every stripper was about ten years past her prime. I think
some of them had been working there since our first album. But the selling
point was that nobody ever hassled us there. It was like...they didn't even know*

who we were. Just some more long-haired weirdos recording over at Huey's come in to ogle the merchandise. It was great.

So, like I said, it was maybe seven or eight years ago now, and Ax and Honeybear and a couple more of us are all in there just shooting the shit, minding our own business, and the emcee announces there's a new girl. Well, hell, we perked right up. Said her stage name was Daisy Fay. And—get this— her intro music was Turkey in the Straw. *No shit. So, me and the boys are cracking up. And she comes out wearing these tiny denim shorts and a red and white checked halter top. Long, blonde hair up in pig tails. Big, blue eyes and rosy cheeks like a China doll. Well, we weren't laughing then.*

Good God. I can see it like it was yesterday. When that spotlight hit her, I just knew an angel had been sent down from Heaven to swing on a pole up in East Nowhere, Alabama. Like she was sent there just for me. Right then and there, I knew I would do anything for that girl.

So, I guess you can figure out I'm talking about Dana. Looking at her now, she's so sophisticated and all, it's hard to believe she was ever a stripper. But, she was. At least, until she met me. Right from the start, I wanted to protect her, take care of her. She brought out this part of me I never knew existed.

She'd had a hard time, grown up really poor, raised by an alcoholic mother who only ever cared where her next drink was coming from. Dana ran away from home at fifteen and, as far as she knew, no one ever even looked for her. That had to be the worst part.

Dana was tough, but...fragile at the same time, you know. I was a goner, man. I fell hard. She came back to Birmingham with me and it was only a couple of months before I asked her to marry me—something I never thought I'd do.

The guys told me I was crazy. I remember Honeybear telling me I was letting my hammer do my thinking for me. He was ready to have me committed when I didn't ask for a prenup.

But she turned me down anyway. She said the only way she'd marry me is if I stopped drinking for good. Her mother, you know. She just couldn't stand it. Nobody thought I could do it, least of all, me. But the heart wants what the heart wants. Ha! Hey, Grace, if you tell anyone I'm quoting Dickinson, say it was Bruce and not Emily, would you? I've got to think about my reputation.

Anyway, I started going to AA meetings, found a great sponsor and, little by little, I started climbing that mountain. It was the hardest thing I ever did, but it helped to know Dana was beside me.

After all this time, Ax still thinks I'm nuts. He thinks I married Yoko, but the truth is, I wouldn't be alive today if it wasn't for her.

And I know she hasn't exactly been what you'd call faithful to me, but hell, I haven't been faithful to her, either. Not physically, anyway. We knew that going in. Neither of us is the monogamous type. We don't flaunt it, but we don't lie about it, either. I guess our relationship wouldn't work for most people, but we're not most people. A middle-aged head banger and a runaway turned pole dancer. God, I love that woman. We'll never be church deacons anyway. Who are we kidding? We're just cut from the same cloth.

Sparks out.

—Sparks Tape Name: ♥

Grace stopped the tape and stared at the computer screen at the words she'd just typed.

Well, damn.

She hated to admit it, even to herself, but now she hoped Dana was innocent. Listening to Sparks pour his heart out about her didn't make Grace

Kelly Adamson

like the woman any more, or trust her even a tiny bit, but she wanted her to be innocent for Sparks's sake.

Grace sat in the darkness of her dining room and read the pages twice more. She started a third time and the barking of her dogs outside broke the spell.

It was a frenzied bark usually reserved for the occasional possum and necessitated Grace's intervention before the neighbor, Mrs. Davenport, called the police.

It was almost midnight and the dogs were usually inside and asleep well before then. Poor mutts. They'd been relegated to the back yard ever since Karishma had temporarily taken over their house. Grace looked at the little Yorkie, asleep in her cushy bed, oblivious to her fellow canines' distress. It wasn't fair.

Grace scooped the dog up, bed and all, and deposited her sleeping form in the guest room. She closed the door behind her and started back down the hall. Before she could reach the back door, though, she heard a different noise. This one sent cold chills up her spine. The sound of chain link and squeaky springs. The fine hairs stood up on her arms. Her own back gate.

This would normally have been the moment when she poked Nick in the ribs to wake him and went back to sleep herself while he went to investigate. But with him two hundred and fifty miles away in Tennessee, she was on her own.

What would Nick say if he were there?

"Situational awareness." She could almost hear his voice in her ear, calm and reassuring.

"Where's your gun?"

"In my purse."

"Where's your purse?"

"In the kitchen."

"Go get it. Make sure there's one in the chamber. Safety off. Finger off the trigger."

She nodded to the empty house and forced her trembling legs to carry her to the kitchen.

The dogs were still barking, a frantic, high-pitched cacophony. Whoever it was had not been chased away.

She heard Nick's voice in her head again, this time not so reassuring. "There's a killer on the loose, Grace."

"Thanks a lot," she whispered, pulling the .22 out of her purse and thumbing off the safety. The kitchen window had a slanted view of the gate. Grace tried to slow her breathing as she edged toward it.

She could make out the fence, galvanized metal glinting dully in the moonlight, and her three furry burglar alarms barking like mad at absolutely nothing.

Nothing there. She wanted to laugh with relief. Whatever had been there was gone now. The dogs were still barking, though, and that told her something had definitely been there, and not your run of the mill field mouse, either.

She made her way to the back door, still walking softly, and slid it open just far enough to stick her head out.

"Lucy! Ricky! Come here, you mangy mutts. Ernie! Hush up, you three, and get in this house!" She called to them in as loud a stage whisper as she dared. Ernie stuck his head around the corner of the house, hesitating. He took a few quick steps toward her, but stopped, drawn back by the call of his comrades.

Lights began to wink on in neighboring windows. Great. Now she had no choice but to go and round up her herd and force them inside before they woke up the whole street.

She kept the pistol pointed at the ground, finger off the trigger, but very close to it. Her bare feet made no noise on the wooden steps, or, if they did, it wasn't audible over the barking.

"When I get my hands on you..." she muttered through clenched teeth, her feet feeling every acorn along the way.

The furious barking continued even as she rounded the corner. "Shut up and get in the house!" she hissed. "You could wake the dead."

Ernie saw her, spun in a circle and slammed his paws on the gate. Ricky and Lucy never paused, so intent were they on their guardianship of the yard.

As Grace reached down to pop the nearest dog on the backside with her free hand, she saw movement just on the other side of the gate.

She froze, staring at the smooth, dark lump barely visible above the ground. The warm August night suddenly seemed cold. It was only then she noticed the loose dirt scattered at her feet. Maybe the dogs had tried to dig under the gate. No, Ricky's white paws shone ghostly in the moonlight as he jumped against the gate. It wasn't them.

But someone had been digging. Or some*thing*.

Grace limped back around the corner and grabbed the garden hose. Cranking the spigot as fast as her fumbling hand would allow, she couldn't help but remember someone telling her the story of surprising his wife in flagrante delicto with a garden hose one time. She smiled in spite of everything and pulled the hose around the corner with her left hand, still holding the gun in her right.

Nick's voice in her head said, "Breathe in. Breathe out. Line up your shot. Steady. Now squeeze the trigger."

The water shot from the end of the nozzle like a fire hose, through the chain link gate and onto the offensive lump.

The dogs hopped back, stunned into momentary silence. The lump, however, shot straight into the air like a demonic jack-in-the-box, a good three feet off the dirt. It hit the ground running and disappeared into the neighbor's front yard at an incredible speed for an animal with such short legs. The moonlight reflected momentarily off its wet, armored shell as it ran.

Lucy, Ricky, and Ernie, having finally routed the enemy, could only run back and forth in front of the gate, sniffing at the damp dirt and emitting a series of noises that combined growls, howls, and yelps, the canine equivalent of, "and don't you come back, either!"

Grace released the nozzle and let the hose fall to the ground. Breathless, she collapsed against the side of the house in relieved laughter. The pistol was still clutched tight in her right hand, finger off the trigger. Nick's voice wasn't whispering in her ear anymore, but she could just imagine what he would say when he found out she'd almost shot an armadillo.

Kelly Adamson

Chapter 23 — Dreamland

Wednesday morning felt irritatingly akin to Groundhog Day as Grace awoke to Karishma's barking, this time from the guest bedroom.

Her own three dogs, expressly forbidden to bark within the confines of the house, were confused by this turn of events, but offered unhelpful whines and yips nonetheless.

Grace opened the back door for them and stood aside while a flurry of fur brushed past her bare legs. When she opened the door to the guest room, Karishma darted to the front door, dancing on tiny feet while Grace clipped on the leash and unbolted the locks.

The dog bounded down the steps ahead of her, but stopped to sniff a freshly turned flower bed where the armadillo must have made a pit stop the night before. Grace squeezed her eyelids shut against the bright morning sunlight, while Karishma whined and dug and got her long hair genuinely dirty. Great. Grace's shoulders slumped inside her Snoopy sleep shirt, and she sat down on the steps to wait.

Thinking of the armadillo made her face flush. She'd let Nick get to her with his "killer on the loose" warnings. She leaned her head against the wrought iron railing and reminded herself for the hundredth time that the killer wasn't after her.

But now what? Grace truly didn't believe Raul was the killer, and she didn't want to believe that Dana could betray Sparks's trust by having anything to do with his murder. But who did that leave? Her fingers itched to dial Shipps's number, but she knew that wouldn't end well. She'd just have to be patient.

Yeah, right. Grace, patient.

She stood and gave a slight tug on the leash. "Come on, meanie. You're done. Let's go back inside. It's hot out here already."

The dog obliged, her little pink tongue hanging out, the one thing on her face not covered in top soil.

A cup of coffee and a honeybun later, Grace settled down to the real business of the morning— the book. She'd start at the beginning, fleshing out some of the early stories she had questions about. She'd call Honeybear and fill in some of the blanks about their humble beginnings. What was Sparks like as a boy? What was the first song they played together? Who did they imagine themselves to be as they rocked out in Honeybear's parents' barn on second-hand equipment?

But when Honeybear's deep, Southern drawl answered her call, she was surprised to hear the first question out of her mouth wasn't about Sparks at all. Indeed every single question she could now think of was centered around the death of Tommy Redfoot, the good-looking bassist all the girls adored, the little boy lost with the gentle soul. She hadn't even realized he was on her mind.

Did Honeybear think it was murder? Did anyone ever accuse Sparks of any involvement or cover up?

"I don't know," Honeybear said, his voice resigned. "They did an autopsy that said he had a ridiculous amount of cocaine in his system and his heart just stopped. After that, they didn't break their backs doing an investigation. He wasn't the first rock musician who accidentally overdosed and he wouldn't be the last."

"What about a motive? Who could have wanted him dead?"

"I've wondered that a million times over the years. Everyone loved him."

"Did anyone act suspicious afterward?"

"Beats me. After that night, everyone who hung around us scattered like cockroaches when the kitchen light comes on. For months, it was like we were too hot to touch. None of the old dealers came around. None of the party girls. They just vanished. Like a magic trick. I assumed at the time they were being extra cautious, but the farther that gets in my rearview mirror, the more I wonder. I don't know. Maybe it was too much of a coincidence."

"Some people don't believe in coincidences."

"Ax doesn't. That's for sure. He always held it against Sparks that he'd passed out and didn't remember anything. I guess he thought Sparks could have done something, called 911 maybe, if he'd been awake. You gotta understand, Sparks never passed out. He said he had a hangover, too, the next day. I remember, because no matter how much he drank, he'd never had a hangover. Whatever he'd had that night was different somehow. Maybe somebody dosed him."

"Do you remember who all was there? Earlier, I mean. You were there, right? Was there anyone out of the ordinary?"

"Nobody different. I have pictures I took that night. I'd just gotten a new camera, a Nikon. I fancied myself a photographer for about fifteen minutes. I was tired of everyone taking incriminating pictures of me, and I wanted to be the one behind the lens for a change. Of course, it didn't occur to me that the key to staying out of embarrassing photos was to stay straight enough to know what was going on." He paused and chuckled. "That was probably the only night I ever used that camera. I still have the pictures, though. They were the last ones of us all together with Redfoot. Kind of personal somehow. It wasn't like nowadays, when everybody has a camera on them 24/7, taking pictures on their cellphones all the time. It was the end of an era, you know?"

She knew.

Photos from Redfoot's last night on earth. Possible evidence of foul play. Grace cleared her throat and tried to sound calm. "Can I look at them? I mean, would you mind?"

Honeybear didn't answer at first and Grace held her breath. "No, I don't mind," he said finally. "It's been a long time. That's all ancient history now. It's time to let it go. Maybe you can even use some of 'em in your book."

Grace arranged to meet Honeybear at Dreamland Barbecue on Southside to get the photos. And eat ribs. There was no way she was going into Dreamland without eating some ribs.

She found a parking spot in front of the small, triangular park that sat directly across the street from the restaurant, unfolded the sunshade into the front window of her car and stepped out into the wilting heat. Two young girls were playing on the swings, squealing as their mother pushed first one then another.

"Higher! Higher," the older of the girls gasped between giggles. Something about the girl reminded Grace of Raul's daughter, Sophia, and she felt a pang of regret that her father had become tangled up with Dana in the first place.

Stepping in off the sidewalk, Grace squinted in the dim light and the smoke from the open barbecue pit. A sweet, spicy aroma filled her lungs and made her mouth water. She could be a vegetarian if barbecue didn't smell so good. Or taste so good. On second thought, maybe she'd shelve the vegetarian idea.

A young woman with a round face gathered up dirty dishes from a long wooden bar that ran along the wall to the right. Every bit of its expansive front was covered in old car tags. Most were vanity plates with combinations of letters and numbers that identified the driver as some sort of sports fan, Alabama, Auburn, UAB or NASCAR. But one, in a prominent spot above the bar, caught Grace's eye. It read simply, "SPARX." Displayed on a shelf beside it was a paper to-go box bearing the Dreamland logo and signed by both Sparks and Honeybear in bold strokes.

The girl behind the bar sported a tight tee-shirt with the same logo and the motto, "Ain't nothin' like 'em nowhere." The girl smiled at Grace and motioned with her ponytailed head toward the far end of the restaurant. "You the girl Honeybear's waiting on," she said, not really a question. "He's up there in the back."

Grace thanked the girl and made her way up the steps, past framed UAB basketball jerseys and photos of Bear Bryant and Joe Namath, past the red neon "no farting" sign that occupied a prominent place on the back wall.

The heavenly, smoky scent of barbecue spices and charred meat covered ten city blocks outside and, depending on which way the wind was blowing, could even be smelled by the undergrads at UAB as they changed classes. Talk about the freshman fifteen.

Honeybear sat at a battered wooden table built for two, his bulk making him look like a giant at a child's table, waiting for imaginary tea.

He hadn't noticed Grace as she approached. All his attention rested squarely on the stack of 4 X 6 snapshots that rested on the table in front of him. He held one of the photos up, studying it.

Grace stood for a moment, unnoticed. Feeling like an intruder, she wondered if she should cough or maybe say his name, but felt silly calling a grown man "Honeybear," even though that seemed to be what everyone else called him. As she toyed with the idea of calling him "Nathan" or "Mr. Ray," he saw her and his bearded face lit up in a familiar smile.

"Ah, Grace, so glad you could make it. Please join me at my tiny table." He gestured with one hand at the other chair, and Grace noticed his left arm was in a sling.

"Funny story," he said, resting his good hand on the sling. "Well, not funny, as such. But a story, nevertheless."

"For the record, I didn't ask. That would be rude. But I'm all about the story, you know."

Honeybear chuckled and looked sheepish. "I've got a daughter named Summer. She's eight. My only child. We thought we couldn't…well, my wife was forty-one when Summer was born." He cleared his throat and straightened up. He smiled again. "Summer used to pretend she was a princess. Can't tell you how many tiaras and scepters I've stepped on barefoot. But now she wants to be the boy from *The Jungle Book*."

"Baloo?" Grace said, uncertain.

"No idea. I wasted too much time learning princess names. There's not room left in my brain for Baloo, or whoever he is." He shrugged his good shoulder. "Anyway, yesterday morning I'm out working on my tractor and Summer's with me, as usual. She decides to climb this big, old shade tree behind the barn, which was fine until she climbed too high and was afraid to climb back down."

The waitress came and took their orders, leaving two big plastic cups of ice water and a roll of paper towels in the middle of the table. Honeybear called the woman "Sugar," and Grace wondered if that was really her name or just a term of endearment on his part. No matter. The woman winked at him and swayed her hips a little more than necessary as she walked away. He pretended not to notice for Grace's sake and continued his story.

"So, I didn't pay it too much mind at first. Hooking the bush hog up to the tractor takes a modicum of concentration, you understand. Took me a few minutes to realize she was crying. And not one of those fake, wailing cries to try to get sympathy, but a scared, sniffling cry." He shook his head, his mouth pressed into a grim line. "Well that was all she wrote. I can't stand my baby to cry. So, my 270-pound ass decides to climb the tree and get her down. Each

Kelly Adamson

limb I climbed on creaked and groaned and made me think it was gonna break. And then one did."

He paused to take a drink from the plastic cup, and Grace found herself leaning forward, mouth slightly open, waiting to hear what happened next. He was a born storyteller, like Sparks had been. Maybe it was a common trait among people who were comfortable on a stage, who craved an audience. Only now Honeybear's audience was usually of the Black Angus variety.

"Next thing I remember, I'm flat on my back on the ground with Summer kneeling down beside me patting my face. I still don't know how she got down. She said she jumped, but it was a good fifteen or twenty feet. All I know is a dad will do all manner of crazy things when his little girl is crying."

He grinned then, triumphant at a story well told. "Dislocated my shoulder when I fell. Doctor says she thinks it'll heal on its own, as long as I don't move it for a while. Unfortunately, farmers and drummers are generally of the two-armed variety. But *adapt and overcome*, as the Marines say.

"Here," he said, motioning to the photos on the table. "This is why you're here, not to listen to me brag about my tree-climbing abilities. Better look at 'em now, before the ribs come. Can't flip through pictures with sauce on your hands."

The photos were better than Grace could have dared to hope. Almost all were in focus and he'd even written names on the backs in a neat, felt-tip hand. Mostly names like Cold Cut and Sweet Pea, but names, nonetheless. He sat quietly while she flipped through them. There was one of Ax flexing his biceps for a buxom admirer. A slightly blurry one of Sparks juggling limes. And a beautiful one of Redfoot and a tall, willowy knockout with big doe eyes and a complexion like a porcelain doll.

"That's CC, Redfoot's girl," Honeybear said. "The one we told you about at the wake."

Grace nodded, transfixed. "The one who disappeared. Did you ever see her again after that night?"

"At his funeral. She laid across the casket and sobbed. I thought she was gonna try and crawl in there with him. I've never heard anything like it." Honeybear shivered, though Dreamland was by no means cold. "A couple of guys had to help her to her seat."

Grace flipped the picture of them over, giving them some privacy.

The next photo was of three men hamming it up for the camera, arms around each other's shoulders, heads up, grinning. She didn't know them, but the tall, skinny one seemed familiar. She tapped his bushy brown hair with her index finger, trying to remember.

Her phone rang, vibrating lightly on the wooden table as it did so.

Honeybear gave a whoop when he heard her ringtone. He slammed his good hand down on the table. "Damn straight! That's the best song we ever did. I knew I liked you."

Grace grinned back at him, chuckling a little until she saw the caller ID. It was her alarm company. Something had tripped the alarm at her house.

Kelly Adamson

Chapter 24 — Broken

"I'm faster (faster),
Faster than the speed of light.
I'll catch you (catch you).
Girl, I got you in my sights.

Faster, higher, louder, harder.
I'll live my life like there's no tomorrow.
— Faster (1994)

Grace's mind spun as she floored the accelerator, her car shaking a little as it gained speed. Someone had broken into her home, the place where she ate and showered and slept, her sanctuary, the place where she was currently residing alone. She wished Nick were there.

It was broad daylight on a Wednesday. Was this usual burglar behavior? Having never been the victim of a robbery before, Grace knew nothing of the average burglar's modus operandi. She ran it over in her mind, her hands tight on the steering wheel, wondering what could have been taken. The TV, of course, maybe a little cash lying around. All firearms were securely locked in a gun safe that was bolted to the floor. Nick was a stickler about that. The few pieces of good jewelry she owned were locked up with the guns. She hoped they hadn't ransacked the place, angry that there was so little worth stealing.

Two black-and-whites were parked at the curb, and Grace had to maneuver her car between them into the driveway.

Her neighbor, Mrs. Davenport, was there, too, spelling her name for a stocky policeman with a clipboard. Grace hopped from the car without a word to either of them, intent on getting in the house. The dining room window was broken, the Venetian blinds twisted and moving slightly in the hot afternoon breeze.

A second officer stood in the doorway, blocking Grace's entrance. A petite woman about her own age, the officer probably weighed one hundred and ten soaking wet. She wore her jet black hair in a tight bun, and the no-nonsense air about her was undeniable.

"I'm Grace Howard. This is my house."

The woman nodded but didn't step aside. "Can I see some ID, please?"

"What?"

"I can vouch for her!" Mrs. Davenport called from the driveway. "She is who she says she is."

"No offense, ma'am, but it's standard procedure," the female officer said. "This is a crime scene."

Grace felt like pushing past her, but thought better of it. To begin with, the woman was just doing her job trying to protect Grace's property. And even though the woman was tiny, the pepper spray, handcuffs and pistol on her belt were all full size. No need to make an enemy.

Mrs. Davenport was on Grace's heels as she headed back to the car to retrieve her driver's license, chattering away as if she was the official spokesperson for the police department.

"I knew something was amiss when I heard your dogs just raising Cain this morning. I thought maybe that danged armadillo was back. Filthy things. Carry the plague, you know. Anyway, I looked out my window and I saw this car in your driveway. It was no one I recognized. And I said to myself, Frances, those people are up to no good."

Grace stopped, ID in hand, and turned to her neighbor. "You saw them?"

"Oh, yes." The older lady nodded solemnly. "As I was telling Officer McInnis here, I was just about to walk over and see who they were when I heard this crash that must have been your window breaking. Then the alarm started wailing like a banshee." She clucked her tongue and shook her head. "My, but that thing is loud. It must have done the trick though, because the man ran back to the car then, lickety-split, with just one thing under his arm. Looked like a big coffee-table book. Odd thing to steal, I thought, but to each his own. He jumped in on the passenger side and the woman peeled off. Not a good driver at all, either. She nearly ran over my mailbox backing out. Can you believe such carelessness?"

"Did you get a good look at them?" Grace asked.

"Oh yes. The driver was a white woman, very thin. Maybe she has one of those eating disorders like what killed Karen Carpenter. And the man was black." She paused and turned toward the female officer. "Is that what we're supposed to say now, black? Or is it African-American? I don't want to be disrespectful, Officer...Thomas, is it?"

The officer took in a deep breath, having probably been asked the same question under less polite circumstances during her career. She sized up the older woman quickly though and her shoulders relaxed a little. It was clear she meant no harm.

"African-American is the standard terminology, ma'am, but I'm not offended by the word 'black,' if that's what you're asking."

Officer McInnis stepped in then, middle-aged, balding and infinitely patient, as career patrol officers tended to be. "Mrs. Davenport, ma'am, can you tell us what kind of car the suspects were driving?"

"I'd be glad to, Officer. It was a silver one."

"Silver?"

"Oh, yes. I'm sure of it. Definitely silver."

"Can you tell me what make it was? Ford, Honda, Chevy?"

Mrs. Davenport waved a heavily jeweled hand in the air dismissively. "Heavens, anything built in the last thirty years looks the same to me. No character anymore. I had a Lincoln Continental back in 1977. Now that was a fine automobile."

By this time, Grace's ID had been approved by the female officer and she hurried into the house, leaving her neighbor in the capable hands of McInnis.

She'd wanted in—*needed* in—but stopped inside the door to her own kitchen, unsure what to do next and not really wanting to move.

She took a few tentative steps and leaned around the corner until she could see into the dining room. Slivers of broken glass sparkled like diamonds on the floor near the window and smaller bits dusted the dining table like the first frost in winter. The only clean spot was a rectangular one where her laptop had been.

Grace jumped as someone touched her arm. Officer Thomas, it seemed, had been talking, but Grace had heard nothing.

"Do you need to sit down, Ms. Howard?"

"What? No, I'm okay I just need…" She didn't know what.

The officer steered her over to the sofa, well away from the glass, and motioned for her to sit. "Take your time," she said, her voice now quiet and soothing. "It can be quite a shock. Just sit here and get your bearings, and then we'll need you to take a look around and tell us if you notice anything missing other than whatever that was." She motioned to the clean rectangle on the table. "I assume it wasn't a coffee table book."

"A laptop." Grace said, feeling a little numb. "I've never been robbed before." Though that was probably obvious considering the sissy way she was acting. Suck it up, buttercup.

Her eyes scanned the open space, living room and dining room. The TV was still there, and the silver tea service that had belonged to Nick's mother. She took a deep breath and stood up. A slow inspection of the house showed a new Makita power drill still in the box in the laundry room. Her diamond earrings lay in full view in a small pottery dish on the dresser, unmolested. It seemed the alarm really had done its job and scared the robbers off before they could do much damage. The guy grabbed the first thing he could get his hands on and crashed back out the same way he entered. Served him right that all he got was a battered, ten-year-old computer that crashed every time the wind blew. There wasn't a pawn shop in town that would give him a dime for it.

"The important thing is that nobody got hurt."

Grace jumped, like someone had stuck a pin in her. "Oh! Karishma. You hateful little mop. Where are you?" She fell to her hands and knees, looking under the sofa and the tables. The officer took a step back in surprise, thrown off guard by the sudden surge of crazy.

"My dog," Grace sputtered. "Well, not *my* dog. But *a* dog. Sparks Westergard's dog. If you see her, don't touch her. She hates everyone and she bites. But in her defense, she's had a rough couple of weeks."

She scrambled down the hall, making kissy noises. Karishma's little bed lay in the middle of the guest room floor, empty.

Grace put her cheek to the floor and peered under the guest bed. There she was, pressed against the wall, as far away as she could get. Grace couldn't reach her, and the dog definitely was not budging.

She'd hidden, Grace realized with a start. Karishma, the seven-pound she-devil who had never hidden from anything.

Grace wedged her leg behind the bed and pushed. It slid out from the wall with a groan just enough for her to reach down and scoop the little dog up with one hand. She yelped in distress as Grace lifted her, not a sound of protest, but of pain. She was hurt. Grace looked her over quickly, but saw no blood, nothing obvious. She was panting, her tiny pink tongue sticking out through her crooked front teeth.

What had they done to her? Grace could only imagine the tiny ball of fury that had met the intruder, surprising him on his way in the window with some quick snaps to the ankles. Had he stepped on her or kicked her? Grace could only hope Karishma had drawn first blood.

"Poor baby," she murmured, hurrying back through the house.

McInnis knelt by a large tackle box, a makeup brush in one hand. One look at the black dust that covered the window frame and parts of the dining table, and it was clear it was a fingerprint kit. Grace didn't pause, couldn't look at her house as a crime scene for one more minute. She needed air.

Mrs. Davenport stood outside, cell phone in hand, giving someone on the other end the grisly details in a scandalized stage whisper. Another twenty minutes and everyone in the neighborhood would know.

She hung up when she saw Grace and hurried over, her Cuban heels tapping on the sidewalk. "Oh, I forgot about your new little one." She extended a hand to pet the dog's head, but was stopped short by the ferocious growl that Karishma offered her in return.

Mrs. Davenport took a quick step back, and Grace clapped a hand over the little dog's mouth, ignoring the muffled snarls from beneath. She leaned down and whispered into Karishma's shaggy ear, "Even hurt and pitiful, you're still a bitch."

"So sorry, Mrs. D. I think she's hurt. I should probably run her up to the vet as soon as the police are through here."

The older woman nodded. "I've just spoken with my grandson, Luke, and he's going to bring a sheet of plywood over and cover up this window. So don't you worry about that. And Luke and I will help you clean all this glass up, dear. So you go do what you need to do." She eyed the dog warily as she

Kelly Adamson

spoke, and Grace sighed. Karishma really knew how to win friends and influence people.

"We've got all we need for now," Officer Thomas said. They'd taken pictures and statements and phone numbers. Her partner had fingerprints, the vast majority of which would prove to belong to Grace and Nick, and there was nothing more she could do here. She handed Grace a card with a case number written on it and told her she could pick up the report in a day or two. Grace wondered how many times she and her partner had gone through these same motions and how many of those times they'd actually caught the culprits.

It didn't matter. Not to Grace, anyway. Her stomach felt like she'd swallowed a baseball and her jaws ached from clenching her teeth. She had to get out of there, away from the broken glass and the fingerprint dust.

She got in her car and sped away with Karishma curled up on the passenger seat, leaving two police cruisers parked in front of her house and her seventy-something-year-old neighbor in charge of the cleanup and temporary repairs.

She felt a twinge of guilt, but not enough to turn around. After all, it could have been worse. The only thing taken was a piece of junk that should have been replaced years ago. It would make a good paper weight.

"But they broke into your home," a tiny voice kept whispering. "Your safe place. Your castle. Your refuge."

Then the anger took over as the hot tears spilled down her cheeks.

Grace had to drive around the block a few times to pull herself together enough to carry Karishma into the veterinarian's office. Her eyes would be puffy and her nose red, of course, but she didn't want to walk in while actively crying, especially when she was not crying for the dog, who whined and fidgeted in the passenger seat, not caring for the drive or the distressing noises Grace was making.

The slight, middle-aged woman at the front desk gave her a disapproving look when she explained that a burglar may have kicked the little dog, as if it was Grace's negligence that had put the furry fiend in danger.

Grace drew herself up to her full five-foot-six inches, looked down her nose at Judgy McJudge and deposited the softly growling dog into her waiting arms.

"Don't let her fool you," she said on the way out the door. "She may look like an angel, but she bites like the devil."

The tall grass on the sloping hillside next to Wal-Mart was all beginning to turn brown, despite the recent rains.

Oppressive, that was the word Grace would use to describe this summer, and not just because of the weather. She felt the sweat behind her sunglasses and trickling down her spine. Summer was far from over.

Wal-Mart wasn't exactly known for its Genius Bar, but it didn't matter. Not now. All Grace wanted was something with Microsoft Word pre-loaded, something that wouldn't crash every five minutes. She'd use her tablet for the Internet and let Nick worry about setting up the rest when he got home. She hated that sort of minutiae and Nick was good at it. Machines liked him, responded well to him. Maybe it was his innate patience and attention to detail. Maybe he liked the challenge. Grace was a "big picture" kind of person, or at least that was the excuse she used.

Either way, all she wanted to do now was go home, plug in and type. She'd do it in a different room than usual, of course. The thought of the dining room with its plywood covered window made her stomach clench. The payoff, of course, would be the chance to listen to Sparks's voice again—part honey and part tiger's growl—while she concentrated on nothing but the keys beneath her fingers. She wanted to lose herself in a story about the time he skinny-dipped at the Waldorf-Astoria or danced on a table at a Grammy's after-party. She needed it to take her mind off her present situation. She'd rock vicariously.

The teen-aged clerk in electronics took her credit card without a word, popping her chewing gum as she rang up the purchase. Grace wasn't in the mood for conversation, anyway.

Instead, her eyes were drawn to the hypnotic wall of televisions mounted at the rear of the store. Twenty or so big screens, usually playing a G-rated movie with superheroes or penguins, now tuned as one to a local station where Barney Fife was stuck in his own jail cell, newly deputized Gomer by his side.

The clerk pushed a keypad across the counter toward Grace and handed her a stylus.

Grace obliged and scribbled her illegible electronic signature on the small screen. She pushed the keypad back across the counter and looked up again just in time to catch the last few seconds of a commercial on the televisions. A tall, thin man in an expensive suit stood in front of a stately antebellum-style home shaded by old growth trees. The man stared solemnly into the camera while a crisp American flag blew in soft focus in the gentle breeze behind him, hanging from a shiny new rod jutting out from one of the massive white columns that fronted the porch.

His name was there too, in a bold font across the bottom of the screen, but Grace didn't even see it, so intent was she on the man's eyes. She didn't know him, but she knew him, had seen him somewhere.

Of course. He was the donor from Inglenook House, the one who'd almost run into her on his way to his chauffeured town car.

"Can you back that up?" she asked the clerk, pointing at the TV's.

The clerk's gaze followed her finger as if expecting to see something different on the rear wall. She shook her head and popped her gum for emphasis.

"Okay, then. Do you happen to know who's running for state senate right now?"

The girl's eyebrows shot up and she leveled a look at Grace as if she'd just made an indecent proposal.

"And not the incumbent—the other guy."

"Republican or Democrat?"

"I don't know," Grace admitted. "But he's the only other one running."

The clerk made a noise of distaste and shook her head, handing the heavy bag across the counter to Grace. "I don't follow politics."

"Then why did you ask what party he was in?"

The girl shrugged and popped her gum, unperturbed. "Just making conversation."

Grace forced a smile, fighting hard not to roll her eyes.

The car's air conditioner made a lot of noise for the amount of cool air it managed to produce, and Grace had to bump up the radio louder than usual for it to be heard over the racket.

It was tuned to a classic rock station and Ax's opening guitar riff from "Faster Than the Speed of Light" came howling over the speakers. Grace felt a familiar rush of excitement at the sound, only now it was tempered with sadness, too. Sparks's music would never be the same to her, the carefree anthems of her youth. It would never make her dance in her seat again without thinking of his lifeless body on the floor of his kitchen.

Her car passed the turn to her street. She couldn't go home. Not yet.

She turned up the radio and headed for the freeway.

Chapter 25 — Wayne

Fifteen minutes later, Grace parked her car at the curb in front of Inglenook House. She hadn't realized this was her destination until the big, square building came into view.

She didn't hesitate, but grabbed her bag and headed inside. For research, or so she told herself.

The front door was unlocked, but the interior was dark and cavernous. Grace blinked, trying to force her eyes to adjust to the drastic change.

"Perfect timing," said a voice from above her. She froze, feeling blind and exposed.

"Who's there?"

"It's me. Wayne. Can you get that light switch for me, just to the left of the door?"

Grace could just make out the shape of a tall, step ladder in the middle of the room, and the voice seemed to come from atop it. She fumbled for the switch and blinked again as the whole room was bathed in a bright fluorescent glow.

Wayne had told her and BJ the building was originally built in 1902 as a brewery. The vast open space she'd stepped into was a communal area of sorts now, with sofas and chairs and the like. It must have held the brewhouse, the tanks and burners and kettles, back in the day. It was certainly large enough. Two and a half stories, with a deep mezzanine running along the back wall.

"Ah," Wayne said, arms extended out at his sides in triumph. "And God said, let there be light, and there was light."

He climbed down from his perch, a faulty fluorescent tube clutched in one hand like a sword, and stepped toward his guest with the other hand outstretched in welcome.

"Grace, right? BJ's friend, the writer?"

"Yes. That's me. I hope I'm not disturbing you. I suppose I should've called first. I just had a couple of questions I hope you can help me with."

"Not a problem." He waved the bulb at the empty room. "As you can see, Wednesday afternoons in beautiful weather aren't usually busy for me. All my tenants are out working, or at least soaking up the sun, so I welcome the distraction. To be honest, when I start changing light bulbs, I'm probably pretty bored."

He smiled his infectious smile, and Grace followed him into his office, charmed anew. He took two bottles of water from the mini fridge, handed one to Grace without asking, and sat down in his battered leather desk chair. "Any friend of BJ's is a friend of mine." There was a sparkle in his eyes as he said it, and Grace couldn't suppress a grin.

"Yes, I can see that," she said.

He chuckled and ducked his head, but not before a blush rose above the heavy beard on his cheeks. "Am I that obvious?"

"Not to BJ," Grace said. "Although I daresay the feeling is mutual."

"You daresay?" He raised his eyebrows and gave her a hopeful look. She nodded and his blush deepened.

He cleared his throat and continued. "Well, that's some very welcome information and I thank you for it, but I'm sure that's not why you're here."

"No, it's not. I just wanted to ask you a few questions, if you don't mind, for the book I'm writing about Sparks."

He spread his big hands out in a gesture of acquiescence and leaned back in the chair.

Grace reached into her bag and retrieved a notebook and pen. "First of all, what's the name of that donor who was here the other day taking publicity photos? Running for senate, right? I can't remember."

Wayne nodded. "Sure. Name's Arthur DeWitt."

Grace scribbled the name on a blank page. Surely it couldn't be the same person. "What do you know about this DeWitt? Personally, I mean."

"Personally? Well, let's see. I know his family is old Birmingham money. His grandfather owned a bunch of coal mines or something. He said he still keeps his family's house here, even though it's just him now. There's a picture of it on his website. It's one of those monstrosities close to the old mill on Mountain Brook Parkway."

"You Googled him?"

"Of course. How else do you learn things these days?"

Grace couldn't believe she hadn't thought of it herself. Of course, computer-wise, she'd been living in the Stone Age, lately.

"Did you know each other growing up?" she said. "You're about the same age, right, give or take?"

"Fat chance. Gate City boy, born and raised," Wayne said with a grin, thumping his chest. "I grew up on the wrong side of the tracks from DeWitt's neighborhood, literally."

"What about later, when you were with your band? Did you know him from the bar scene?"

"No. Not that I recall, but I've already told you there are big chunks I don't remember from those days. Still, I don't picture DeWitt as a part of the punk fan base."

"People change," Grace said. "Look at you."

She pulled the envelope of blackmail photos from her purse and poured them out on the desk in a haphazard pile. She zeroed in on one and pushed it across the metal surface toward Wayne.

"Does this jog your memory?"

He leaned in and scowled. It was Witty with an outstretched handful of cocaine, frizzy hair and all. "What? Is this supposed to be the same guy?" He held the photo up for a closer look and chuckled. "It would appear our presumptive senator was a drug dealer in his younger days. I never would have guessed. No wonder he chose this charity. Maybe he's trying to atone. But you wanted to know if I knew him. I don't know. I'm sure we crossed paths at some point back in the day, but I don't remember him specifically. Sorry."

Wayne tossed the photo back on the desk and paused, then took another from the pile and held it up, his smile as wide as Grace had seen it.

"Now her, I know."

It was CC, making a silly face for the camera, a half-empty bottle of rum in her hand.

"You know her?"

"Sure, we grew up together. Well, practically. We were next-door neighbors all through school."

Grace held her breath. Finally.

"What's her name?"

"Everyone called her CC, but her name is Connie Carnaggio."

"Wow. Seems like everyone knew her as CC or Tommy Redfoot's girlfriend, but you're the first who's known her real name. What else can you tell me about her?"

Wayne leaned back in his chair and held up the photo to catch the light from a grimy window. "Well, we were both raised by our grandmothers, our only family. We sort of gravitated together early on, out of necessity. I don't know how much you know about Gate City, but it's a rough area, even though it's not that far from Mountain Brook as the crow flies. CC and I went to Jefferson Heights High School. I'm not even sure it's there anymore, but back then it was the epitome of a failing school. They said the principal carried a

Kelly Adamson

pistol. I never saw it myself, but I'm not saying it wasn't so. I learned to fight and CC learned to run." He chuckled, never taking his eyes off his old friend.

"The first time I ever took a drink was with her. I was nine, I think, ten at the most. CC'd swiped a bottle of Boone's Farm from this little shop on the corner. Probably cost a buck and a half, but it might as well have been a million. We never had a dime between us. I remember thinking it was the most wonderful thing I'd ever tasted. She must've felt the same, because drinking became our new pastime, whenever we could get our hands on it, and she could always get her hands on it."

"You seem quite fond of her. Were you ever boyfriend and girlfriend?"

Wayne laughed. "No, no. Nothing like that. We were more like brother and sister."

"But you lost touch?"

He sobered at that and hesitated before replying. "I was there the night she met the bassist from Sparks's band, Tommy Redfoot. We were all hanging out down at Louie's, this bar that used to be a couple of blocks up from the fountain."

Grace knew Louie's—it was something of a legend in the local bar scene—though it had closed before she was old enough to get in.

"We walked in and boom! There's Redfoot swooping down the stairs like a hawk on a field mouse. I've never seen two people hit it off so fast. It was ... I don't know. Is it corny to say electric?"

"Electric?"

"Like a bolt of lightning." Wayne sighed, his broad shoulders slumping. "It was never the same between us after that. And that's okay. All her time was for Tommy, and I had just joined Downward Spiral. We practiced almost every night. With all that practice, you'd think we would've been better. Gotta have a dream, right?"

Grace smiled and waited while Wayne sorted through the rest of the photos on the desk. The only ones that held his interest were of CC.

"They say she disappeared after Tommy died," she said.

Wayne nodded. "Her grandma passed just a few months before Tommy did. It was a real blow to her. Double whammy. Guess after he died, she just wanted to get out of Birmingham and never look back. Too many bad memories."

"Honeybear and Ax said she wanted to be a model. There was talk that she might've moved to New York."

"Maybe. She had the looks, that's for sure. But wherever she is, she's off the grid. I tried to find her a couple of times, but no luck. She must've changed her name."

Grace cleared her throat and began slowly stacking the photos into one neat pile, avoiding Wayne's eyes. "They said they heard a rumor that she was so distraught after Tommy's death that ... that she may have killed herself."

The last thing she expected to hear was Wayne's laughter. She looked up to see him shaking his head.

"Absolutely not."

"Oh? You seem pretty certain."

"I am."

"And why is that? How can you be so sure if you haven't heard from her in all these years?"

Wayne slid the photo of CC back across the desk toward Grace and tapped it with a broad finger. "Because of this," he said.

Grace leaned forward and peered at the photo. A tiny, gold crucifix hung around CC's slender neck.

"She was a devout Catholic. I know it sounds funny, but I've seen her go straight from an all-night bender to Sunday Mass. Heck, I even went with her sometimes, both of us so drunk I don't know how we got there. Someone would have to wake us up at the end of the service and make us leave.

"I look back at that now and can't help but be ashamed of myself. I must have been a sight in my torn clothes, my hair all starched up in liberty spikes. I'm sure I reeked, too. Beer and cigarettes and stale sweat. Very respectful."

"I'm sure you were just what the ladies in their hats and gloves wanted to see on Sunday morning," Grace added with a grin.

"At the time, church was somewhere with cushioned pews and air conditioning where I could sleep for a while. That's all it meant to me. But for CC it was a promise. Like some sacred law she was not going to break, no matter how many others she might have thumbed her nose at during the week. By God, she was going to Mass on Sunday, come hell or high water."

Wayne finished off his bottle of water and tossed the empty into a blue bin with a hand-drawn recycle symbol on the front.

Grace waited a moment, but that seemed to be the end of the story. "So, you think because she went to church, that she wouldn't have killed herself?"

Wayne chuckled and leaned forward in his chair until the worn ball bearings protested with a squeal. "I take it you're not Catholic yourself?"

"No."

"Well, Catholics and Protestants share a lot of common ideas, despite all the wars that have been fought over the centuries that say otherwise. One of the main beliefs they share is that God will forgive repentant sinners. And even though their stance has relaxed a little in recent years, there's one mortal sin old-school Catholics in particular believe you can't ask forgiveness for, because it would be too late. You know the one I mean?"

Grace nodded. She was far from being a theologian, but this much she could figure out. "Suicide."

Chapter 26 — Ax to Grind

Got some ass to kick
Got a fight to fight
Got a bone to pick
Got an ax to grind
Gonna even the score tonight.
Gonna give you a helluva fight.
— Ax to Grind (1994)

When Grace pulled into her driveway that afternoon, her stomach clenched. Mulling over what she'd learned from Wayne, she'd temporarily forgotten the robbery. The sight of a new sheet of plywood covering her dining room window brought it all crashing back down.

She gingerly lifted a groggy Karishma from her passenger seat—the vet had to give her a sedative to examine her bruised ribs, and it would take a few more hours to get completely out of her tiny system—and unlocked the door to her house.

True to her word, Mrs. Davenport and her grandson had gotten rid of all the broken glass and fingerprint dust and left everything shipshape. If your ship has a gaping hole in its hull, that is.

Grace stood in the dining room and stared at the plywood blocking out the sunlight, a tangible reminder of her vulnerability. She wasn't going to be run off from her own house, but there was no way she'd be able to work at this table until the glass was replaced.

Kelly Adamson

She settled Karishma among the sofa cushions and went back outside for her new laptop. She turned on some music to combat the quiet while she unboxed it. Sparks's *Secret Keeper* was in the CD player, and *Creep* cut through the silence with a welcome wail.

"You know me. I'm the creep on your corner, the dirty little secret, the thing you want to forget," Sparks sang, and it made her think of the album cover, the *Creep* in the trench coat with the frizzy hair, getting ready to flash the *Iowa Farm Girl*.

Grace kicked off her shoes and settled down in the recliner, the computer on her lap. But before she could open her cookie tin of tapes and get to work, she just had to go through the blackmail photos one more time. Something was gnawing at her, nipping at her heels like a tiny, mean-spirited dog. Karishma was still asleep and she certainly didn't want to wake her, so she spread out the photos as quietly as she could. The ones of CC were on top, thanks to Wayne, but what she was looking for wasn't there. Whatever it was.

She pulled out the photos from Honeybear instead. The last known images of Tommy Redfoot. There they were, the beautiful rock and roll couple, looking so much in love. Electric, Wayne had said. Grace could see it.

CC really was stunning, the type of woman who would turn heads in a room full of supermodels. Grinning up at Tommy, her pale, well-manicured fingers wrapped around a bottle of Grapico, she practically glowed. In sharp contrast, the future senator stood behind them in the shadows, arms folded, looking about as morose as a rejected suitor could look. Why did he keep hanging around? Why did he put himself through it, when he knew he had no chance? The money must've been very good. When Tommy died, Witty probably lost one of his biggest clients.

Grace jumped when her cell phone rang. She peeked quickly at Karishma. Still asleep.

"We got a problem."

"Well, hello to you, too, Cindy. It's lovely to hear your voice," Grace said.

"Whatever. Pleasantries are a luxury of people who don't have anything else to worry about," the housekeeper replied.

"Consider me chastised. What can I do for you?"

"I was finishing up at the Westergards' and their phone rang."

"I thought you weren't ever going back there."

"I said when I was finished, I wasn't going back. I'm not finished. Anyway…." Cindy drew out the last word to highlight the interruption.

"Sorry."

"Anyway, the caller asked for Dana, but of course the Queen of Sheba was out getting her highlights lowlighted, or some other such nonsense. But the woman sounded upset, so I asked if I could help her. She said her name was Lakeisha Tyler and that she's Raul's neighbor. He gave her Dana's number as an emergency contact because she keeps his little girl for him after school. Problem is, the kid didn't get off the bus today, and she can't get in touch with Raul."

"What did you tell her?"

"Well, I told her Raul turned himself in, and that he probably left Sophia with some relative. When she got over the shock of hearing her neighbor was a murderer, she told me if he was going to leave the girl with anyone, it would've been with her. Said he told her a dozen times that he didn't have any family at all, other than Sophia. It was just the two of them."

"Sophia's probably with Child Protective Services," Grace said.

"That's what I thought, too, so I called the police. They wouldn't tell me a dang thing. Then I thought of you. Maybe you can call your friend who did security at the wake and find out from him."

Grace made a pained face at the bright welcome screen of her new laptop and closed it.

"He made it quite clear to me that he was not my friend when he threatened to have me arrested for obstruction," she said. "But I'll see what I can do."

Grace had Shipps's private number and worried he wouldn't pick it up if he was on duty, especially if he saw her name on the caller ID, but his irritated voice answered after four rings.

"What do you want now?"

"Don't hang up. I'm not calling for information; I'm calling to give some to you."

"Are you calling to report a crime?"

"What? No. Well, maybe."

"Then you should be calling 911."

"Wait. Just listen." Grace told him about Lakeisha Tyler and her concerns for Sophia as quickly as she could get the words out.

"Is this Sophia a missing person?"

"I don't know. That's why I called you. If the cops picked her up after Raul turned himself in, then I guess she's not missing. But I have no way of knowing that."

"So, you do want information from me."

"Oh, for crying out loud! We're talking about a five-year-old here. An innocent little girl. I just want to make sure she's okay."

A dramatic sigh came through the line. "All right. I'm sure that everything's under control, but I'll make some inquiries about the girl."

"That would only be thorough police work," Grace said, reclaiming her calm.

"Mm-hmm. Don't try to butter me up. It won't work."

"I wouldn't dream of it. As a matter of fact, I was remarking to my sister-in-law, Leah, just the other day that you are the kind of upstanding officer who could never be swayed by flattery or coercion. I said, 'Leah, that Louis Shipps is an honorable man, the kind of man who—'"

"Are you finished?"

"I suppose so."

"Some of us have work to do."

Grace bit her lip. "I appreciate your help. And I am legitimately worried about Sophia. I wasn't trying to be flippant. I'll let you get back to work." Someone had told her once that it was the curse of a Sagittarian to keep talking well past the time for quiet. She wasn't sure about that, but it seemed to be hers more often than not.

"Grace. One more thing."

"Yes?" She fully expected to hear him tell her not to ever call him again.

"Tell Leah I asked about her."

Grace hung up the phone and closed her eyes. She didn't have the inner clock that some people had, but the drone of the cicadas outside could be heard over Sparks's great love ballad, *Love You in Leather*, currently playing on the stereo. It was enough to tell her evening was approaching, whether the sun admitted it or not. So, before it got too late, she set the new laptop aside once more and went about the business of feeding her dogs.

They were thrilled as always to see her, even more so when they spotted the three food bowls she balanced on the way to the deck. She filled their water bowls and sat in the swing to watch them eat. It was a breezy evening, noticeably cooler that it had been, not even breaking ninety, according to the Coca-Cola bottle-shaped thermometer hanging by the steps.

She leaned back and surveyed the yard. The young dogwoods she'd planted looked shriveled from the heat. They could use some water. She headed down the steps and dragged the hose around to the saplings. The overspray felt wonderful on her bare legs and feet. She wriggled her toes, the nails painted a cheerful aqua for summer, and noticed the trail of disturbed earth that led under the gate. The path led to a decent-sized hole—not as big as a bread box—briefly inhabited by the armadillo. It seemed so much larger in the dark, with her pistol leveled at it.

It might be funny now, but what if it really had been an intruder? Would she have been able to shoot? If the time came, would she have the presence of mind to pull the trigger to defend herself, or would she freeze like a deer in headlights? She thought she knew the answer, and fervently hoped she never had to find out.

The dogs wagged in appreciative acknowledgment as she passed by them on her way back inside, their noses buried in the food bowls. The buzz of the clothes dryer met her on the way in, and she stopped to get the clothes before they wrinkled.

She pulled open the dryer door. A pair of red lips and a tongue stared out at her from the top of the load. Sparks's Rolling Stones tee-shirt. Grace pulled it out and hugged it, still warm, and she felt her throat tighten. The rest of the clothes could wrinkle for all she cared. She pushed the door closed.

She stripped off the tank top she was wearing and dropped it on the floor of the laundry room, replacing it with the tee-shirt, warm and soft against her skin. Any thought of returning it to Dana vanished with the memory of Cindy packing all of Sparks's clothes for storage. She would consider it payment for boarding his temperamental terrier.

Grace peeked in on the little dog, snoring softly among the throw pillows on the couch, and decided sleeping was the way she liked her best. She settled back into the recliner with the laptop on a pillow and picked a tape at random from the cookie tin. She'd given up trying to decipher Sparks's labels and enjoyed the surprise. This one had a drawing of a feather on it.

I always seemed to end up as the designated Tommy-sitter, because I was usually the only one who remembered my own name once the night got going. When we were on the road, we had a tour manager for that, and we had a few good ones, too. Their main job, as far as I could see, was to make sure Redfoot didn't O.D., disappear, inject shit he got from strangers, or get the keys to anything with an engine. Rule No. 1: Never, ever let him drive anything. Sad to say, but after Redfoot died, our tour manager's job got a lot easier.

One thing they didn't have to worry about was keeping him out of fights. He was the type of guy who thought everything was funny when he was stoned. The only fight I ever remember him in was one time when Ax loosened a few teeth for him, if you can call that a fight. You see, Redfoot had a bad habit of being late for rehearsal. It started out bad, and it only got worse. It drove Ax abso-freaking-lutely crazy, and this one day, he'd just had enough. We were supposed to be recording a new album, so his tardiness was cutting into our studio time. Anyway, Redfoot comes strolling in two hours late and Ax said, 'Where the hell have you been?' And Redfoot looks up at him with that dumbass grin of his and says, "Taking Latin lessons. Tempus fugit." Well, Ax just had a meltdown. He had a short fuse, anyway. That was no secret. But this was different. You know in cartoons when they show steam coming out of somebody's ears like a tea kettle? Well, I'm pretty sure I saw steam that day.

Ax shoved Redfoot, and Redfoot just laughed. Ax said, "Everything's a joke to you, you pretty boy son of a bitch. See how funny this is." And he punched him in the stomach. When Redfoot doubled over, Ax came in with a knee to the mouth.

Redfoot hit the floor but he was still laughing, like it was the funniest thing he'd ever seen. There was blood all over his face and a couple of his teeth were loose, but he was too high to feel it, I guess. Ax jumped on him, had his hands around Redfoot's throat. It was crazy. Honeybear had to stop him. Got him by that stupid red leather vest he used to wear, and threw him across the room. Just missed crashing into the drums.

I remember in that split-second thinking that was the end for us. But Ax grabbed his guitar and said, "What's everybody staring at? Get up, you lazy assholes, and let's make some rock and roll."

You know what song we recorded that afternoon? Ax to Grind, the best and most ferocious bit of guitar work that Ax ever laid down, no question. Even he admitted it. He always played better when he was pissed off. Adrenaline, I guess. But he usually had the good sense not to aim it at one of us. But, whatever. That's water under the bridge, right?

Grace heard a sigh and the sound of ice clinking in a glass before Sparks continued.

The two of them would have made up eventually. I'm sure of it. But Tommy died that same summer and it turned out that was the last studio album we ever recorded with the original lineup. After that, we had Dix Dixon or Malcolm Smith. Good musicians, both of them, and good guys, but it was never the same. Not to me.

Tommy was my best friend, and the first person close to me who died, though he sure wasn't the last. You know my mom died a couple of years ago, and that was worse, no denying. But Tommy was the first, and unexpected. You can't really understand it until it happens to you, but when someone you love dies, your world is different from that moment on, like it or not, and there's not a damn thing you can do about it. There's no going back. Your debts to that person are left unpaid. Any words you didn't get a chance to say are left unsaid. Money, fame, power—none of that shit matters, because it won't buy you another second with them. You just have to keep on living.

The tape kept running, playing nothing but static. Sparks had said all he would ever say on the subject of Ax and Redfoot, but it left Grace with an uneasy feeling, and the memory of a moth and a flame.

Her first instinct was to pace, but she didn't want to risk waking Karishma, not to mention she was incredibly comfortable reared back in the La-Z-Boy with the laptop nestled right in front of her. The CD had finished. The room was quiet. Even the cicadas had hushed for the evening.

It had been a long day, and Grace was bone tired. She'd been treading water these past few weeks, and the break-in was really trying to pull her down. Her arms and legs weighed a thousand pounds and her eyes burned with the effort to keep them open. The temptation to let them close and forget everything, let sleep carry her under for the next eight hours, was powerful. But the need to put this new information into perspective was even more powerful. Her body needed rest, but fireworks were going off in her brain, flashing and shimmering on the dark water where she floated, bobbing up and down between consciousness and oblivion.

She jumped, startled, as a low, grating noise sounded close to her ear. It took a few seconds to realize it was the sound of her own snoring. She forced her eyes open and pushed the chair into the upright position. Relaxation time over.

The light on her cell phone was blinking. A text message from Nick. *At dinner with the flooring guys. Text u when I get in if not too late. Early morning tomorrow to listen to keynote. Love u. Miss u.*

It had come in half an hour before, and she hadn't heard the chime. She replied with a quick *I love you, too* ☺, knowing she should tell him about the break-in, but all too aware that it would just ruin his trip. Knowing Nick, he would probably leave dinner and come home immediately, driving all night, even though there was nothing he could do to change things once he got home. It was in his DNA to be a protector.

Kelly Adamson

She shifted in the chair and the computer screen popped back on, illuminating the room. *You just have to keep on living* stared back at her in black and white. Redfoot was dead, Sparks was dead, and someone needed to find out who was responsible. It was in her DNA to want answers. She needed to find a witness.

It was full dark outside and even though farmers were early to bed and early to rise, there was only one person who might shed some light on this. Grace hoped he was awake.

Honeybear picked up on the fourth ring, giving Grace ample time to realize that she couldn't just come right out and ask him if he thought one of his best friends killed the other. He seemed genuinely happy to hear from her, and swore he wasn't asleep. Still, she started off slow, after a few apologies and pleasantries.

"I was looking at your photos again," she said. "The ones you took at Tommy Redfoot's house. And I just had a couple of questions."

"Sure. I'll see what my old, addled brain can recall for you."

"Okay. These were taken in L.A., right?"

"Yep. We all kept places out there for a couple of years, and we'd stay out there when we were recording or rehearsing for a tour. I can't say it was ever really home."

Grace made an "I-heard-that" noise of agreement before she continued. "It's just that this Witty guy, he's in some of the photos, and I was just wondering what he was doing there. Did he work for you guys?"

"Lord, no. He was there on his own accord. It wasn't unusual for hangers-on to follow us around the country. Some of them just hung around to soak up our vibe. Apparently, we had quite a lot of vibe." He chuckled. "But Witty was our hookup. He made a lot of money off us."

"Okay. Correct me if I'm wrong, but drug dealers in the movies tend to be extremely territorial. I can't imagine the dealers in L.A. bowing out gracefully and letting you bring your own guy from Birmingham. That seems crazy to me. A good way for him to end up dead."

"Naw, he was just the go-between. He acted as our buyer out there. He'd buy from the L.A. dealers so we didn't have to get our hands dirty. Then he'd take a finder's fee from us, I assume. God, we had more money than sense back then."

As Grace pondered the volatility of that setup, Honeybear said, "He made a lot of us money off of us, but the real reason he was there was CC. After she left, we never saw him again."

"Guess a lot of things changed then."

"You said it, sister."

Grace paused, picking through the mine field of questions she wanted to ask next. "I was wondering, too ... well, I've heard that Ax used to have quite a temper back in the day. And one of Sparks's tapes said he played much better when he was angry."

"Yeah, that's true."

"Do you ever remember him picking a fight just to play better that day? You know, at a concert or rehearsal or whatever." Smooth.

"I don't ever remember him picking a fight with me."

Grace thought of Honeybear's six-foot-four-inch bulk and was not surprised.

"But I'm not saying he never took advantage of it. You know how some people say angry sex is the best? Not me personally, you understand. I'm a lover, not a fighter. But I think Ax subscribed to that theory. His idea of a hot chick was one who rode a Harley and had more tattoos than he did. Sparks used to say Ax wasn't interested in any girl who couldn't kick his ass. You know his ex-wife, Toni, used to box when she was young? True story."

"Interesting," Grace said, and it might have been, if she wasn't looking for a different story. "But as far as you guys? He never fought with any of the band members?"

"Naw. Well, I do remember him getting mad at Redfoot a few times, there towards the end. And he hit him once in the recording studio, bloodied his nose or something. But, you gotta understand, Ax wasn't the only one angry at Redfoot then. We all were; we just didn't express it with our fists."

"Oh, yeah? Why is that?"

"Well, Tommy had gotten to where he never wanted to practice. He was always late and I mean *really* late. He spent all of his time with CC. Nothing else mattered to him. And I mean, I get it, you know. They were young and in love and all that bull. But he wasn't taking the band seriously anymore, and that was hurting all of us."

Grace thought of the moth at the wake and took a deep breath. "I can't find Ax in any of the photos that you took that last night at Tommy's."

"Oh? Well, he might have been there and left early or something."

"Early to bed and early to rise?"

Honeybear chuckled. "With a companion, I'm sure. Or he might not have been there at all, what with it being Redfoot's house."

"What do you mean by that?"

"Oh, nothing."

"Was he still mad at Tommy for the incident at the recording studio?"

"No, no."

"What then?"

"It's nothing, and certainly nothing that needs to go in a book."

"I'm not a tabloid reporter. I'm not trying to make you guys look bad."

Honeybear made a frustrated noise. "Look, it hadn't been that long since all of that happened, and the two of them were still on the outs. That much I remember. And if that ever got out, it would just make Ax look like a suspect, like he had a motive."

"And you don't think he did it?"

"Of course not. That's ridiculous."

"Did you ever ask him?"

"What? Ask Ax if he killed Redfoot? Why the hell would I do that? Besides, Redfoot OD'd, remember? It wasn't murder. And Ax wasn't even there. You said so yourself."

"If he has a good alibi, then he wouldn't have anything to worry about. Did he have a good alibi?"

Silence.

"Nobody ever asked him about his alibi?" Grace said.

"He didn't *need* an alibi. He didn't do it. Redfoot was his friend."

"Who do you think did it?"

"I don't think anybody did it. I think it was an accident. Redfoot finally snorted more coke than his heart could handle. That's what I think."

Grace held the line, returning his silence.

"Look," Honeybear finally said. "He may have had a temper, but Ax is not a murderer. He was as broken up as the rest of us when Redfoot died. I know he always felt guilty that he didn't make up with him before it was too late."

Or, thought Grace, maybe he felt guilty because he'd just killed a man.

Chapter 27 — Passport

"We got another problem."

Grace rubbed her face hard with her free hand and tried to sit up. Disoriented and stiff, she'd fallen asleep in the recliner again, only this time daylight was streaming in the windows.

"Oh, God, we've got to stop meeting like this," she mumbled at the cellphone.

"Grace, are you listening to me?" Cindy's voice came in loud and demanding.

"What time is it?" Grace stretched and yawned, glad to see she'd put the laptop safely on the coffee table at some point during the night.

"It's almost eight-thirty. You weren't asleep, were you?" The voice sounded incredulous, as if no normal human could ever sleep past sunrise.

"Me? No way. I just got back from a jog. Made myself a nice kale smoothie." In truth, she had answered the phone from sheer muscle memory and was currently stumbling barefoot to the kitchen for a semi-stale doughnut and a cup of coffee.

"Good. You need to get over here as quick as you can."

"Wait. Where's here? Don't tell me you're back at the Westergards' house. Dana's going to think you're stalking her."

"I forgot something. And it's a good thing I came back, because I caught her in the act."

"The act of what?"

"Absconding. Vamoosing. Running away. I saw her passport sitting on Sparks's desk."

"Why would she be leaving now? She's not even a suspect."

"Maybe she's leaving the country with Raul's kid."

"I thought she didn't even know her name."

"Who cares? Maybe she'll call her 'Hey You' or maybe she was lying. Ever heard of lying?"

"Okay. I'm on my way. But I don't know what you expect me to do about it. Beat her into submission and make her confess?"

"If that's all I wanted, I could do it myself. No, we've got to keep calm. We don't want to spook her. Thought maybe you could stall her for a while. We've got to find Sophia."

"Wait a minute. What's my excuse for coming over there? I don't want to look suspicious."

"I don't know. Make something up. Do I have to think of everything?"

Before Grace could reply, Cindy hung up.

"Okay, well, thanks for calling," she said to the dead line.

She crammed half a doughnut into her mouth and cast a longing look at the empty coffee maker.

Sleeping in your clothes was usually a bad thing, but at the moment it was a time saver. All she needed was shoes. Grace retraced her steps to where she'd kicked them off the night before. She peeked at Karishma, who had changed positions during the night, but was mercifully still sleeping, this time on a stack of clean bath towels. That's what she got for not putting them away.

Grace groaned quietly. She really needed to wake the little dog and take her outside to avoid spending the afternoon cleaning carpet and/or upholstery. But there wasn't time. She picked up the stack of towels, dog and all, and deposited them in the bathroom, then came back with a saucer of soft dog food and some water. Karishma wobbled over to the bowl as Grace pulled the door closed and hoped it wouldn't be too bad.

Twenty minutes later, she stood at the Westergar hand poised to knock. The heavy, wooden door swung o' still in the air, was hauled inside unceremoniously by C

"What are you—?"

"Shh!"

"You're shushing me? You weren't exactly quiet on th. you know."

"Dana was in the shower when I called earlier. Now she's out and she's got hearing like a … well, like some animal with great hearing." She shooed Grace to the kitchen that looked out onto the pool, before she continued in an exaggerated whisper. Grace didn't catch the first few sentences, because she couldn't pull her attention away from the spot where she'd found Sparks lying dead, not so many weeks ago. It looked so innocent now, just another patch of cheery blue tile, but Grace could still see him perfectly, the image burned into the backs of her eyelids.

"Grace, are you listening to me?"

"Hmm?"

"I said, what's your excuse for being here?"

Grace turned, eyes wide. "What do you mean, my excuse? You woke me up and *insisted* that I drop everything and rush over here."

Cindy waved her hand in the air like Grace had just blown cigar smoke in her face. "No, no. I mean, your *excuse*. What are you going to tell Dana?"

"Oh, that." Grace patted her purse and smiled. "Don't worry about that."

"You packing?" Cindy said, her eyes narrowed.

"I'm always packing, but that's not what I was talking about." Grace set her purse on the island and pulled out Sparks's ancient address book, held together by rubber bands and now protectively encased in a gallon Ziploc bag. "I'm returning this."

.odded approvingly.

, fill me in. You said you saw her passport. What else? Did you see or plane tickets? Anything like that?"

"Nope. After I called you, I started for her closet to have a look around, it that's when I heard the shower turn off, so I high-tailed it back here. Dana came out once since then and saw me, but I just pretended to be dusting. She didn't seem surprised. Guess she forgot I said I was quitting. Shows how much she listens to me."

"I'm still not sure what you want me to do." Grace purposefully turned her back on the offending patch of tile. "Even if she comes out rolling a big suitcase behind her and waving a plane ticket, I can't stop her. Well, not legally."

A door closed at the far end of the hallway, the only indication so far that Dana was home. Grace turned toward the sound, and when she looked back, Cindy had a bar rag in her hand, vigorously polishing the granite surface of the island. Grace wondered where the rag had come from. Maybe Cindy pulled it from her sleeve, like a magician producing a bouquet of flowers.

"Oh, Grace. What a wonderful surprise." Dana floated into the kitchen on pedicured bare feet. Grace put a hand over her thudding heart and reflected that Dana would make a fine ninja.

"I was just thinking about you. Were your ears burning?" Dana seemed genuinely pleased with the unannounced visit. She crossed to the refrigerator and pulled out a bottle of liquid that resembled pond scum, then took a sip like it was fine champagne. Luckily, she didn't offer one to Grace.

Never having been confused for a ninja, Grace fumbled Sparks's address book and the plastic bag slipped through her fingers, hitting the floor with a slap.

"I just came by to return this." She ducked awkwardly to pick it up.

"What a coincidence. I have something for you, too. Wait right here." Dana took the address book and the pond scum and hurried from the room.

As soon as she was out of earshot, Cindy threw down the rag and grabbed Grace's arm. "What if she comes back with a gun?"

"Good grief. You don't seriously believe she's going to come out here and shoot me in her own house?" Grace said in a stage whisper. "She'd have to shoot you, too, you know. Then who'd clean up all the mess?"

Cindy made a sour face and let go of Grace's arm. "Don't underestimate her. If she kidnapped a kid and talked her boyfriend into killing her husband, what makes you think she won't kill us?"

"It would have been awfully nice if you'd told me you thought your life was in danger *before* I came over here, you know," Grace hissed.

Dana stood in the doorway, a look of surprise on her pixie face. "Your life's in danger?"

Damn it. Her bare feet hadn't made a sound in the marble hallway. Before Grace could formulate a response, Cindy fell into a coughing fit, going so far overboard that Grace finally pounded her on the back.

"I'm taking a cold, that's all. But Grace here is a germophobe and she's convinced I've got the plague or something."

All three women looked unsure about what to do next. Then Cindy produced a dust mop, seemingly from thin air, and started mopping with a vengeance, making a beeline for the door of the kitchen and continuing down the hallway.

So much for backup.

Dana watched her go with a puzzled look, giving Grace ample time to see that Dana was not holding a gun, but something small and flat.

"She's been working too hard," Dana said of the housekeeper. "She needs a vacation from this terrible mess. We all do."

Remembering what she was carrying, she waved it in the air with a half-smile. "Speaking of vacations, I found this in Sparks's personal papers." She held it out, open to a small photo of an unsmiling Sparks, blond hair pulled back over his shoulders, no makeup, no jewelry. It was his passport. "I think it would be a great addition for your book. Take it and make some scans. It might be a fun way to show some of the places he played. There are stamps in there from all over the world."

Her pretty nose turned red as tears shimmered in her blue eyes. "I never needed a passport of my own until I met him. He took me everywhere." A single tear spilled down her cheek, but she maintained her composure, even managing a shaky smile. "I know what some people said about me, but Sparks was never ashamed of me, of what I had been. He was the best thing that ever happened to me."

Grace took a moment to admire the world's most melancholy adulteress and wondered once more how many of her tears were genuine. She remembered vividly walking around the corner and finding Dana and Raul locked in an embrace she'd never seen in any fitness class. And just a few weeks before Sparks was poisoned, no less.

While she may not have shared Cindy's conviction that Dana was a murderer, the girl was definitely no angel. Grace had the sudden, overwhelming desire to call her on it.

"What about Raul?"

"Raul?"

"I saw the two of you together a couple of months ago."

Dana looked puzzled.

"Maybe you didn't notice me. I think you had your hand down his pants at the time."

Dana's shoulders fell. She slumped back against the island. They let the silence grow for a minute until Dana looked up at Grace with a weak smile and a shrug, her hand caught firmly in the cookie jar.

"What can I say? Raul is a very nice guy. He has the body of a twenty-five-year-old kick boxer, and his accent is sexy as hell. But he was a fling, nothing more." Dana took a fortifying sip of the pond scum and continued. "Sparks had flings, too. I knew he wasn't a one-woman-man when I met him. It never bothered me. We didn't keep secrets from each other. Our one rule was to keep it discreet. And we did. Raul knew up front it was never going to be anything serious and was happy with that. He didn't want any strings. That's why I don't understand all this business about him saying that he ...." She couldn't finish, her blonde hair forming a curtain as she leaned forward and covered her face. "Raul didn't kill Sparks. Why would he?"

Sparks had said it himself, on the tape about Dana, and she had just corroborated it. They'd had an open marriage and both were okay with it. Pretty darn weird in Grace's eyes, but true nonetheless.

"Have you talked to Raul since he's been in jail?"

Dana shook her head. "No. I tried, but they wouldn't let me. They told me he was refusing to talk to anyone, but that sounds like a load of crap. Why wouldn't he want to see me?"

Grace wanted to say, "Maybe he couldn't bear to look you in the eye after killing your husband," but she refrained. In truth, she was inclined to agree that Raul was innocent, but why would he confess to a crime he didn't commit unless he was covering for someone? The obvious choice was Dana, but no matter how hard Grace tried, she just couldn't figure out why Dana would want her husband dead and her lover sent to the electric chair for it.

There was no indication that either man had been abusive in any way, and both seemed crazy about Dana. Sure, money was always a popular motive for murder, but, although Sparks lived comfortably, he was no Wall Street mogul. If someone wanted to kill him for his money, they should have done it twenty years ago. Not to mention the fact that he hadn't asked for a pre-nup, and Dana could probably have taken him to the cleaners simply by divorcing him. No need to go to all this trouble.

There just didn't seem to be any clear motive, and every murder has a purpose, even if it doesn't make sense to anyone except the murderer. If Grace could find the reason, then maybe, just maybe, she could find the killer.

"Look, I'm sorry I brought it up," Grace said. "I wasn't trying to accuse you of anything. If that arrangement worked for you, then ... whatever."

Dana nodded but didn't meet Grace's gaze.

"Why don't we go outside, sit by the pool and get some fresh air?" Grace said. Anything to get out of that kitchen and away from that patch of tile.

Dana obliged and Grace followed her through the double French doors onto the patio. Dana seemed smaller now, all the pep gone out of her step, her dancer's grace abandoning her in her time of need.

The two of them sat in silence at a round table near the pool. Grace sat in the shade of the big, striped table umbrella, while Dana and her tan sat on the sunny side.

It was still hot, at least ninety. Summer wasn't going anywhere yet, but a breeze made it almost tolerable, and the sun stayed mostly hidden behind fluffy cumulus clouds.

From her vantage point, Grace could see the semi-circle of lawn and garden that Sparks had considered his private oasis. The bird bath was dry and the Freddie Mercury rose bush needed dead-heading. The cushion on the lounge chair had been removed, and the metal framework looked sickly and fragile without it.

She forced herself to face her hostess, who was still and quiet and looked pretty fragile herself at the moment. Time to change the subject.

"So, how well did you know Ax and Honeybear?"

Dana cleared her throat and shifted in the chair. A sign of life. "Not well. Until the wake, I hadn't seen them in years. There was no love lost there, though."

"Oh? Why do you say that?"

Dana studied Grace for a minute, her eyes narrowed against the sun. "I'll tell you, but only if you swear you won't put it in the book."

Grace nodded, thinking that if one more person told her to keep something off the record, there wouldn't be much of a book left to write.

"Ax and Honeybear say I broke up the band, but the truth is the band was broken long before I got there. Their bass player O.D.'d. Their lead guitarist had anger issues. Their drummer was playing Billy Budd, wearing those rose-colored glasses and trying to pretend it was still 1989. And their lead singer had his head in a bottle of scotch."

Dana saw Grace's expression, and smiled. "I would never have said anything like this while Sparks was alive, but let's face it, by the time I met them, they were recording a Hail Mary album up in North Alabama. They hadn't had a top 40 song since OJ Simpson was only famous for playing football."

"*Eat. Sleep. Rock,*" Grace said. "That's what they were recording, right?"

Dana nodded. "They came in the club where I was dancing, a place called Peachy's. I'd only been there a couple of weeks, just moved up from Pensacola, trying to get away from a bad situation, an ex who thought I was his punching bag." She looked right at Grace and said, "At least you're not pretending you didn't know I was a dancer."

Grace gave a little shrug, but said nothing. She thought about mentioning that Rooster Hathcock had told her that Dana had been fired from her job in Pensacola because she put Visine in bad tippers' drinks.

"I didn't know who they were that first night, just some rockers recording in the studio a few miles away. I grew up listening to the Opry," she said in answer to Grace's raised eyebrows. "You know, pickup trucks and hound dogs. My stage name was Daisy Fay. The only rock and roll I knew was Elvis.

"Anyway, I could tell right away Sparks was different. He had a good heart, you know. I think I fell in love with him that very night. And after that, I did my damnedest to save him from that bottle."

Grace thought of the tape Sparks recorded about Dana, where he'd said she gave him an ultimatum. It was her or the booze. If Dana had wanted him for his money, it seemed like it would have been a lot easier to marry him when he was still a raging alcoholic, then let him continue to drink himself to an early grave.

"If Ax and Honeybear want to blame me for the band's decline, fine. I'm a big girl. I can take it," Dana said. "But what I can't forgive is them not even pretending to care about Sparks. If they thought his sobriety killed his creativity or whatever, then it's obvious they would have gladly traded his life for another number one. If he'd kept on drinking like he was when I met him, he would have been dead ..." her face clouded when the words registered, "years ago."

This was a side of Dana that Grace had never seen. This was the plucky little runaway who'd grown up fast and taken care of herself just fine until Sparks came along and swept her off her feet. She liked this persona much better than the vapid centerfold model Dana usually hid behind.

"They were supposed to be his friends, but they never came around. They never called after he got sober. And Honeybear didn't even live that far away. It would've been easy for him to come by."

"But they're clean, too, now, right? Or at least Honeybear is."

"I guess. But ... how can I put his? Honeybear wasn't exactly the sharpest tool in the shed, you know. And he believed everything Ax told him. Without question. If Ax had said I was a vampire and he'd seen me change into a bat, Honeybear would have run right out and bought garlic and a crucifix."

"So, you think Ax hated you because he was looking for someone to blame when the band was past its prime?"

"I don't know. That's the only thing I've ever been able to come up with. But I don't suppose it matters now, anyway." Dana shrugged one delicate shoulder and looked away. "Ax was hard to read. He loved to make people laugh. But he was just as happy to fight. Maybe he just craved attention so much, that he didn't care if it was good or bad."

When Grace left the Westergards' an hour later, Cindy was sweeping the tiled front steps with a straw broom that looked more decorative than functional. As Grace passed, she let the broom fall where she stood and hustled down the steps in Grace's wake.

"What did you find out?" she called in a loud whisper. "Did she say anything about Sophia?"

"I found out Sparks's band spent two months on tour in Japan in 1988," Grace said without stopping. "I found out you can keep your expired passport as a souvenir as long as they punch a bunch of holes through it. And I found out you read way too many murder mysteries."

Grace got in her car and buzzed the driver's window down. She looked at the housekeeper and tried to smile. "You need a break from this," she said, echoing Dana's sentiment. "Maybe we all do."

Instead of getting on I-65 and heading for home, Grace drove over Red Mountain and straight down University Boulevard to Southside. She needed the unbiased, unvarnished truth about Ax Royce and barring that, she needed to talk to BJ.

She took the steps two at a time and pounded on the door to BJ's apartment, maybe a little harder than was strictly necessary, and waited.

She hadn't bothered to call first. She didn't want to give BJ a chance to formulate answers. When Grace asked her about Ax, she wanted to be looking into that cherubic, guileless face and get an instant reaction.

As BJ opened the door, the aroma of freshly baking chocolate cake embraced Grace like an old friend. She inhaled and smiled automatically. Her eyes went to the spatula of frosting in BJ's left hand and her mouth began to water.

"Oh, Grace, come in. Come in. You're just in time to join me for lunch. I hate to eat alone."

Grace nodded and made an unintelligible noise. Damn chocolate cake Kryptonite.

After a lunch consisting of a glass of whole milk and a huge slice of chocolate cake, Grace watched as BJ flitted around her like a mama bird. She wouldn't have been surprised if her hostess brought her a blanket so she could stretch out on the dainty floral couch for a nap. It looked like such a comfortable couch too, with all those pillows.

Grace shook herself and sat up straight. Lulled by buttercream, she'd almost forgotten why she was there.

"Um, hey, BJ, I actually came by because I wanted to ask you a question."

"Of course." There it was, the cherubic, guileless face, looking straight at her.

Grace cleared her throat and plucked a chocolate crumb from her shirt. "Did you ever think that, maybe, just maybe, Ax could have killed Tommy Redfoot?"

She expected shock, horror, disbelief. Or at least vehement objections from the leader of the band's fan club. What she got instead was a half shrug and a nod.

"Sure," BJ said. "I guess you can't be a hard-core Sparks fan without pondering that possibility at some point over the years. Given their history and all."

It was Grace, instead, who looked shocked.

"It's ridiculous, of course," BJ hastened to add. "But it's fun to speculate, like the death clues from the *Secret Keeper* album cover. We all knew it was fake, but it was like finding a four-leaf clover when you spotted a new clue. Like playing detective, except without a real crime."

"But Tommy's death wasn't fake. And by speculating on it, you are admitting that there was a possibility he was murdered."

BJ made a pained face. "I know. It sounds macabre in retrospect. But it seemed so surreal at the time, almost like it was part of the show. Very theatrical. At first, there were even rumors that Tommy faked his own death, that he and his girlfriend were living down in the Caribbean somewhere, happily ever after. That was my personal favorite."

"But there were also people who thought Ax killed him? Why?"

"No particular reason. Just stories. Ax had a reputation of being sort of a bad boy. I'm sure you remember that."

Grace nodded.

"Mostly prankster stuff, trashing hotel rooms and public indecency, that sort of thing. And there was something about him beating up a photographer once." She shook her head, her soft brown curls bouncing around her head as she tried to recall.

"What? How come I never heard about that?"

"They paid the guy off, I think. I don't remember exactly, but if you'll wait right here, I'll go get my book."

BJ hopped up and scurried down the hall to her Sparks shrine, which also served as her bedroom. She came back with a fat, 12 X 12 scrapbook held together at the spine by three silver posts. The cover started its life as a plain, black book, but was now hidden by an elaborate collage of photos of the band—all big hair, ripped jeans and eyeliner—protected by a shiny layer of decoupage glue.

She opened the book and began turning pages. It was filled with newspaper clippings and magazine articles from the days before the Internet, when people still got the bulk of their news delivered by the paper boy.

Grace's mouth fell open. It was like the chocolate cake all over again. "You've been holding out on me."

"This?" BJ nodded toward the book. "Oh, this is all public record stuff. There's nothing in here that hasn't already been published somewhere."

Grace gave the woman her best admonitory glare and BJ said, "You can borrow it if you want, of course."

She turned a few more pages before pointing a stubby finger at a short newspaper article. It was two columns, maybe four inches long, topped by a grainy, unflattering black-and-white photo of Ax. It was from a Minneapolis newspaper and gave an account of an altercation between the guitarist and a freelance photographer, who had been waiting for him outside a local nightclub one early September morning in 1987. According to several eye-witnesses, the photographer was blocking the sidewalk in front of the club and wouldn't let Ax and his female companion du jour pass, but continued to take photos of them the entire time. Heated words were exchanged, at which point Ax picked up the man's camera bag and tossed it into the street, whereupon it was immediately run over by a passing taxi. The bag reportedly contained another camera and some very expensive lenses. The photographer then pushed Ax, who responded by ripping the man's camera from his hands and breaking his nose with it. When the photographer fell to the sidewalk, Ax proceeded to kick the man with his custom-made alligator boots, resulting in two broken ribs and a bruised kidney.

A second, shorter article was dated less than a month later and taken from the same Minneapolis newspaper. The headline read, "Heavy Metal Guitarist Settles Assault Charges." It simply stated that the photographer had agreed to drop the charges, and Ax had agreed to pay for his medical bills, his legal fees, his ruined camera equipment, and an undisclosed amount for "pain and suffering."

"Wow," Grace whispered. The spider web kept getting bigger and stickier.

"Yeah, wow is right," BJ said with a disapproving shake of her head. "Can you believe they called him heavy metal?"

Grace ignored the quip and said, "Was this an isolated incident?"

"I wouldn't go that far, but most of the other stories I heard weren't documented, so they were just that—stories. There are a few other things in here about trashed hotel rooms and such, like the time he drove the motorcycle through the casino, but it was mostly chalked up to the rock and roll lifestyle. There was a lot more tolerance for this sort of thing back then. It was almost expected. It gave them street cred."

Grace nodded, carefully turning the pages and marveling at the hours and hours of work that had gone into compiling this time capsule.

"And you say I can borrow this?"

"Sure. Anything you need," BJ said. "Would you like some more cake?"

It was late afternoon before Grace got back home and dealt with the aftermath of Hurricane Karishma. The bathroom wasn't as bad as she'd feared—nothing a gallon of Lysol and some elbow grease couldn't cure. And the work did her a world of good, cleared her head and got her blood pumping. Manual labor really was the poor man's workout.

The good news was that Karishma was back to her usual feisty self. The bad news was … well, the same.

Grace tethered the dog's leash to the post at the bottom of the front steps and sat down to watch her sniff her way around a twelve-foot circle in the front yard. The breeze was almost constant now, thanks to the storm front that was rolling in from the Great Plains. The local weather man had been yapping about it for two days, predicting damaging winds and flash floods. Grace looked at her neglected flower beds and welcomed it.

She checked her phone. Nick had left a message while she was cleaning the bathroom. "Hey, sweetheart. I'm sorry I missed you. I'm about to go into the exhibit hall, and I know I won't be able to hear if you call me back. I'll try to call you later. I really miss you. I can't wait to get home. Only two more days. I love you." Then he made a few kissy noises before he hung up.

Grace smiled. Nick's messages always became sweeter the longer he was away. Absence really did make the heart grow fonder. And she missed him, too. She was tired of sleeping alone, of eating alone, of listening for noises that weren't there. But most of all, she wanted to see his sleepy, grinning face first thing in the morning instead of Karishma's.

The little dog came over and sat at her feet, panting. She was done with the great outdoors and ready to go back inside, an indoor dog if ever there was one. A fine mist of rain was beginning to fall, so it was just as well they should head inside. With some luck, Grace would get another tape transcribed before Nick called back.

She made a cup of coffee and turned on the new computer. It was wonderful to watch the machine boot up so fast, ready to go before she even had time to take the USB drive from the chain around her neck. The computer was state of the art, at least in comparison to the technology Sparks had used to record the tapes. With a start, Grace remembered Sparks's Dictaphone in her purse. She grabbed her bag and upended it on the dining room table. She picked up the recorder and headed back to the computer, leaving everything else behind. Sparks's last words were on that tape, at least his last words to her. And she was finally about to hear them.

Chapter 28 — Unmarked

Funny thing about the truth. If you live without it long enough, you make up your own. Your mind fills in the gaps and you start to believe it, rely on it, get really attached to it. And somewhere down the line, if some asshole comes along and offers to give you real *truth ... well, let's just say I'm not sure I want to hear it anymore.*

Let me back up. I'm getting ahead of myself. About an hour ago, I got a phone call, a real blast from my past, this lowlife named Arthur DeWitt. He said he's running for state senate now. He's says he's being groomed for the Presidency. I find this to be an incredible crock of monkey shit because back in the day I knew him as Witty—which he never was—a small-time drug dealer who latched onto the band's teat like a big, frizzy-haired leech. I couldn't stand him, and I'm pretty sure the feeling was mutual. After all, I was never his customer.

So, I was pretty surprised when he called me out of the blue and said he wanted to talk. He said he heard I was writing a book and he had something I needed to hear. Said it wasn't the kind of thing you should tell over the phone. But he said he'd kept it to himself too long, and now he's going to tell me and I can do whatever I want with the information, as long as I keep him out of it. That whole grooming-for-the-Presidency thing, I guess. Bullshit.

Honestly, I'd almost forgotten about Witty, except when I hear Creep, *of course. That song from* Secret Keeper. *He was the inspiration for it. Only use I ever had for him.*

Anyway, I tried to blow him off, told him I was busy. Then he drops the bomb. Says he wants to talk about Redfoot. Says it was murder and he knows who did it. Can you believe this jackass? I asked him why he didn't go to the cops with this information and he said he was too scared back then and now he can't afford to be associated with it. Bad for his career. Says he wants to come over tomorrow afternoon. Then he said he doesn't think I'll be surprised when I find out the truth.

But, like I said, I'm not so sure I want to hear it. What if the killer turns out to be someone I always thought I could trust? Someone who stood beside me at Redfoot's funeral, who helped me carry his casket, somebody who grieved with me, with the world?

Sparks was quiet for a minute, but Grace waited, knowing there had to be more.

I'm not saying it never crossed my mind before. We all knew Ax had a temper and he was sick of Redfoot's attitude, but he never would have killed him, not on purpose. A few loose teeth and a bloody nose, sure, but poison? That's straight-up premeditated shit. I don't ... I don't want to know if one of my best friends killed one of my other best friends. God, how chicken-shit is that, Grace? Huh? Crazy, I know. But to think that Ax could kill him and then go about his business like nothing ever happened. Just live his life.

And, why in the hell is Witty just coming forward now, after all these years? If the little prick had evidence, he should have brought it forward a long time ago. The fact is, in the great punchbowl of life, Arthur DeWitt is nothing but a cockroach turd. Damn it, I should never have answered the phone.

There was the sound of footsteps and ice clinking in a glass. Sparks never hit the pause button. It was either on or off, just like his life.

Well, um, Grace, I suppose it goes without saying that I don't want any of this to go in the book. I don't even know why I said it. It's just hearsay, after all. Not even that, yet. He didn't even come right out and say Ax's name. Guess I should erase this. Where's the erase button? How do you...? Damn it. Sorry piece of shit.

The next sounds were all fumbling and static, then a sigh of technical resignation.

Hey, Grace, don't forget to erase this, okay? I can't find the button and I sure don't want this in the book. Thanks. Ciao, baby. Sparks out.

—Sparks Tape Name: Unmarked

Grace stopped the tape and sat, stunned, staring at the computer screen.

So, Ax Royce had murdered Tommy Redfoot in a fit of professional rage. No, she reminded herself, it was not a fit of rage. It was poison, cold-blooded, calculated murder. And then he pretended to mourn with everyone else while comforting his remaining bandmates. What a scumbag.

And somehow their drug supplier, Witty, had found out. He'd overheard or witnessed something that he wasn't supposed to. It scared the crap out of him, so badly that he left town and hadn't been seen or heard from in the past fifteen years. It scared him so much that only now was he willing to share what he knew, now that he was running for senate and wanted to clear his conscience.

This was too much. Grace sprang from her chair and scrambled for her cell phone. She had to report this. She couldn't just sit on this information. She'd call Shipps and tell him…

Tell him what? To put out an APB on Ax Royce, guitar god, for a decades-old homicide that had been ruled accidental? And all this based solely on the speculation of another murder victim—who, incidentally, believed Ax was innocent.

Grace's finger hovered over the screen of her phone. Shipps would go ballistic if she called him with this new, wild theory with, as usual, not a thread of evidence. How could she convince him? Aside from the killer, there was no one who knew the truth.

Kelly Adamson

Except.

Except for Arthur DeWitt, presumptive senator, who'd had a deep, dark secret to tell Sparks Westergard.

Less than an hour later, Grace was in the car on her way to his house. He said he had the truth. Sparks may not have wanted it, but she sure did.

Grace had called Wayne to find out how to get in touch with DeWitt's people. He did her one better and gave her his personal cell phone number.

"He called me from the car the day they came to take publicity photos," Wayne said. "Acting like we were old pals or something. Well, he can call me *bro* as long as he brings me a donation check."

"Do you know where his house in Mountain Brook is?"

"Sure. It's that big monstrosity on his TV commercial."

"I haven't been watching much TV lately."

"Well, it's a looker, that's for sure. Most politicians show off the wife and kids on TV. Witty doesn't have either of those, but he does have an old-money mansion with two-story columns across the front. Looks like something out of *Gone With the Wind*. Maybe he thinks that house makes him look like some honorable old Southern gentleman. But it just makes him look like he's out of touch with his future constituents. He should've kidnapped a wife and kids to show instead."

It took several tries before Arthur DeWitt finally answered his cell phone. Grace's hands shook as she shoved her scattered belongings back into her purse and listened to the phone ring again and again. The thought of finally finding someone who could give her some answers was overwhelming. The questions ran through her head in a jumble.

What happened to Tommy Redfoot all those years ago? Did Ax Royce have any suspicions that Witty knew the truth? Had he threatened him? Bribed him?

"Yes?" The voice on the phone sounded anything but pleased.

"Mr. DeWitt?"

"Yes. Who is this?"

"My name is Grace Howard and I'm doing some research for a book I'm writing. I have some questions I was hoping you could help me with if you have a few minutes."

"No, I don't have a few minutes. You should call my office. I'm sure my assistant could answer any questions you might have."

"I doubt that very much, Mr. DeWitt."

"I don't know where you got this number, Ms. Howe, and I'm not going to ask. But I would appreciate it if you didn't use it again. It's my personal number. Now, if you don't mind, I'm very busy."

"Howard."

"Pardon?"

"My name. It's Howard, not Howe. Grace Howard."

He paused for a moment and then said, "What did you say your book was about?"

"I didn't," Grace said, her mouth feeling a little dry. "But it's about Sparks Westergard."

There was another pause, this one much longer. Then DeWitt said, "Why don't you come over to my house, Ms. Howard, so we can talk in person. Any friend of Sparks Westergard is a friend of mine."

He gave her directions to his house and even gave her the code to get in the main gate, and when she pulled up twenty minutes later, he was waiting for her. He stepped out onto the front porch with a drink in his hand and motioned her to drive around back.

The rain was coming down steadily now and the wind had picked up to the point that it had taken all of Grace's concentration to navigate through the dark and winding Mountain Brook streets.

She pulled around the house to find a large, covered carport structure, built well after the main house, and was happy to pull out of the rain. She parked beside a white Mercedes coupe and turned off the engine.

The lights were on at the rear of the house, illuminating a large, stone patio and a well-established, if a trifle neglected, flower garden. Old-growth azaleas and hydrangeas higher than Grace's head lined the edges of the property and, if there had been houses nearby—which there weren't—they would have been hidden from view. There was no pool, but the back of the yard disappeared off a rocky embankment and the dark woods swallowed up everything beyond. It was probably beautiful in the daylight, a slice of old-money Birmingham, and Grace made a mental note to ask if she could come back some day and tour the grounds.

The house itself did indeed look antebellum, but Grace didn't think there was anything older than a hundred years or so in the area. It was a looker, though, just like Wayne said.

Arthur DeWitt stood under the rear portico, framed in the light of the open back door. His silhouette was tall, whip cord lean, and imposing, perfect for a political figure, Grace decided. She wasn't about to vote for him, but it was easy to envision him standing on the senate floor, striking fear into the hearts of the opposition.

He approached her car and called to her as she stepped out. "Ms. Howard, I presume."

Grace grabbed her purse, locked the car door and turned to face the small-time drug dealer turned possible senator, wondering again who the hell could ever make that leap. In this day and age, the media could and would out a public figure if they'd ever had so much as a parking ticket, and this guy had the brass cajones to think he could escape that? And he had the nerve to tell Sparks he was being groomed for the Oval Office? She wasn't sure whether she was about to meet a genius or an idiot.

He stood a few feet away, right hand outstretched, his smile revealing a gleaming mouthful of capped teeth. He wore gray silk suit pants and a starched white dress shirt with no tie, and the sleeves rolled up just enough to reveal tan, muscular forearms. There was little resemblance to the slovenly young man in Honeybear's photos, the inspiration for the Creep in the trench coat. "I'm your dirty little secret, the one you want to forget," Sparks's voice sang in her head.

She shook his hand and returned his smile. "So nice of you to see me on such short notice."

"Nonsense. I'm happy to help."

"This is beautiful," Grace said with a nod toward the darkened property and woods beyond. "Reminds me of a storybook."

Her host smiled. "Thank you. Yes, I love it here. My grandfather built this place in 1932. Some people thought he was being pretentious, building a place like this at the height of the Depression, but he focused instead on all the people he was putting to work—carpenters, stone masons and the like. He made his money in coal mining, and he was always looking out for the working man. Now I'm trying to keep that alive."

Grace smiled and nodded and wondered how many times he'd given some version of that speech while campaigning.

A gust of wind blew rain under the carport where they stood and he said, "Let's get out of this weather, shall we?"

The inside of the house was even more incredible than the outside, a time capsule straight out of *The Great Gatsby*.

"Wow. This place is … exquisite."

DeWitt chuckled and moved around to a bar in the center of the room—a den, or keeping room, or whatever rich people called the place where

Kelly Adamson

they sat, sipped brandy, and warmed their toes by the fire. She had the urge to take pictures, but pushed it down. She was here on more important business.

Her host stood patiently at the bar, sipping from a highball glass. The crystal sparkled and winked as he moved. "May I pour you a drink? Bourbon? Scotch?"

"Scotch, thanks."

A silver ice bucket sat amid the crystal decanters on the bar, and DeWitt plucked a cube with a small pair of tongs and held it up to her with raised eyebrows. She nodded.

"I'm a bourbon man, myself," he said, motioning for Grace to sit. She did and he handed her the crystal glass, which was much heavier than it looked.

"What can I do for you, Ms. Howard? You say you're writing a book?"

"Yes, about Sparks Westergard. I understand you knew him when he was just starting out here in Birmingham."

He nodded and studied his drink. He moved his hand minutely, just enough to swirl the bourbon over the ice. "Seems like a million years ago," he said. "We were all so young."

"I believe you may have been one of the last people to speak to Sparks before he was killed."

"Me? No." He looked surprised. "I'm afraid I haven't seen Sparks in many years. Our lives took very different paths."

"Oh? He said you called him and wanted to talk. He said you were planning to come to his house the day after he died."

"He said?"

"Yes, well, he said it on an audiotape that I transcribed."

DeWitt leaned his head back, practicing his thoughtful pose. "Ah, well, I did speak to him on the phone a month or so ago and indeed had planned to call on him. It's campaign season, you know. Do you follow politics, Ms. Howard?"

"Not much," she admitted.

"Well, I can use every vote I can get. I was hoping to get an endorsement from Sparks. But at the last minute, something came up. So, I never made it to his house. You say that was the day he died?"

"He was killed the night before. Not too long after he talked to you on the phone."

"Such a shame."

"Such a shame," she echoed. She'd let her hopes get too high about this meeting and thought for sure she was going to get answers about Sparks. Shot down with a simple, "Something came up."

Well, he'd said he had information. And she certainly had questions. She wasn't leaving this house until she found out who killed Tommy Redfoot.

DeWitt got up and moved behind the bar again. He lifted a crystal decanter and said, "May I freshen your drink?"

"No, thanks."

"How do you like it? It's a twenty-five-year-old single malt aged in oak barrels."

Grace looked down at the glass in her hands, the amber liquid untouched so far. She had no intention of drinking any of it, then driving home in this crazy weather, but didn't want to appear rude, so she lifted it to her lips and inhaled. The smell of scotch was half the enjoyment anyway.

He freshened his own drink and took his seat again in the buckskin leather club chair facing her. She looked up and he was staring at her expectantly, a half smile on his thin lips, waiting for the verdict on the scotch.

"It's very good," she said, and it probably was.

"You taste the honey?"

"Oh, yes. The honey's good."

"And the smokiness? It's not too much?"

Grace shook her head. "Oh, no. Just the right amount of smokiness."
Whatever.

He seemed satisfied, settled back in his chair and crossed his long legs.
He was a man very much at home in his own skin. He must know that she
knew how he earned his money as a teenager. How else would she have known
of his involvement with Sparks? Yet it didn't seem to rattle his cage in the
least. He took another sip of his bourbon and smiled, waiting for her to begin.

She cleared her throat and shifted in the leather chair.

"So, you knew Sparks and his band back at the beginning, when they
played The Nick and hung out at the fountain?"

He nodded.

"They were pretty wild even then, weren't they?"

DeWitt's smile stayed in place, but seemed to stiffen. He held her gaze
as he replied. "I'm sure I know where this is going, Ms. Howard. Anyone who
knew me as an eighteen-year-old knew a foolish, arrogant, self-centered child,
seemingly destined to become a career criminal."

Grace was a little taken aback by that and was sure it showed on her
face.

"I did some things I regret," he said, "and some things I'd very much
like to forget. But, haven't we all?" He stared at her as if he knew her deepest,
darkest secrets. She wondered for a moment if he knew what she had done the
year before in Las Vegas, then reminded herself, as she had done so many
times since then, that it had been self-defense.

"But, I've changed." He broke eye contact and took a long sip of
bourbon. "I'm not the man I used to be, and I say good riddance to him. I
believe everyone deserves a second chance. Don't you?"

Grace nodded. She did. She just couldn't help wondering how many
second chances Arthur DeWitt had had.

"Don't worry," she said. "I'm not here to air your dirty laundry or derail your political career. My book is about Sparks and, to a lesser extent, his band, but not about you." It wasn't a complete lie. If she found out what she was after, the information was going to the police, not to her manuscript.

He raised his glass to her in a salute. "To journalism."

"I'm not a journalist."

"But you still have questions for me."

"I do."

"I'm an open book now, a servant of the people. What do you want to know?"

She put her glass on the marble-topped coffee table and pulled her notebook and pen from her purse. "You knew Sparks's original bassist, Tommy Redfoot, and his girlfriend, Connie Carnaggio?"

DeWitt's smile vanished, as did most of the color from his face. After all these years, her name still evoked such a response.

He didn't speak, but stared instead at a spot a foot or so above his Persian rug.

Grace waited what she considered a respectful length of time and continued. "I've seen photos of you at Tommy's house in L.A. the night he overdosed. Did you see anything out of the ordinary that night? Did Tommy argue with anyone?"

DeWitt made no move to answer, just continued to stare at nothing.

"Did Tommy seem anxious that night? Worried about anything?" And then, in an effort to see if he was even still listening to her, she said, "Have you seen CC since that night? Do you know where she is now?"

He looked at her then, blinking his eyes like he was just waking up. But he still didn't say anything. This must have been a record for a politician keeping his mouth shut. He was going to make her work for this.

Finally, he muttered, "That was so long ago. It's hard to remember," which was clearly a lie, judging from the look on his face.

"You were around them a lot, even went to California to be near them. Do you ever remember seeing Tommy arguing with anyone, maybe one of the other band members?" Grace was pretty sure this was "leading the witness," but she was no lawyer and he didn't seem to be listening anyway.

She made a show of checking her notebook, flipping pages and scribbling a few words, giving her host time to regain his poise. The rain was pelting the rear windows of the house. It sounded like someone was throwing pebbles against the glass. She was glad she'd taken the time to shut Karishma in the guest room and let her own dogs inside. Ricky hated thunder.

She looked around the room but didn't see a clock and wondered how rude it would be to pull out her cell phone and check the time. The weather was getting worse and this show needed to get on the proverbial road. May as well get on with it.

"Sparks said that you told him that you had some information that might prove Tommy was murdered."

DeWitt's face lost what little color it had left. His dark eyes looked like two coals on a snowman's head. All he needed was a carrot for a nose.

Grace waited for a reply, but after a minute he turned away again and held up an open palm toward her. "CC was … very special to me. Can you give me a minute?" It was quiet and polite, but it was not a question.

"Of course," she said. "May I use your powder room?"

He motioned to the hallway and Grace shouldered her purse and headed to the bathroom, wondering if she had ever used the term "powder room" in her life. It was this grand old house that was doing it, making her say things like "exquisite" and "powder room." She felt a trifle out of place. A "trifle."

The hallway was dark and narrow, surprising considering what she'd seen of the house so far. There were two closed doors on either side of the hallway and at the other end was a large, open foyer. The front door was straight ahead, and the staircase leading to the second story was on the right. She knew it was wrong to look around someone's house without permission, but she'd file that in the same category with the leading questions. To the left of the foyer was a formal dining room and, presumably, a kitchen beyond that. There were no lights anywhere that she could see. Occasional flashes of lightning from outside were the only illumination. The leaded glass of the front door shone bright as a bolt struck nearby and thunder shook the house.

She turned back to the hallway and tried one of the doors. A guest bedroom, from the looks of it. Directly across the hall was another, almost identical. The third door led to a bathroom in working order, thankfully, but in need of a little modernization.

As she returned to the study a few minutes later, she passed by the fourth door and tried it on a whim. It opened to another staircase, narrow and steep, barely wide enough for an average adult. This one went down instead of up. Maybe used by servants in days of yore to access the cellar? It seemed a poor design to put the entrance so far from the kitchen.

She eased in and put her foot on the first step. She felt something soft under her shoe and reached down to pick it up. A flash of lighting came in from the end of the narrow hallway and she could see a loop of elastic wrapped in purple ribbon embellished with sequins. Like something little girls wore in their hair. Odd to find such a thing behind a door that was probably rarely used.

Grace took the ponytail holder back into the sitting room where DeWitt stood staring out of the rain-spattered rear windows into the darkness.

"I opened the wrong door looking for the bathroom," she said, "and found this. I don't think it's yours. It's not your color." She held it up and smiled, trying a little humor.

Kelly Adamson

He crossed the room in three strides and took the bit of ribbon from her outstretched hand. He smiled as an afterthought. "Oh, my niece must have dropped that the last time she visited."

"Your niece?"

"Yes, adorable child, but you have to keep your eye on her all the time. You know how little children can be, always getting into something."

He pocketed the hair ribbon and turned, picking up Grace's glass from the coffee table as he passed it. He'd definitely regained his composure.

"Have you ever had port?" he said. "I'm always surprised by the number of people who have never tried it. I have a bottle here that is really incredible. I'd love for you to taste it."

A thought was bouncing around in Grace's mind like a pinball in a machine. Too fast to catch. She'd seen a ponytail holder like that somewhere before, but couldn't place it. She closed her eyes, trying to concentrate on the pinball, or maybe it was a soap bubble. Then another thought rushed in, rudely bumping that one to the ground. It was the memory of Wayne in his office saying, "Witty is an only child. Maybe his parents didn't want to run the risk of having another one like him."

DeWitt pulled two short, fat glasses and a bottle of dark wine from underneath the bar.

"Does your niece belong to your brother or your sister?"

"My sister," he said without hesitation as he poured the wine. "They live in Oregon. I don't get to see them as often as I'd like."

"Oh? I'd heard you had no siblings. I must've gotten some bad information. What's your niece's name?" She leaned over to retrieve her notebook and pen from the coffee table and in a flash it came to her, the first memory, the soap bubble, and this time it was being chased by an animated puppy. A little girl sat cross-legged in Sparks's guest bedroom on the evening of his wake. She could still hear the girl saying, "My daddy is a friend of Ms.

West-er-gard." Grace suddenly felt a little light-headed. The sequined hair ribbon belonged to Sophia, Raul's daughter.

There must be some mistake.

She looked up to see Arthur DeWitt leveling a pistol at her and knew there was no mistake.

Chapter 29 — Witty

"You ask too many questions, Ms. Howard."

Grace froze. Her heart pounded frantically, but seemed to be the only part of her able to move.

"I'd hoped I would get what I needed from Sparks's computer. I should've known he wasn't literate enough to write his own memoirs. Then I found out about you and thought stealing your computer would be enough. But no such luck."

His eyes moved to her chest and he smiled. "Is that what I think it is?"

Grace looked down to see the orange USB drive that hung from a chain around her neck. It had fallen out of her shirt when she leaned over to pick up her notebook and she hadn't moved to tuck it back in. DeWitt stepped forward and grabbed it with his free hand. He jerked downward and the chain snapped, but not before almost pulling Grace off balance.

"How nice of you to bring it to me." He pocketed the little thumb drive with the scrunchy and took a peek at his watch, then motioned with the pistol for her to sit. "Make yourself comfortable, Ms. Howard. Or may I call you Grace?"

"No, you may not."

He laughed then, and it sounded quite genuine. "I like you," he said.

"So, let me guess. You like me so much that you're really going to hate having to kill me." Her voice said the words, but she wasn't sure where this unexpected bravado was coming from.

"Maybe, but that doesn't mean I'm not going to do it. Sit," he said again, more forceful this time.

"Or what? We both know you won't shoot me on your expensive Persian rug."

"You think not? Well, the fact is, this is a Chinese knock-off, and I won't hesitate to shoot you on it, roll your dead body up in it and dump you in the middle of Smith Lake with a couple of cinder blocks for good measure. It's two hundred feet deep in some places, you know. I sincerely doubt yours would be the first body disposed of there."

She shivered involuntarily, and he smiled when he saw it.

"But then you'd have to burn this place to the ground to get rid of all my DNA. I don't think you want to do that."

"Not if I don't have to, true. Besides, it really is a two-person job. That's why I called someone while you were snooping around my house."

"Who? The police?"

"A friend."

"You have friends? I never would have guessed."

"Well, *friend* is too strong a word in this case. *Business associate* is more precise."

"You mean the mugger who stole my doughnuts, or are you referring to his crack-head accomplice?"

"It might take him another half-hour to get here in this bad weather, so we've got time to relax and have a drink," he said, ignoring her question. "Sit." This time it was a command.

This time, she sat.

They stared at each for a minute, listening to the rain pounding against the rear windows of the house.

If she was going to make a move to escape, she had less than half an hour to do it. Part of her knew she had to keep the guy with the gun talking, lest he get bored and his trigger finger got itchy.

"If you're going to kill me anyway, why don't you go ahead and answer my questions? It'll pass the time."

He tilted his head to one side and made a show of considering her request. "All right. I'll grant your last wish. But only because I like to talk about myself. What do you want to know?"

Thunder boomed, the lights flickered, and DeWitt looked concerned for a moment. He found some votive candles under the bar and lit them with a wand lighter, never lowering his pistol.

"How did you get Sparks to drink the whiskey?"

"With this, of course." DeWitt nodded at the gun, then rolled his eyes in exasperation. "Imagine my surprise when Sparks Westergard said he stopped drinking. That's like saying a shark stopped swimming. I didn't know it was even possible. But, of course, he didn't know the bourbon was poisoned, so the threat of being shot was all it took to get him to cooperate."

He smiled, pleased with himself.

"Why did you kill him?" Other than the fact that you are a raving lunatic.

He looked at her like she was a simpleton. "Are you really going to pretend you don't know?"

"I don't," she said. "But I can guess."

"Oh, good, a game," he said. "Be my guest. I'll stop you if you get something wrong." He leaned back and waited, the perfect example of a polite audience, if you like your audience armed.

Grace cleared her throat, which was incredibly dry, but she refused on principle to drink anything in the house. "I think you killed Tommy Redfoot, and you thought Sparks knew about it and was going to expose you in his book, so you killed him, too."

He studied her over the rim of his wine glass, but said nothing.

"Of course," she continued, "you're a big, important man now. You had to find someone to frame for Sparks's murder. Sending the fan club president the bottle of bourbon to get her fingerprints on it and then stealing it back was pretty inspired, I'll admit. You just never imagined that mousy little BJ Knox would have an airtight alibi all by herself in her apartment."

"God bless the Internet," DeWitt said with a smirk.

"So, you had to come up with Plan B. You found out Sparks's wife was having an affair and that could have worked, except she was out of town at the time. But then you found out that her boyfriend's only family was his five-year-old daughter. I'm sure you thought you'd struck gold. So you kidnapped the girl and hid her—here, judging from the ponytail holder—and used her as leverage to make Raul confess to a murder he didn't commit. How am I doing so far?"

"I didn't stop you, did I? Although I'll assume you hadn't connected these dots until after you found the ribbon. Otherwise, you would've brought the police with you."

He waited for her to deny it, but it was pointless. She felt completely foolish knowing that an hour ago she was convinced that Ax Royce was the killer. What a sorry excuse for a detective she'd make.

"Why did you come here, anyway, Ms. Howard?"

"I wanted the truth."

"Well, you came to the right place for that." He chuckled, obviously finding the whole affair entertaining. The four glasses of bourbon and wine probably had some bearing on that as well. "You haven't asked me what I plan to do with the girl. Don't you want to know?"

Grace's stomach lurched.

"I thought this part was pretty ingenious," he said. "After all, I had to do *something* with her. It's not as if I could just keep her for the rest of her life. But, if I killed her, there would be no incentive for Raul to keep his mouth

Kelly Adamson

shut. He had to believe she was okay, or he could always retract his statement and start feeling truthful."

"My, we couldn't have that."

"Obviously. So my plan is to sell the girl. It's entirely up to Raul who I sell her to. If he plays ball and keeps quiet, I know a lovely couple in Miami who can't have children of their own. They can't adopt because of his criminal record, but they would make wonderful parents. They have plenty of money. They'd send her to the finest schools, make sure she never wanted for a thing. They could give her a better life than Raul could. I'd make sure he got to see photos of her now and then. On her polo pony, on their yacht, et cetera. You get the idea. What do you think?"

"You don't really want to know what I think."

He cocked his head to one side, considering. "Don't you want to know what happens if Raul gets a sudden urge to tell the truth and nothing but the truth?"

"Not really."

"I'm glad you asked," he said. "I have a business associate who lives in Chicago. He likes young girls. He likes them *very* much. And he likes them *very* young. I told Raul if he felt compelled to come clean, I could arrange for him to get some photos of his daughter with my Chicago friend instead. He didn't seem too keen on the idea."

The lights flickered again. Grace fought the wave of nausea that washed over her. DeWitt was a sociopath, and he needed to be stopped. But he still had the girl.

"Where is she now?"

"She's safe. She's in the basement. I told her that her daddy had to go away for a while and wanted her to stay with me. Eventually, I'll tell her he died in a plane crash or something. I haven't decided. Do you have any suggestions?"

"You don't want to hear my suggestions."

He laughed, showing a mouthful of white teeth, and looked charmed and amused by her revulsion. The fact that he could sit there so serenely while sharing his plans to traffic a five-year-old was just too much. Grace felt the rage bubbling up inside her like lava in a volcano.

Somehow, the fact that he was about to kill her hadn't made such an impact. Denial, most likely. But this was different. She wanted to hurt him. She wanted to claw his eyes out. But how could she hurt a man holding her at gunpoint?

She looked from the gun back up at his tranquil face, and for a second she could see a ghost of the young man who stood in the shadows in Tommy Redfoot's kitchen on the last night of his life. And in that moment, she knew exactly how to hurt him.

"How old would CC and Tommy's baby have been now if you hadn't killed her?"

His peaceful smile vanished, and Grace felt a moment of triumph.

"Yes, I know about her—or him, I suppose. It could have been a boy. That's why CC wasn't drinking that night. And why she and Tommy were so blissfully happy in the photos. They did look blissfully happy, don't you think? I've never seen two people look so much in love."

"I don't want to play this game anymore," DeWitt said evenly.

"Is that why you killed her, because you couldn't stand the thought of her having someone else's baby? It all makes sense now," she said with a nod. "You killed Tommy thinking you would have a shot with CC when he was out of the picture, but of course she was physically repulsed by you when you approached her after he was dead." She was playing with fire here and knew it. There was a fine line between making him lose his concentration and making him so furious that he went ahead and shot her in his fine leather chair. She grinned. "Oh, God. Maybe you even offered to help raise Tommy's baby as your own, like you were doing her a favor. Is that it?"

He didn't answer, but his face had gone from white to red and there was a vein pulsing in his forehead.

"Did the beautiful woman laugh at you? Did she tell you that you made her sick to her stomach? Maybe she said she'd rather die than be with a greasy, two-bit drug dealer like you, so you obliged her. Is that it?"

DeWitt lurched to his feet and Grace flinched in spite of her swagger. "Shut up. You don't know what you're talking about."

"Oh no? Well, where is she then? Living happily ever after as a runway model? Or did you sell her to one of your business associates?"

"Shut up."

"Or maybe her body's at the bottom of Smith Lake, rolled up in another fake Persian rug."

"Shut up! Stop talking about her." He raised the pistol and pointed it straight at Grace's face. His hand was shaking. She stared at the barrel, barely breathing, while he ranted.

"Tommy Redfoot was a low-born, low-class drug addict. He didn't deserve her. He didn't deserve to touch the hem of her garment. Every time I saw him touch her, I wanted to puke. That was supposed to be me." He hammered his chest with his left hand for emphasis. "She was *mine*!"

The last word came out through clenched teeth, as a snarl. He was showing her the animal that he was. Maybe this is what they all saw before he killed them—Tommy, CC, and Sparks.

"Yes, I killed her. I did her a favor. She's better off dead than with him."

He grabbed his wine glass from the coffee table and threw it at the wall behind Grace. It crashed into a mirror and a console table that held bric-a-brac that probably came over on the Mayflower. Or, hell, maybe they were Chinese knock-offs, too. Maybe everything about him was a lie.

He spun around and crossed the few feet to the bar, grabbed one of the crystal decanters and hurled it at the nearest wall.

The heavy crystal bounced, unbroken, off the wall, landing at DeWitt's feet. The stopper had flown in a different direction and the smell of whiskey immediately engulfed the room. DeWitt stared for a few seconds at the perfect spider web of cracks that the bottle left in the old plaster, his rage momentarily interrupted.

A few seconds was all Grace needed.

When he turned back to face her, he was breathless from the adrenaline rush, and his face was slick with sweat. But now it was his turn to stare down the barrel of her gun. It had just been a matter of getting it out of her purse and flipping the safety off.

He looked at it, uncomprehending at first, and then actually smiled. "You're not going to shoot me."

"Is that what you think?" she said. "Well, I don't give a shit about your Persian rug."

He raised his gun. Grace squeezed the trigger on her .22.

It was louder than she remembered.

Witty's right arm jerked back and up, and the pistol flew out of his hand. It looked like a trick shot, except Grace had been aiming for his heart.

He grabbed the bloody arm with this good hand, stared at it, and then at her. Then he let out a howl of pain and rage, and lunged. She tried to jump back, but the leather club chair was behind her, blocking any retreat.

She fell, scrambling, clawing, up and over the chair. But he managed to get his left hand—already covered in blood—around one of her ankles and pulled. She kicked frantically at him with her other foot. He didn't seem to feel it. He pulled again and her body slid back down into the chair.

"You'll pay for this, bitch," he hissed, pinning her to the chair with one knee. "You can find out how deep Smith Lake is for yourself."

Grace felt Witty's hand close around her throat. Then she remembered what was in her own hand and heard Nick's voice in her head. "Be prepared to empty the magazine."

She pointed her pink and black .22 at him and fired ... again and again and again until it was empty and DeWitt was finally still.

She stumbled away from his blood-soaked body, shaking and gasping for breath. She hit the back door full force and scrambled to turn the knob with her left hand, her primitive brain refusing to drop the empty gun in her right.

The door swung open, and she fell through into the darkness, out of one storm and into another, landing on her hands and knees on the slate pavers. Water rushed over the patio in a shallow river underneath her while rain pounded on her back with enough force to bring her back to the present.

She felt deaf and blind, a sensory overload. But she had to get up. If DeWitt's lackey hadn't mercifully driven off a cliff on the way over, he could be pulling up any second. She had to run, get as far away as possible.

No. If she ran now, she'd be abandoning Sophia to the hired hand. It wasn't an option.

She struggled to her feet and tried to push wet hair out of her face with an equally wet hand.

The open door to the house mocked her. Car keys, phone, purse, and Sophia all demanded she go back inside, the last place on earth she wanted to be.

Pausing long enough to let out a string of every curse word she could think of, she took a deep breath and stepped over the threshold. The beautiful, Gatsby-esque room was wrecked. It reeked of burnt gunpowder and whiskey, with just a hint of something more vile. Broken glass and bits of plaster were scattered on the floor. The centerpiece of the scene, of course, was the dead man sprawled grotesquely over the fake Persian rug, now tinted crimson along with his fine white dress shirt and his dove gray slacks.

Grace headed for the hallway, staying as far away from DeWitt's outstretched arms as possible, but keeping an eye on him as she scooped up her purse and threw it over her shoulder.

There was a light switch on the wall inside the door of the narrow basement stairs. A bare low-wattage bulb hung from the wall, but it was enough. She scrambled down the stairs to find a newly installed metal door with a heavy deadbolt. Luckily, it wasn't the kind that required a key from the inside. The thought of having to go back upstairs and rummage through DeWitt's pockets for a key made her queasy.

She knocked on the door before opening it, feeling a little foolish for doing so. "Sophia, honey? Are you in there? I'm here to take you home."

There was no answer, so she pushed the door slowly, terrified of what she might find.

The light of a television winked and flashed from atop a dresser. It was a cartoon and the characters were stuck in a giant snowball, rolling down a hill, yelling and laughing as they went. Silly sound effects played over the top of the scene. The room must have been soundproofed, because Grace heard none of that through the door. Luckily, that meant Sophia hadn't heard any gunshots either.

There was a bed in the room as well, and Sophia sat up groggily, rubbing her eyes with her hands, confused by the late-night visitor.

Grace felt a sob of relief coming on, but pushed it aside. There was no time to celebrate yet. She crossed over to the bed. "My name's Grace. I met you at Mrs. Westergard's house once. You were playing a video game. Do you remember me?"

The little girl hesitated, then nodded, and then, miraculously, blessedly, she smiled. "I remember."

"Good. Well, I'm here to take you back there. To get you out of this basement. But we've got to hurry, okay?"

She held out her hand and Sophia scrambled out from under the covers. The blanket was printed with baseballs and footballs, and Grace wondered if it had belonged to DeWitt in his youth. Maybe this had even been his old room. The thought made her shudder.

Sophia bounded into her arms and hugged her tight, burying her face in Grace's neck. "You're wet," she said, but she didn't cry, thank God.

Grace squeezed back up the narrow steps with her new friend and listened carefully at the top. Hearing nothing but the rain outside, she stepped out into the hallway and turned left toward the front door so as not to have to pass DeWitt's body again.

A clap of thunder made them both jump and Grace laughed a little uneasily. She stepped into the big, open foyer, and her voice echoed as she said, "That's the angels bowling, you know. Someone just made a strike." Sophia nodded into Grace's neck, but didn't look up.

Grace reached for the front door, and her breath caught in her throat. Through the heavy, leaded glass and the driving rain, a pair of headlights was pulling up to the gate.

She spun around and headed back down the hallway. "Hey, do you know how to play hide and seek?"

Sophia nodded.

"Good," Grace said, as she pushed open the door to one of the bedrooms. Without the lights, she could just make out the shape of a huge bed with a canopy and headed for it. She pulled back the hangings and deposited Sophia in the center of the frilly bed. "Oh, this is a great hiding place. No one will find you here," Grace said, trying to inject some enthusiasm into her voice as she pulled back the mountain of decorative pillows at the head of the bed.

"Climb up here and I'll pile these on top of you. It'll be just like when E.T. hid in the middle of all the stuffed animals? Remember?"

"Who's Eat Tea?"

"Um, I guess that's before your time. But trust me; he had a great hiding place. Just be very quiet and still, and don't come out, no matter what you hear, okay?"

Sophia nodded, curling into a ball as Grace piled the pillows on top of her.

She closed the hangings and tiptoed to the door.

"Grace," a small voice called from the bed. She turned to see Sophia's tiny, moonlit face peeking out from the pillows. "Don't forget to come find me, okay?"

"I won't forget. Cross my heart." Grace shut the door behind her, then hurried back into the den. She was out of bullets. She needed DeWitt's gun. He was lying face down on his Persian rug, and she took a perverse bit of satisfaction in knowing it was ruined.

His left arm was stretched over his head, where he had grabbed her. Ten shots to the chest before he let go of her throat.

His gun was nowhere in sight.

Grace groaned, realizing he must have fallen on top of it. A shiver of revulsion ran through her at the prospect of having to touch him, but there wasn't time for hesitation.

She pushed the coffee table out of the way so there was room to roll him over. Already breathing heavy from the adrenaline, she grabbed his outstretched arm and heaved. The very definition of dead weight, his body lolled and rolled and finally fell over onto its back. Trapped air escaped his lungs when he landed and Grace jumped, afraid for a second he might still be alive. Then her eyes fixed on his chest. At such close range, all of the bullets—

Kelly Adamson

with the exception of the one in his arm—had hit him center mass. Nice grouping.

His eyes were open and so was his mouth. Bloody foam covered his perfect capped teeth. His expensive white shirt was turning red, but the bullet holes were still perfectly visible.

She shivered. She'd just killed a man, and all she could think of was, "nice grouping."

Another clap of thunder rattled the windows and brought her back to the task at hand. The gun. But it wasn't underneath him. Instead, a bit of chain hung out of his pants pocket and Grace wound it around her finger and pulled until her USB popped out in her hand.

She dropped to her hands and knees and felt under the club chairs and the coffee table, blindly groping for the weapon, but her hands found nothing.

The wind caught the open back door and slammed it against the outside wall. Grace jumped, her heart hammering so fast that it hurt. When DeWitt's man saw the open door, he'd know something was wrong. She scrambled around behind the bar, and crouched down with her back to it. She tried to slow her breathing, tried to think. The first order of business was a weapon. Without a weapon, she was as good as dead. She reached up blindly behind her head and felt the port wine bottle. She grabbed it and pulled it down into her lap.

This was ridiculous. How did she get into this situation? She'd just wanted to help an aging rock idol write a book. Was that so much to ask?

Blocking out everything outside, her ears picked up the sound of glass crunching under heavy boots. He was in the room. He was saying something in a low voice, talking to someone else, maybe on the phone, maybe right behind him. She couldn't make out the words over the rushing sound in her ears.

Her breathing came in shallow gulps. Her arms ached from holding the wine bottle so tight. It only lasted a few seconds, but it seemed like an hour. She couldn't take it anymore.

She jumped up from behind the bar to see a man in black with a gun. She screamed like a banshee, and threw her makeshift weapon at him with all the force she could muster.

The wine bottle whizzed past his ear so close that the man's eyes widened in shock at the near miss. The bottle bounced off the plaster wall behind him, fell to the ground unbroken, and rolled to a stop at his feet. The man stared down at the bottle, giving Grace the second she needed to grab a crystal decanter from the bar and wind up for another pitch.

This time, the man was prepared. "Whoa!" he said. "Police. Drop your weapon and get down on the ground!"

Chapter 30 — This Party Never Ends

The girls all want me for themselves,
Don't want to share with their friends.
But I got enough for everyone.
And this party never ends.

They tell me rock is evil
and my lifestyle's just a sin.
But I got enough for everyone.
And this party never ends.
—This Party Never Ends (1990)

Three weeks had passed since that night. It was early October, and fall was nowhere to be seen in the deep South. The car's thermometer showed ninety-one degrees in the shade of the massive oak tree that stood in front of BJ's apartment building.

Karishma sat with her face right in front of the air conditioner vent, her fur blowing back like a supermodel's hair.

"I'm glad you could make it," Grace told Nick for the third time in the last hour.

"You know I wouldn't miss this," he said. "What kind of a husband do you think I am?"

She knew what her real answer to that would be, but she didn't want to get sappy, not today, so she shrugged and said, "The only one I could afford at the time."

He grinned and leaned over the console to give her a kiss. Karishma growled at him without moving her face from the vent.

He gave the dog a piercing look. "One of these days, rat, I'm gonna make a coon-skin cap out of you."

"I'm sorry," Grace said, putting a hand around the dog's muzzle, "but I thought it only fitting that she come, too."

Karishma's neck was saved by the arrival of BJ and Wayne, who held her door like a proper gentleman before walking around the car to climb in on the other side.

Nick pulled away from the curb and made a left on Sixth Avenue.

BJ talked most of the two-mile drive, but even she was subdued and quieter than usual. It wasn't a day for witty banter.

They passed the Birmingham jail on their left and Grace was glad that at least she had been taken to the relatively posh Mountain Brook precinct instead of here. Birmingham's was a stark and foreboding complex by nature and design, and she hoped she never saw the inside of it.

Still, the ordeal in Mountain Brook wasn't one she'd soon forget. And although everything was eventually sorted out, there were a few hours there where she was simply a murderer.

She'd killed a man in his own house, a public figure, filled him full of holes without his ever firing a single shot. Oh, and she assaulted a police officer.

None of this shone a favorable light on her as she waited that night, exhausted and frightened, in an interrogation room at the Mountain Brook Precinct. They'd brought her there directly from DeWitt's house and left her in this windowless room. At least they hadn't chained her to the table, she reflected, and they gave her a towel and a paper cup of coffee. It could have been worse.

And then Detective Morton came in carrying his own cup of coffee. He didn't look much happier than he had the first time she'd met him at Sparks's house. But maybe that was just a side effect of the job. He sat down opposite her with a yellow notepad and sipped his coffee.

"Ms. Howard, you seem like a relatively normal woman at first glance, so why is it that every time I see you, it's because you're in a dead man's house, with the dead man?"

"I can explain," and she did. It took over half an hour and several more cups of coffee to tell the whole story. She tried hard to keep the chronology right, but it was almost impossible with Morton asking questions that triggered other lines of thought.

In a stroke of luck, Detective Morton had been a fan of Sparks's music in his younger days. Grace tried to picture him with long hair, teased and sprayed into a proper glam rock mane, or to picture him with hair at all. Still, it saved her a lot of time explaining who was who. He was well aware of Tommy Redfoot's death and the fact that it had been ruled an accidental overdose. He even remembered seeing photos of Tommy's gorgeous girlfriend, although he hadn't known her name.

He didn't seem at all surprised to find out it was poison instead, or even that it was over a girl. He'd probably seen worse in his day.

"Too bad you killed him. I'd like to have seen him stand trial for that," was all he said.

Grace understood. For a man like DeWitt, the scandal and prison would have been a fate much worse than death.

"I didn't mean to kill him," she said in a soft voice. "But it was him or me."

Morton nodded and she finally relaxed a little.

He flipped a few pages in his notepad and said, "So, you have a tape in your possession where Sparks Westergard says he witnessed Arthur DeWitt poisoning Tommy Redfoot?"

"Well, no, not exactly."

"Not exactly?"

She shook her head and took a sip of cold coffee.

"So what *exactly* does the tape say?"

"Well, it says that DeWitt was the inspiration for the song, *Creep*. Did you know that?"

Morton closed his eyes.

"And it also says that DeWitt had contacted Sparks and wanted to come over and talk to him. Said he knew who murdered Tommy Redfoot."

"But Sparks didn't suspect DeWitt of Redfoot's murder?"

"No. As a matter of fact, I think Sparks expected DeWitt to tell him that Ax was the killer."

"Ax? Ax Royce? Then what made you suspect DeWitt?"

"I didn't. Surely you don't think I'm stupid enough to have gone over there alone if I thought he was a cold-blooded killer?"

"So, let me get this straight," Morton said, choosing to ignore that question. "If what you're saying is true, DeWitt killed Sparks for absolutely no reason at all. And if he had just left well enough alone, he would've gotten away with the first two murders."

"He'd gotten away with them all these years," she said. "Sparks wasn't going to expose him. He didn't know anything to tell."

They sat in silence for a minute. It seemed even worse now, laying it all out like that. It seemed even more tragic knowing it was all for nothing.

Morton was still scribbling in his notepad when Grace said, "How's Sophia?"

"She's good. She's a tough little cookie. She got to see her father, and he gave us the number of a neighbor who keeps her after school. The lady came up and got her and took her home. We posted a car outside her place for a couple of days, just to make her feel better. I don't think there's anything left to worry about."

This was probably true. On Grace's insistence, the officer she tried to hit with the wine bottle called for backup and hid his cruiser on the far end of the house. Sure enough, DeWitt's thug entered the back door fifteen minutes later with a loaded gun in his hand, one he had no right to possess as a convicted felon. There were three more in his car—all stolen, along with a roll of heavy plastic, duct tape, nylon rope, and two cinder blocks. And if that wasn't damning enough, Sophia ID'd him right away. His name was James, she said, and he came up to her while she was waiting on her bus after school. He told her that he was a friend of her father's and he had been sent to give her a ride home. She was wary at first, but then James said something about getting ice cream.

Sophia was five. Ice cream trumps logic when you're five.

"What about Raul? You didn't let him go?"

"Not yet. He's got a lot of talking to do. He's the key to this whole thing. And he did sign a false confession statement."

"But—"

"Don't worry about him. He'll be out by this afternoon." Morton smiled under his bushy moustache. "You should have seen him. As soon as he knew his daughter was safe ... Well, I shouldn't be telling you all this. I'm getting worse than Shipps."

He leaned back in his chair and studied her for a minute. "You're one of those people, aren't you?"

"What people?"

"The kind everyone confides in. You know all the secrets, don't you? People just tell you things."

She shrugged. "Maybe. You feel like telling me your secrets, Detective Morton? Maybe I can write your memoirs someday."

He laughed at that and his dark eyes flashed, remembering. "I don't think there would be much of a market for the crazy shit I've seen."

"Oh, you'd be surprised," she said. "People love to read about other people's crazy lives. Makes them feel normal. Makes them forget their own problems for a while."

He nodded. "I saw Sparks once at Boston Garden, you know. I was almost thirty, a beat cop in a rough neighborhood. I had responsibilities and debts and problems. I was going bald already, and my ex-wife was trying to turn my kid against me. But that night at the Garden, I was a head banger."

"Rock on," she said quietly.

"Rock on," he echoed, like an answering amen.

He drank the last sip of his coffee, crushed the cup in his hand and tossed it at the wastebasket in the corner. He missed. "Who knows? Maybe I'll look you up after I retire so you can write that book."

Morton stood and extended his hand to her. She shook it and he said, "Officially, don't leave town. Unofficially, thanks."

He opened the door to the small room and motioned for her to go ahead of him.

"Can I go home now?"

"Yes."

Her shoulders slumped, realizing her car was probably still at DeWitt's house.

"I don't have any way to get home."

"Oh, I think you do," he said, nodding toward the front of the lobby, where Nick was pushing through the glass doors like zombies were chasing him.

He'd driven all night through a solid wall of thunderstorms, and arrived in Birmingham just as the sun was coming up. The storm front had finally passed, gone on to march through Atlanta on its way to the sea.

He threw his hands out in exasperation when he saw her. "What the hell?" he said. "I can't leave you alone for five minutes. Are you trying to give me a heart attack? I'm going to have to post a twenty-four-hour guard on you ..."

He was still talking when Grace reached him and pulled him in for a kiss.

Grace had fourteen missed messages on her muted phone that night. The texts were mostly from Officer Louis "Loose Lips" Shipps. The first one came in at 8:09 pm and read, "Girl not under police protection. Not reported missing. Call me."

The sixth came in at 8:54 pm and read, "Do not go to Arthur DeWitt's house. Call me."

The voicemails were mostly from Nick. The first one was calm. The second, not so calm. The third one was just a bunch of mumbled cursing, with the sound of his truck's engine whining in the background.

It turned out Grace had a long line of guardian angels that night, beginning with Shipps. When he couldn't get her on the phone about Sophia, he called Nick. When Nick had no luck, he called BJ, who was still bubbling with excitement, having just gotten off the phone with Wayne. Thanks to Grace's encouragement earlier in the day, Wayne had called to ask BJ out on a date.

During their conversation, Wayne happened to mention that Grace thought Arthur DeWitt had answers about Tommy Redfoot's death, and how she'd asked him for his phone number. And if he knew where DeWitt lived.

When this information made its way back to Shipps, who was not on duty that night, he was none too pleased. He'd heard rumors about Arthur DeWitt and his recent rise in state politics, despite his misspent youth. He had a car dispatched at once.

For his part, Nick remembered seeing the photos of Witty holding the baggies of cocaine in the blackmail photos. He was already heading south, crushing the speed limit and pissing off the other drivers by the time Shipps called him to tell him Grace was safe.

Three weeks had passed since then. Seemed like a lifetime. Seemed like a minute. Grace looked over at Nick, hands on the wheel of her car, winding through the streets of Elmwood Cemetery. He caught her staring and smiled.

Elmwood was huge, a true city of the dead, over four hundred acres just west of downtown Birmingham. It was the final resting place of Alabama legends like football coach Paul "Bear" Bryant, Eddie Kendricks of the Temptations, venerated politicians, decorated war heroes, and even the woman who invented the windshield wiper. And, of course, Donna Westergard, Sparks's mother.

They had gotten directions from the office, but it still wasn't easy to find. There was no red stripe painted on the road to guide you, as there was to Coach Bryant's grave.

But they found it eventually. They were in no hurry, after all.

They walked through the graves, Grace holding Karishma's leash in one hand and the partial remains of her master in a plastic bag in the other. All four mourners wore Sparks tour tee-shirts donated from the vault by Dana for the occasion.

Wayne and BJ walked ahead of them, holding hands. If one good thing came out of this tragedy, it was that.

There was a granite bench that read, "Westergard," and the foot marker for Donna read, "Beloved Mother." They all stopped and just stood and stared at it for a minute.

Grace hadn't thought about what she would say, or even the need for words at all. But there was a definite void here. They couldn't just dump his ashes and go back to the car. It seemed indecent.

"Wayne," she said, "Would you mind saying a little prayer?"

"I'd be honored."

They all bowed their heads and he said, "*Make a joyful noise unto the Lord, all ye lands. Come before his presence with singing.* That's what the Bible tells us. And it tells us that the Lord loves us all, the beggars and the prostitutes, the thieves and the head bangers. Even the lawyers."

That drew a little chuckle and he went on.

"So, I know Sparks is up there now with his mother, and with Tommy Redfoot, and they're all making a joyful noise and wondering why we're sad. Thank you, Lord, for letting us borrow him for a while. Now, we give him back."

That seemed to be Grace's cue, so she handed the dog's leash to BJ and opened the bag. There wasn't much more than a cupful in it, having been divided into half a dozen portions, and she was glad of it as she sprinkled the contents over Donna's grave.

Everyone was quiet, even Karishma, and then Wayne said, "Amen."

They walked back to the car after a respectable few minutes, and when BJ got into the back seat, Karishma jumped right in after her and settled in her lap.

The woman began to rub the little dog's head, as if she were any other cute, little lap dog. Grace stared at this scene, open-mouthed. She felt like crying. Two burdens lifted off her in one day. No more ashes in her living room and no more beastly little dog in her guest room.

"BJ," she said, "You just got yourself a dog."

"Really? Oh, that's wonderful!" She hugged Karishma to her cheek, and the dog did not even try to claw her eyes out.

"There's no return policy on that," Nick said. "You take her, you can't bring her back."

"Oh, I won't."

"Seriously," he said. "I'm changing the locks and taking out the dog door."

Grace smiled and leaned her head against the passenger window as they drove away. She could just make out the Westergard bench about fifty yards back, through the rows of markers, under a big shade tree. It was a nice enough place to be buried, she thought. But maybe Sparks had it right. Part of him here, part of him in his garden, part of him in the great rock and roll halls of Europe and on Sunset Strip. All the places he loved.

"Rock on," she whispered.

The End

Kelly Adamson

Made in the USA
Monee, IL
13 January 2020